END OF DAYS
AN APOCALYPTIC ANTHOLOGY

OTHER LIVING DEAD PRESS BOOKS

BOOK OF THE DEAD: A ZOMBIE ANTHOLOGY
THE ZOMBIE IN THE BASEMENT (YOUNG ADULT)
FAMILY OF THE DEAD
DEAD WORLDS: UNDEAD STORIES VOLUMES 1, 2, 3 & 4
REVOLUTION OF THE DEAD
KINGDOM OF THE DEAD
THE MONSTER UNDER THE BED
DEAD TALES: SHORT STORIES TO DIE FOR
ROAD KILL: A ZOMBIE TALE
DEAD MOURNING: A ZOMBIE HORROR STORY
DEADFREEZE
DEADFALL
SOUL EATER
THE DARK
RISE OF THE DEAD
DARK PLACES
VISIONS OF THE DEAD: A ZOMBIE STORY
THE LAZARUS CULTURE: A ZOMBIE NOVEL
RANY AND WALTER: PORTRAIT OF TWO KILLERS
THE DEADWATER SERIES
DEADWATER
DEADWATER: Expanded Edition
DEADRAIN
DEADCITY
DEADWAVE
DEAD HARVEST
DEAD UNION
DEAD VALLEY
DEAD TOWN
DEAD SALVATION
DEAD ARMY (coming soon)

COMING SOON

BOOK OF THE DEAD 2: NOT DEAD YET
BLOOD RAGE by Anthony Giangregorio
DEAD WORLDS: UNDEAD STORIES 5
DEAD CHRISTMAS: A Zombie Anthology

END OF DAYS
AN APOCALYPTIC ANTHOLOGY

EDITED BY
ANTHONY GIANGREGORIO

Table of Contents

THE LOCUSTS

KELLY M. HUDSON

The locusts came on a bright April day, choking the sky with numbers so thick that some say the sun was blotted out for two days straight. They came over the east coast of the United States and swept westward until they reached California, eating and destroying nearly every plant, tree and crop in their path. By the time they finished and turned southward towards Mexico and Central America, the entire agricultural economy in the U.S. was utterly destroyed.

They worked their way through Mexico down to the southerly tip of South America. The rain forests were devastated and countries were thrown into upheaval.

After that, they went north, to Canada, and then turned to Asia, Europe, and Africa. In the course of a year, the world's food sources were destroyed and starvation ran rampant.

In the U.S., grain stores held for most of the year, finally depleting and giving way by the next spring. But hope was high for the new crops being grown and cultivated, even though large populations of humans and animals had perished from riots, lawlessness, and a harsh winter.

Another swarm of locusts, larger than the previous year's, came again the next spring and destroyed all the new crops, speeding through every province on the planet until not a tree or bush stood that wasn't completely devoured but for its branches.

Turmoil was too small a word to describe what happened next. Cities fell and people died of starvation, murder, and cannibalism. There was nowhere to run; no place that anyone could go for relief from a relentless, beaming sun and no food. In the matter of a month, most cities and towns were barren. For humans and animals alike, there was nothing much to do other than sit and starve to death. That or go insane. There were plenty who did, and cannibal clans roamed the country sides of U.S., seeking victims as meat for food and blood for drink. Some people banded together, though, for protection.

Thomas Paterson, forty years old, fat and squat, and a career librarian, was certainly not a person anyone could expect to survive much less thrive in such an environment. But survive he did, his fat providing him with stored energy until the weight was lost and he was trim and lean. He fought though; he had to. Many were the men and women who saw in him a lovely feast, and in the glare of their insane eyes, he could see them imagining him on a spit, his fat roasting over a blazing fire. Thomas wasn't much in the old world, an unimpressive man with a fancy imagination and lots of book smarts, but in this new world, he blossomed. He was part of a group that got together and left Lexington, Kentucky, and headed southeast, traveling through the mountains to the ocean, where they hoped to find fish to eat and a place to build a new life for themselves.

When they left Lexington, they saw spires of smoke in the distance behind them. One of the women in the group, a skinny girl with long straight hair and a nose like a vulture's beak, looked at the smoke and blinked with tears in her eyes.

"Locusts," she said. Thomas thought she'd lost her mind.

Thomas killed his first man, Ken Jackson, a former college baseball player and part of the group Thomas was traveling with, when Ken had slugged him early one morning when the group had packed up and was ready to leave. It was part of a plot hatched amongst their group of survivors. They were hungry, all of them, and the night before, when Thomas went to sleep, they discussed what to do.

Ken got the idea to kill Thomas in his sleep and would have, if Thomas hadn't woken from a terrible and strange nightmare. He stayed awake all night and Ken decided to wait until morning, when Thomas would be more tired, to attack and kill him. Thomas was ready, though. He'd picked up a large rock earlier in the day when he noticed their furtive glances as they walked down Interstate 75, weaving through abandoned cars and dead bodies long since picked over by crows and wandering animals. He knew, instinctually, they were going to come for him; he just didn't know when. Ken paid for the plan with his life when Thomas cracked

2

Ken's skull open with the rock he was carrying. Ken fell to the ground, twitching, blood pouring from his ears as his eyes rolled back inside of his head. Thomas didn't stop, he pummeled the top of Ken's head until it was crushed and his brains spilled out through his ears like cheese through a grater. He didn't stop even then; he kept hitting Thomas even after his body stopped twitching.

When Thomas backed away, the other people in the group looked upon him with awe and fear, even as they descended on Ken's corpse, ripping free meat and drinking the blood until they had their fill. Thomas wandered in among them, stealing Ken's backpack full of empty, plastic water bottles and a change of clothes, and then he slipped away and disappeared. He couldn't trust them or any other man, he realized. It would be better to go out and die alone than at the hands of a betrayer. In that moment, he came up with a new idea. Instead of heading for the ocean, he would go into the mountains of Eastern Kentucky. Surely there were caves there that could provide shelter, condensation for water, and insect life to eat. It was a solid plan and Thomas reckoned that if anyone else had the same idea about finding a cave, then they'd head west towards Mammoth Cave and not think of the small caverns that dotted the hillsides to the east.

Initially, this appeared to be a mistake. Thomas wondered alone for days, the sun beating down on him, turning his former jellyfish-colored skin a bright, burning red. He occasionally found a stream or a brook to quench his thirst but he didn't linger long, often chased off by roving packs of dogs or wolves that came around, sniffing but not attacking. Not yet, they sensed that Thomas was still strong enough to fight back. But they followed him for two more days, keeping their distance like circling buzzards, waiting until they knew he was weak enough to be easy pickings. And Thomas probably would have died, torn apart by their fangs, had he not stumbled upon a group of people, women and children mostly, that sat in a barren valley.

They were mentally handicapped, half naked, and starved. How they'd made it out here in the middle of nowhere without being killed already was a minor miracle. There was nothing he could do for them, however, when the twin packs of dogs and wolves raced past him, ignoring him as if he were just another tree stump, and swarmed the people, tearing them limb from limb. Thomas stood and watched for a moment; he gazed upon the new law of the world that was really the old law: kill or be killed. If you were weak, you were dead. This was the world he lived in now, and with each passing day, the one he'd come from faded into his memory.

To stay alive, he ran into the carnage, stealing an arm here, a leg there, and carrying them off. He roasted them later that day, using two sticks and a pile of dried grass to start a fire, and he ate heartily. There were no pangs of conscience in his heart. He did what he did to survive, and that was it. His entire existence had been boiled down to that one thing, to putting one foot in front of the other and to finding food enough to last another minute, another second.

In the middle of the night, when his belly was full and sleep hung heavy on his brow, Thomas saw a pair of glowing eyes appear in the darkness just outside the flickering of his fire. Then another pair appeared, then another, until dozens of animal eyes gazed at him from the deep night. It was the wolves and the dogs, joined together now. They stood there and observed him for a time, judging him. And then, one by one, they disappeared until none were left.

Thomas never saw them again.

The next day it rained and Thomas counted it as a blessing. He was tired and thirsty and stood in the rain with his mouth open and let Mother Nature nurture him. It only took a half hour before the ground at his feet, once hard and crusty, turned to mud and slime. He slid and fell and the next thing he knew, he was slipping down the side of the mountain he'd climbed, slamming into leafless trees and tumbling through barren bushes. He stuck out a hand and caught the root of a big oak tree and held on for dear life, the rain pouring from the skies like the judgment of God.

Thomas held tight as a flash flood gushed down the side of the mountain, sweeping weakened trees and tearing out brush and bushes. He climbed up the oak and sat and watched the devastation just a few feet under him. The rain kept coming and then there was lightning and pretty soon it had turned into a full Kentucky thunderstorm. Thomas worried about being in the tree with the lightning that streaked the sky like a freak science experiment, but there was really no other alternative for him. If he got down, he'd get swept away and probably drown. So he clung to the tree for dear life and prayed to a God he no longer believed in to help the oak stay strong and for the lightning to stay in the sky and not strike the ground. In the distance, he heard a train whistle and thought it odd. Then he realized it was a tornado he was hearing. Thomas ducked his head, too afraid to look. He held to the tree and cried for mercy. After a while, impossibly, he fell asleep.

Hot, humid air and burning sunshine woke him the next morning, his arms still locked around the tree. He back hurt and his shoulders were full of cramps, groaning when he moved them. Below, the ground was a soupy, gunky mess. Thomas got down from the tree and dipped an empty water bottle into one of the puddles, filled it with muddy water, and then used his shirt to strain the water into another bottle. Once he filled his three bottles up in this way, he headed back up the mountain, continuing east.

His mind turned over in his head, full of confusion and tumult. Why had any of this happened? Why did the locusts come and destroy not just one region, but practically the entire planet? Was it truly God judging humanity? Or was it nature itself, fed up with mankind's waste and filth? Or was it just rotten, dumb luck?

Thomas had no answers but one: he would keep heading east, through the mountains, until he found a cave, any cave, that was suitable for habitation.

Surely out there, somewhere, he could find shelter and food.

He climbed up the side of the mountain, fearing that the flood had washed enough mud and dirt over any cave entrance and thus hiding them from him. When he reached the top of the mountain, he paused and looked back to the west, towards the cities where he and so many others had come from. He saw smoke rising in the distance, high and tall, and he wondered if the cities were burning. He shrugged his shoulders and headed down the other side of the mountain, walking between fallen trees and mud-swamped bushes, searching for any openings in the side of the mountain.

Two days later, he struck gold.

He walked, on and on, the hot sun beating down, turning the top of his head pink and his nose and cheeks rosy. Every day was like this, walking, keeping low, staying alert at any noise, any movement, skittish and fearful.

This day was like any other; except when he came over a rise and stumbled on a field of dead bodies.

There were twenty of them, best as he could tell, and they were bloated and black, a foul, rotten smell hissing from their mouths. How long they'd been dead he couldn't tell, but it was long enough for the meat to spoil because they'd been untouched by any animal.

Thomas stood and studied them from a distance for a moment, deciding what to do. He could move around them or he could search through them, see if he could find anything useful. He had nothing better to do, other than to continue walking, hoping to find something to eat or some more water, since he'd run out of the muddy water he'd gotten after the thunderstorm. So he walked amongst the corpses, working his way past each body, lifting a swollen arm here, a rotten leg there, checking for anything he might be able to use. Halfway across the field, he hit pay dirt. A knife, clutched tight to a dead man's chest, glittered in the sunlight. How it hadn't been found yet Thomas didn't know nor did he care. It was his now, even if he did have to snap the putrid fingers to pry it loose. He cracked each knuckle of the dead man's hand, pulling them back and breaking the bones, the fetid skin sliding off in his hands, until he freed the knife and held it to his chest. He didn't blame the dead man for holding it like he had, for this was a precious thing to own. After the first wave of locusts, people went gun crazy, grabbing every pistol and rifle they could find, eventually turning them on each other.

By the second summer, when things finally got as bad as they could get, there were still guns around, but the bullets were spent, and since there were no more plants to manufacture them, the guns became useless. A knife, though, that was something special to have. And now Thomas had his.

He left the field behind, looking over his shoulder one last time, and then climbed another hill. He wondered what had happened to those people, how they'd come to die like they did and why they'd rotted so quickly that no other animal had anything to do with them. Were they diseased? Was the knife Thomas stole carrying a sickness? It didn't really matter to him; he was dead anyway, no matter what. Another day or two without water and that would be it for him.

Where were the caves? He knew they were out there, somewhere, and he should have spotted one by now. Bowing his head, Thomas trudged on, his eyes scanning the barren earth before him, hoping and praying for some more good luck.

None came that day, or the next.

He was barely standing now, stumbling and falling to his knees for every step he took. His head buzzed, he couldn't think straight, and his eyes weren't working right, his vision blurry; his eyes raw and bloodshot. His tongue was swollen in his mouth and it was so thick he was afraid it was going to choke him to death if his head tilted the wrong way. He fell to his knees, gazing up at the hill that loomed ahead of him, and realized he no longer had the will or the strength to keep going. This was it; this was to be the place where he died, from dehydration and exhaustion.

He blinked and something glittered on the hillside and he blinked again and saw that behind the sparkle lay a big, black empty space. Thomas gasped and dared not hope, sure that his eyes were betraying him, that he was seeing a mirage.

There was only one way to know for sure. Thomas marshaled what strength he had left and climbed the hill on all fours, his feeble and cracked fingers clawing the dirt. He passed out dozens of times before reaching the entrance to the cave and then another three times before he actually crawled inside. It took him most of the day, but when he reached the cool, damp dimness of the cave, he felt better. There was something about the chill coming from the black rocks beneath him that seeped into his muscles and skin and gave him whatever extra he needed to keep on going. He crawled into the cave, night falling behind him on the rest of the world, and slipped into a sleep fueled by exhaustion.

When he woke, he was lying next to a trickle of water pouring from between two rocks. The cool water dripped next to his head, so close that all he had to do was shuffle over less than a foot and it was splashing into his open mouth. He drank deep but he drank slow, afraid he might puke if he took it too fast. He moved his head and let the water beat on his forehead, cutting a clean spot through the dried dirt and mud on his face. Eventually it ran down in rivulets through what was left of his balding scalp and down the sides of his head, cooling his burned skin.

He fell asleep smiling with a full stomach, even if it was just water.

He slept through the day, exhausted, and rose the next morning as sunlight carefully crept into the opening of the cave. Thomas sat up and drank some more, the water never seeming to end, and then washed the rest of his face off. He was still weak from lack of food, but the water had brought something back to him, giving him hope in the face of the utter loss of expectations and dreams, and now he was ready to explore.

There wasn't much to the cave, it hung low so he could only get through by crawling. It went deep into the mountain; disappearing into darkness so thick he couldn't see his hand in front of his face. It was damp and there didn't appear to be any animals about, but plenty of water. His hands fell into several puddles as he worked his way forward, deeper and deeper, feeling his way along with his hands in front of him. He wondered how far he should go before turning back around, when his hands found a pile of loose rocks blocking the way in front of him. He gave them a light push and two of them fell back and he was blinded by a shaft of bright sunlight. He winced and covered his eyes. He waited a few moments, letting his vision adjust, and then peered between his fingers. The rocks had been piled in such a way to make it appear as if the cave had ended but it hadn't. Instead, it opened up on to something that Thomas, in all his wild imaginings, had never thought could be conceivable. He pushed his way through the rocks and slid out into the sunlight, blinking rapidly because he simply couldn't believe what he was seeing.

At his feet lay a valley, full of lush, thick trees and teeming with wildlife. It was what Thomas could only call the Garden of Eden, and it was hidden away somehow from the rest of the world, untouched by the locusts.

He found he could stand and then, that he could run, dashing down the hill that the cave spilled out of and scampering on his wobbly legs to a pool of water some thirty yards away, giddy as a boy who has discovered sex for the first time. He plunged into the water and it was cold, but a good cold, and he exploded from the

8

surface, yelling with glee. Thomas looked around and saw that the pool was fed by a small waterfall that ran down the side of the mountain. He swam over, found footing at the base of the fall, and let the water beat down on his head, washing him entirely clean for the first time since he could remember.

Thomas spent a long time in the pool, soaking and enjoying the sensation. He finally got tired and dragged himself up one of the banks and laid down, sunning dry. It felt good, like somehow he'd died and gone to Heaven and Thomas figured if he truly was dead, then let him stay that way, because this was too good to ever let end.

He blinked when the shadow in the shape of an adult human fell across him and he barely had time to raise an arm in defense when a rock slashed the air and thumped his skull, knocking him unconscious.

Thomas woke hours later, hands and legs tied together behind him. It was night and he was lying next to a small campfire being stared at by a boy who couldn't be older than ten. The kid was scrawny but healthy, and he wore a t-shirt with the Kentucky basketball logo on it and a pair of cut-off jean shorts. His feet were bare but a pair of sandals sat next to him. The boy had brown hair and eyes and a long scar down his left cheek that had healed poorly and was still puffy. The boy had Thomas' knife in his hand and he was running the blade lightly over his right palm. He blinked and stared at Thomas for a long time before he opened his mouth and spoke.

"He's awake, Donna," the boy said.

Thomas looked at the boy and then craned his neck when he heard leaves rustling off to his right. A woman, barely twenty-five years old, slipped through the woods and stood over him, her tall, skinny frame dancing with the shadows of the flickering firelight. Thomas stared up at her, taking in her long auburn hair, tied back with a shoestring, her crooked nose that looked like it had been broken more than once, and her glittering black eyes. The woman stared back at Thomas, deciding what to do with him.

"Can you speak?" the woman said.

Thomas nodded.

"Then speak," she said.

Thomas tried. All that came out was a croak. The woman snapped her fingers and the boy brought over a small flask and pressed it to Thomas' lips. He drank deeply of the cool water inside of it.

"Now," the woman said. "Speak."

"Hello," Thomas said. How long had it been since he'd spoken a word? He couldn't remember.

"How did you get here?" she said.

"Through the cave," Thomas said.

She looked at the boy, anger in her gaze. The boy shrugged and looked at the fire to avoid her stare.

"I'm sorry," Thomas said. "I didn't mean to do anything wrong. I just, I'm lost. I need food, I'm dying."

"Who isn't?" the woman said.

"How did this place come to be here?" Thomas asked. "I thought the bugs ate everything."

The woman ignored Thomas and turned again to the boy. "In the morning you go and seal the cave again. And do it better this time."

The boy nodded and disappeared for a moment on the other side of the fire. When he returned to Thomas' line of sight, he was holding three bass fish, cleaned and run through with long, thick sticks of wood. He held them out over the fire and cooked them. The smell of the sizzling fish slapped Thomas' nose and he nearly vomited. His stomach roiled and screamed and pleaded to be fed.

The woman heard his stomach growl and smiled down at him.

"How long has it been?"

"I don't remember," Thomas replied.

"I'll feed you tonight. Tomorrow, we'll decide whether to kill you or not," she said.

Thomas ate the fish and thought it the finest he'd ever had in his entire life. It was always like that when a person was hungry and finally got a bite to eat; whatever it was they ate turned out the be the most delectable thing they'd ever eaten. Thomas remembered a time, back in the old world, when his father took him out one night when he was just ten years old. His father refereed high school football games and their crew was minus a guy to hold the downs marker.

Thomas' dad took him that night, trained him on the job, and Thomas stood out there in the cold, rainy night, shoes filling with wet mud, and had a grand old time. When it was over, his dad took him out get burgers and Thomas remembered how he was starving like never before in his life. When he first bit into the burger it was the best he'd ever had before or since, and the memory of sitting there at that table, eating a burger with his dad after a job well done, was one the happiest of his life.

The fish the boy made for him was almost that good.

He ate, felt sick to his stomach, drank some water, and fell fast asleep. He didn't care what the next day brought. This day had been the greatest he'd had since the locusts swept the Earth.

*   *   *

The boy kicked Thomas in the side to wake him up but Thomas didn't mind. He'd slept well at the foot of the pine tree he was lying under, the pillow of shed needles providing a comfortable cushion for his body and head. He didn't even mind the cramping in his arms and legs from being tied up all day and night. He looked up at the boy and smiled. Morning sunlight shone in shafts through the leaves of the trees, creating thousands of tiny spotlights on the ground.

"I don't mean either of you harm," he said. "I'll go, if you want."

The woman walked through a stand of bushes, slipping up next to the boy with the stealth of a ghost. She stared down at Thomas and studied him for a few minutes. When she said nothing, Thomas finally spoke again.

"Thank you for the food and the water," he said. "It was the best day of my life. I can die now, if you want, and I can die a happy man."

The woman craned her neck as if she couldn't believe what she was hearing.

"You're crazy," she said.

"Who isn't?" Thomas said. "I just have one request for you: if you're going to kill me, do it in the shade, like the one under this tree. I've had enough sun to last two lifetimes."

The boy looked up at the woman. "He's nuts."

11

"Quiet, Tommy," she said.

"Tommy?" Thomas said, a huge grin spreading across his face. "That's my name. Well, it was until I got to be fifteen years old or so. Then I went by Thomas because it sounded more grown up."

"I like Tommy better," Tommy said.

"Well, nice to meet you, Tommy," Thomas said. He looked at the woman. "What's your name, if I might ask?"

"None of your business," she said.

"You're going to kill me anyway," Thomas said. "So what does it matter?"

She considered this. Finally, she said, "My name's Donna."

They didn't kill Thomas that day, nor the next. Soon the time stretched into a week, and by then, Thomas had earned their trust. They untied him and taught him to fish and which berries to gather in the wild. But Donna always kept a suspicious eye on him and when night fell, she insisted that Thomas must submit to being tied to a tree, the same tree he'd slept under the first night, until morning.

Finally, one night, she didn't insist. Thomas slept by the fire with Tommy and Donna.

The next day, the boy gave Thomas his knife back without saying a word. Thomas used the knife to show the boy how to fashion spears out of some saplings near their camp. They made six spears and caught many fish that day.

That night they ate well and Thomas watched Donna as she ate and moved about the area. He tried not to, but he couldn't help but stare at the way her thighs moved, the way her butt shook, and her breasts swayed. It had been a long time since he'd been with a woman, but he stayed honorable and stayed away from her.

A week passed.

In the middle of one evening, Donna came to him when the boy was asleep, the fire dim and the stars shining bright on a cloudless evening. She slid next to him, naked, and Thomas found out that it had been a long time for her, too. He was not honorable that night.

Or the next.

Another week passed. They were like a family, close and tight. Food and water was plentiful and they had no worries. Occasionally, off in the distance, a wisp of smoke would appear over the mountains and Donna would stare up at them, worry creasing her pretty face. Thomas always meant to ask what was bothering her, but he never quite found the courage.

That night, when Tommy fell asleep, Donna lay close to him and kissed his neck.

"The boy isn't mine," she said. Her voice was soft against the darkness as her eyes reflected the glittering firelight.

"I know that."

"I came upon him outside of Atlanta. There were these men and they had him surrounded and they were kicking him. One of them took a rock and smacked Tommy on the head. I was sure they were going to eat him," she said.

"Cannibals," Thomas said.

"Yes. They're everywhere," she said. "I felt for the boy, and even though I was afraid, I had a baseball bat I carried with me back then, so I charged them. I guess I was crazy. I broke the ribs of one man and the knee of another before they scattered and ran off."

"You were very brave," he said.

Donna shrugged. "They were stick men, so skinny a breeze could fold them up and carry them away. That's how feeble he was," she pointed at the sleeping Tommy. "Anyway, we were together after that. And in a way, I became his mother and he became my son."

"It makes sense."

"The cannibals followed us," she said. "We ran and fled and hid as best we could. But they were going to get us, and they would have, if not for another group of cannibals. They ran into each other and stood across a barren field, just staring. And then somebody screamed and both groups charged each other. It was like something out of a movie. They slaughtered each other. I've never seen so much blood in one place."

Donna's face went slack with the memory and her eyes glazed over. Thomas was sure she was speaking of the group of dead bodies he'd stumbled over when he found the knife. Now the mystery was solved.

"We ran up the mountain and found this cave and we crawled as far as we could in it until we saw daylight and came through the other side. And we found this place," she said. She looked all around, the images of horror gone from her eyes and replaced by wonder. "I sometimes think we really died and are in Heaven."

Thomas smiled. "I thought the same thing when I first came here."

Donna snuggled against him. "I'm glad you're here."

"Me, too." He kissed her forehead and they lay in the quiet, enjoying each other. Finally, Thomas gathered his courage.

"Sometimes, when we see smoke in the sky, I see you get upset. Why?"

Thomas felt Donna stiffen by his side, like she was suddenly frozen. Her skin rippled with goose bumps so large Thomas could feel them pop from her and poke his side.

"Locusts," she said.

Thomas remembered the woman in his group when they left Lexington. She's said the same thing about the smoke, but it made no sense to him then or now.

"I don't understand," he said. "The locusts are gone."

"No," she said. "They're humans. They call themselves the Locusts."

Thomas stared at her, his eyes blank.

"I saw them in Atlanta. It was why I left. They're a cult; an evil, evil cult," she said. Her voice cracked and she cried softly against his chest.

"It's okay," he said. He stroked her hair.

"They preach destruction. They say God sent the locusts on us as a curse for what we've done to the Earth. They were environmentalists at first and then they became a religion and their numbers grew."

She shook and shivered. Thomas kept running his fingers through her hair and wishing he'd never brought it up. He didn't like seeing Donna so terrified, like she was reduced to a whimpering child.

"They say that for the Earth to become truly clean, we must finish what the locusts started. They called themselves the Locusts after the insects. They seemed harmless at first. You know how it was; people were scared and lost and dying and they were looking for anything to help them through their misery. One day, though, the Locusts rose up and set fire to the camp I was staying at, killing dozens of people."

"Good God," Thomas said. Could such madness be true?

"They marched out and burned everything behind them. I watched Atlanta burn, just like Sherman did so long ago. And as they grew, more and more people joined them. They broke into packs and carried fire in every direction."

"That's insane."

"I got away and I hop I never see them again," she said. Her teeth chattered and she shuddered.

"And you think that smoke is from them?"

"It gets closer everyday."

"We're safe here," he said. Thomas ran his fingers over her cheeks and caressed her skin.

"No one's safe. Not from them," she said.

A tiny squeak slipped from between her lips and Donna fell hard against his chest, sobbing so loud he thought she might wake the boy.

Thomas didn't know what to say. He held her close and tight and didn't speak again. He kept rubbing her hair and wiping the tears from her cheeks until she eventually fell into a deep, troubled sleep, her body twitching as she moaned from terrible nightmares. Thomas held her and looked up at the sky, blinking back his own tears, until, he too, fell asleep.

*　　*　　*

The next day he rose early, took the knife, and traveled to the cave entrance. He inspected the rocks, tested how well they were shored up, and ended his examination with a frown on his face. They would hold, but not under intense pressure. Reluctantly, he moved several key rocks away, opening up the back end of the cave, and squirmed through the hole. He crawled on his belly in the dank dark, brutal memories of his life before the valley flashing through his mind. It was a horrible and cruel world out there beyond the cave and he'd almost forgotten completely about it. Now he was reminded, through Donna's pain and tales, and he had to make sure that she and the boy were never threatened again. He moved slowly and carefully until he saw daylight from the opposite end of the cave filter around a sharp turn. Thomas stopped and sighed. He didn't really want to go out there, but he had to make sure. He rounded the corner on his belly and froze when the pungent smell of smoke clogged his nose and lungs. He rolled over, spat, cleared his throat, then blinked his eyes against the cloying smoke. It was thick and heavy in the cave and he could feel the heat from burning fires in the near distance.

Flickering shadows played across the floor of the cave up near the entrance and Thomas slid back around the corner. He could hear them, the murmuring of voices, as people moved cautiously into the cave.

"This could lead somewhere," one voice said.

"Praise God," another said.

He heard more murmuring and decided it would be a good idea to get out of there. Thomas slid back, turned around, and made his way towards the hidden valley. On his way, another voice, this one female and angry, spoke, and her words clawed at his bare feet like the teeth of pursuing rats.

"Go to the end," she said. "Find us something to burn."

Thomas slid out of the cave and put the rocks back into place, hoping they'd be enough to hide the valley for the moment. As his feet touched the cool ground and soft grass, he heard a movement behind him and he spun, knife raised and ready, to see the boy standing twenty yards from him, staring intently.

"They've come," Thomas said to the boy. "Go tell your mother. Tell her to hide."

The boy didn't move.

"There's no time," Thomas said, his voice hissing between clenched teeth. "Go!"

The boy dashed away, crying.

Thomas went to work piling every rock he could find up against the stack already assembled, trying his best to keep them out. He hoped that they would come up against the back wall and give up, but something nagged at him, tugging the edges of his heart and mind, and that something told him that it wouldn't be that easy. He heard a branch snap behind him and he spun. The woman and the boy were standing and staring at him over by the edge of the woods.

"I went into the cave and saw them," he said. "You were right. They're crawling through there right now. You need to hide, both of you."

The boy grunted and shook his head. Donna stumbled forward and then ran, as hard as she could, and threw her body into his arms. She was shaking, but at least there, wrapped in his embrace, he could calm her. Thomas took Donna by the hair and gently tilted her head back so she could see him.

"We need water," he said. "Go to the pond, get as much as you can, and wet down the entire area. The fire won't burn if the grass is too wet. Take the boy with you."

She blinked and tears slid down her cheeks.

"It's okay," he said. "We'll be okay."

Tommy tugged at her arm and Donna let go. She turned and ran down the hill as fast as she could. She and the boy returned time and time again with leaves full of water, splashing it all about, trying to drench the surrounding area. Thomas climbed to a spot over where the rocks were piled to hide the entrance to the cave and stood guard. He held his knife in one hand and waited. It should be any minute now.

One rock tumbled, clacking against the others. Then another. Then two more then three and they cascaded down, rumbling, clicking and clapping.

Thomas dipped down as the first Locust head poked from the hole.

"You won't believe this!" the man said.

Thomas yanked him by his hair up and back and then slid the blade along the man's throat, slicing it open. Blood spurted and splattered on the rocks as the man gurgled and choked. He wouldn't last long. Thomas let go and watched as the man flopped, groaned, and then died.

At the bottom of the hill, Donna and the boy had stopped dousing the grass with water and looked up at him and the dead man. Donna's face was white as bone and the boy was crying.

"Keep at it!" Thomas told them.

They jumped, jolted by his yell, and ran off to gather more water. He hated for them to see this, but there was no choice. It was back to the old law, to kill or be killed. And Thomas would clog the hole with dead bodies if need be, to protect those he loved.

He heard a scream from below him and suddenly the dead man he'd killed surged forward and dove from the hole. His body tumbled down the rocks, bones cracking and extremities flopping in unnatural angles.

Another head stuck through the hole, this one belonging to another man. He had curly hair and his face was caked with dried blood. The man looked up at Thomas just as Thomas jammed the knife in the man's right eye. The man screamed as Thomas dug the knife in deeper, twisted it, and then wrenched it out. Blood and eye goop bubbled from the eye socket and he kept screaming, his hands pulling free of the hole and clawing at his wound.

Thomas kicked him in his face and the man, shoved by the people inside the cave, fell and rolled down the rocks. Like his comrade before him, his bones shattered from crashing along the rocks, and he was dead before reaching the bottom of the hill.

Another torso popped from the cave and Thomas stabbed him in the back of the neck and ripped the knife down and to the side. Blood gushed from the wound but the man Thomas cut barely had time before he, too, was shoved through. He fell down the hill and the snap of his neck when his head hit a rock reverberated off the surrounding trees like a thunderclap.

Another man slipped through. This one was too quick for Thomas. He slid and then dove to the side, tripped on a rock and fell over, cracking his ribs on the jagged rocks and screaming in pain.

Then they pushed through, two at a time, and Thomas could do little but slash at them and hope to injure them enough so they couldn't fight. But there were too many. The four turned to six turned to eight and suddenly Thomas was on his heels, the members of the Locusts finding their footing on the rocks, turning and moving to encircle him. He slashed his knife in the air in front of him in an attempt to keep them back, but he knew it wouldn't hold them for long.

Each one of them were naked but for a pair of shoes and their bodies were caked with human blood, dried and crusted in their body hair so that they looked like men struck with some kind of rust disease. Their loins were clumped with dried feces and they stunk like copper and manure and each one of them, all male, growled and howled like madmen, their mouths twisted in lunatic grins.

Finally, the tide stopped, twelve men in all, and a woman, last to come through the hole, a flaming torch in one hand, as naked as the men, with blue eyes that shone of a tighter madness, controlled and evil. She stepped out and looked around, saw Thomas and her followers that surrounded him now, and smiled, wicked as murder.

"You," she said. "You killed my men. Good. All were born to die under the sky."

"If you leave now, you'll live. If you don't, I'll kill you all," Thomas said coldly as he glared at her.

She licked her lips and grunted. A laugh slipped from her mouth as three of the Locusts charged him. They held no weapons in their hands but they were quick and fueled by insanity and religious fervor. One punched Thomas in the shoulder and another dove to the ground, skinning his legs and back on the jagged rocks as he wrapped himself around Thomas' legs to try and trip him. And as Thomas stumbled and nearly toppled over, the third moved in, fingers clawing Thomas' face, scrabbling for his eyes and mouth.

Thomas went down, landing on top of the Locust on the ground, driving his knee hard into the man's feces-thick groin. The man screeched and Thomas plunged the knife into the man's stomach as the one who punched Thomas kicked him in the ribs.

Thomas pulled the knife out of the man on the ground and rolled across the rocks, feeling their jagged tips bite into his skin, and came up on his knees next to the Locust who had clawed his face.

Thomas thrust the knife into the man's knee. The man fell over, his screams joining those of his fellow Locust. The third one, the last one standing of the initial attackers, jumped over the rocks and bounded towards Thomas. The Locust kicked at Thomas' head but Thomas ducked, came up with the knife, and gouged the man's left calf muscle. Thomas stabbed the blade in deep, twisted and then pulled it out. The Locust shrieked and fell, the side of his head cracking on a rock just at his temple. The man went silent.

The woman, the Leader of the Locusts, skipped down the rocks, laughing and pointing at the scenery of the lush valley as she made her way towards the grass and trees at the bottom of the hill. She shouted her madness at the top of her lungs.

"God has brought us here to destroy!" she yelled. "What out brothers the insects couldn't or wouldn't finish, we shall! Glory be to God!"

Thomas got to his feet. He had to get down there and stop her. But the nine Locusts left glowered at Thomas and slowly close ranks around him. They were going to move in and kill him and, despite the advantage of his knife, he knew he didn't stand a chance.

"So be it," Thomas said. He looked over the valley and was thankful for the short time he spent there, for the pleasures it brought him and the life it had restored to him. For a brief moment, Thomas had known life as it was meant to be, filled with hope and love and purpose. That moment had passed, and now, so too would he.

"It's a good day to die," Thomas said.

Four Locusts rushed him. Thomas stabbed one and punched another before they threw him onto his back and pummeled him with fists and feet. He kicked and rolled and slashed with the knife but one of them hit his hand and the knife flew away and clanged on the rocks. Thomas saw it spin and fall between two rocks and he closed his eyes because he knew that this was it. His time had come.

The Leader screamed at the bottom of the hill and her followers, the Locusts, froze and turned. Thomas, bleeding from his ears and mouth and nose and a dozen other places, lifted his bruised head and followed their gaze.

At the bottom of the hill, the Leader stood impaled on one of the fishing spikes. At the other end of it stood Donna, holding the spike firm and resolute.

The moment seemed froze in time.

Hope surged in Thomas' chest as he rose off the ground and kicked the Locust closest to him, sending the man tumbling down the hill of rocks. Thomas clawed another man's legs and kicked and punched as the Locusts spilled away from his sudden and furious assault.

Thomas risked a glance down the hill to see Donna push the Leader aside and pick up another spear, eager to climb up and help him. He smiled and struggled to get to his feet. Perhaps there was a chance, after all.

A roar shook the cave below him and the entrance vomited another dozen men, all covered in dried blood and feces. They poured from the opening, torches in hand, and marched down the hill. It happened so fast. One moment it seemed that the day was winnable, that life could go on in this paradise, and then just like that, more Locusts came, and still more, until there was four dozen with more still coming through the cave.

Thomas stopped and stared. He watched as the Locusts, men and women alike, strode down the hill. They walked past the grass wetted by the boy and Donna, and on into the woods. They put their torches to the leaves and limbs of the trees, the bushes catching fire as sparks caught and flared up in a matter of moments.

Angry flames licked high in the air as smoke clogged the valley.

Donna stabbed at one of the Locusts as they bristled past her. Hardly affected, some of the men grabbed Donna, disarmed her, and threw her to the ground. One man each grabbed her arms and legs and another sat on her chest as they tore her apart, yanking each limb from its socket and then twisting and ripping until nothing remained of her but a twitching torso on the ground.

Thomas sank to his knees, a small squeak sliding from his throat, as he watched them take Donna's arms and legs and bash her skull in with them.

When they were finished, they dropped the limbs and joined their brethren in setting fire to the surrounding area.

Thomas wondered where the boy was. He hoped he was safe. A rock struck his head and Thomas pitched forward, shattering his teeth on the pile of stones before him. Another rock cracked his head and his vision went blurry, then sideways. Blood poured from his scalp down over his face and into his eyes. He blinked it away. Pain wrenched his head and body as he forced himself to turn over and look up into the sky. He wanted his last sight to be of the blue, cloudless day and not the horror that was unfolding around him. His vision was crimson and disjointed, like he was looking through a fractured windshield, the image of what he was seeing broken in two and distorted.

The boy stepped into his vision. Tommy. That was his name. Just like Thomas. He was a fine boy and Thomas would have been proud to call him his son.

The boy stood before him, looking down on him and Thomas could see something was wrong in Tommy's eyes. There was now something broken and beyond repair swirling in the dark orbs.

Tears flowed down the boy's cheeks as the Locusts closed in around him. Thomas could see them as they swam into his vision, crowding in and staring at the boy. Thomas didn't want it to end like this. Anything but this.

The boy had found the knife and held it out before him. He moaned and raised the knife and drove it into Thomas' stomach. Thomas coughed blood as the boy reached inside the wound, scooped out a palm full of blood, and then smeared it across his naked chest. The Locusts howled their approval as the boy took off his pants and bent down and scooped more blood from the wound and wiped it over his body from head to toe. The boy kept bending down, dipping out more blood, until he was filthy with it.

Thomas looked at the boy. This was what the world had come to. He was glad to be leaving it. Thomas turned his head to the side, saw the burning paradise, and then shut his eyes and lived no more.

The boy plunged his hands into the feces Thomas vacated when he died and scraped out two handfuls. The boy took them and slapped them on his groin, covering his genitals in the warm waste of his former mentor.

Tommy leaned back his head and cried to the sky, "The Earth shall be cleansed!"

The Locusts roared.

Tommy gazed down at the valley below him and watched as the fire spread, the smoke rising high into the air. It was good to see it burn. It was good to see the old world finally pass away. It was good for the woman and the man to have died because they were of the old world and not fit for the new one. The zeal of this belief made his heart soar as he looked out on the land where he once played, hunted, and fished, now burning, made right in accordance to what God desired.

Tommy walked down into the valley, took a torch from a fellow Locust, strode to his former campsite, and set fire to it.

The tears on his cheek dried, mingling with the fresh coating of blood as the heat of the flames licked the air.

Tommy turned and walked away into the new world.

His world.

THE FEVERS

JESSY MARIE ROBERTS

The shuttle sputtered and hissed, blowing hot, harsh smoke onto the dead earth. Samantha's view of the take-off was blurred by tears, sweat and exhaust fumes. She fell to her knees, broken and sobbing, clutching her *Exodus* boarding pass in her hands.

With a scream, she wrinkled up the useless paper and threw it skyward. A gust of wind tangled with the scrap of paper and ink and blew it back toward her. An hour earlier she would have fought tooth and nail to keep that paper. Now it was scattered across the barren land, useless and forgotten.

Samantha took a deep breath, and stumbled to her feet. Night would fall soon, and she had a three mile walk to the closest shelter. Food was scarce, and only available on a first come, first serve basis.

Raised in an upper-middle class family, Samantha never imagined that the term 'born lucky' would constitute a small meal and a safe place to sleep, but things had changed when The Fevers spread out from Africa, suffocating and blistering nine out of ten men on each continent.

There were some isolated cases of The Fevers infecting females, but they were few and far between. For the most part, women were immune to the ailment. Men were not so lucky, falling victim to the illness and dying within days of contracting the virus.

After her father and three brothers had been taken by the plague and her mother's subsequent suicide, Samantha was left a small inheritance and the family's gun shop.

People were willing to trade anything for a gun or ammunition when the world was ending. Safety was a commodity, traded for canned peaches and bottled water. Samantha stored her resources in the basement of her parent's two-story Victorian, and slept with her hoarded guns, ammo and supplies.

Then she had traded most of it for a one-way pass onto *Exodus*.

"I thought you had a ticket off this planet," a voice called from behind her.

Samantha turned, recognizing the voice. "Looks like they left without me. Think I'll get a refund?" she joked with a fake, stiff laugh.

Amanda laughed in kind. Real laughter was a thing of the past, the joyous sound burned out by The Fevers.

"Probably not, Sammy. You're screwed. Just like the rest of us."

Samantha wondered if Amanda took pleasure in pointing out their commiserate state. Amanda's mom had been a stripper-turned-cocktail waitress, her dad out of the picture before she had been born. Cursed with bad teeth and splotchy, oily skin, Amanda had been ridiculed on a daily basis throughout school.

Samantha wished she had stood up for her.

She looked around at the charred ground. The fire pits the control team dug to burn the diseased bodies spread out of control, raging untended until most everything in its fiery path was destroyed. Trees were black and mangled, acrid puffs of smoke stinking the air.

"At least I'm in good company," Samantha answered, swinging her arm around Amanda's shoulders. "Maybe things will be peaceful on Earth without men."

Amanda stared at her, incredulous. "I know you don't mean that, Samantha Yeager. They're gone. They're all gone, shipped away in a spaceship. They're the lucky ones."

"Maybe you're right, Mandy," Samantha whispered as they walked, side by side, to the nearest shelter.

* * *

The shelter was an old elementary school, and it was over capacity. The stench of unwashed bodies and chicken soup assaulted Samantha's nostrils as they entered the cafeteria.

"Think there'll be any food left by the time we get through this line?" Amanda asked, squeezing her shoulders together in an effort to make them smaller. Still, other women bumped and elbowed into her stocky body, vying for a better place in the slop line.

"I hope so," Samantha replied, worried. The portions got smaller every day, and the line grew longer. She glanced over her shoulder, and saw more downtrodden women and girls filing into the building.

An hour later, the harassed cook announced that there was no more food. Groans of disappointment were punctuated by the loud, desperate wails of hungry children.

Girl children.

The boys had been ripped from their mother's bosom and herded into quarantine until they could be safely stowed aboard *Exodus*.

Looking around, Samantha was amazed what mankind would do to save its only sons, even if it meant leaving its daughters behind to mourn them.

"Might as well find a place to sleep," Samantha suggested.

Her sullen friend nodded her head and walked out of the food hall. The classrooms were set up with cots and sleeping bags. The overspill of people slept on the blacktop playground or lawn, exposed to the weather and the smoke from the fires.

Samantha was grateful when she found a quiet spot in the corner of a third grade classroom. Small hands cut out of colorful construction paper dangled from the ceiling like a baby's mobile, reminding Samantha that she would never bear a child, never hold a tiny hand in her own.

Tears slid down her dirty face, and she turned toward the wall, pretending to sleep. She didn't want Amanda to see her cry.

* * *

Hours later, Samantha awakened to shouting and fighting. The harsh glare of the fluorescent light illuminated two women attacking each other, pulling clumps of hair from scaly, dry scalps, slapping and biting each other in a fierce struggle for dominance.

Amanda was gone, her sleeping bag wrinkled. Samantha scanned the room, but didn't see her friend.

A circle of women cawing and cheering surrounded the fighters, blocking Samantha's view. She reached up and grabbed a red paper hand and stuffed it in the pocket of her jeans, desperate for a memento of youth and hope, then shuffled to her feet.

The brawling women broke through the circle and fell into Samantha, knocking her against the wall with a painful thud. Her head cracked against the plaster and she saw stars for a moment or two. She lifted her arms over her face as misplaced and furious fists missed their mark and slammed into her lip, splitting it wide open.

Enough was enough.

Her frustration with The Fevers, being left behind on a doomed planet, and hunger was festering within her until she lost control of her temper and struck back against her attackers.

Samantha screamed and wedged herself in between the fighters, forcing them apart. "Stop fighting!" she yelled at the bruised lady she faced, leaving her back exposed to the other party. She felt teeth go through the back of her shoulder, the pain muted by adrenaline and rage, though she knew it would hurt like the devil after she calmed down.

Samantha spun on the balls of her feet with her small fists clenched, and was taken aback by the snarling hate fused into the dirt-caked wrinkles of her assailant's face. The men had been gone for less than a day and already the fairer sex had evolved into primal, aggressive animals. Survival brought out the beast, and the beast fed on humanity. Soon there wouldn't be any left to feed it, and they would die, alone and broken, with nobody to burn them or bury them or give a damn they ever existed.

"Get out of my way," the woman spat, blood and spittle spraying Samantha's face.

Samantha crouched low to the ground, ready to defend her body. "No."

She saw the swing coming out of the corner of her eye and raised her left forearm to block the blow, leaving her right fist free to connect with her opponent's jaw. A sickening crack warbled through the air. Then silence, thick and raw, enveloped the room.

Samantha, through an adrenaline-soaked haze, watched her challenger fall backward onto the large oak teacher's desk. Pencil and ballpoint pen tips pointed straight out of a mug that read *Teachers Have Class*. The insidious instruments slid up into the back of her adversary's neck and the base of her skull on impact, rendering her still and soiled.

It took a minute for Samantha to register that her rival was dead, and had become a lackey for Death.

Uncomfortable silence was replaced by hushed, muted tones as the other women in the classroom whispered to each other behind cupped hands, pointing and gesturing, in turn, from Samantha to the dead lady staring at the ceiling impaled on Ticonderoga number two pencils and multi-colored Bic pens.

Amanda broke through the crowd, coming to a shocked stop next to Samantha. "What happened?" she asked, surprise and fear hitched in her tone. "Somebody just ran into the bathroom and told me that my friend killed someone."

Samantha watched Amanda step close to the body and slide her hands over the corpse's eyes, shutting them for eternity.

"I didn't mean to kill her, Mandy. I just wanted them to stop fighting."

Amanda shook her head, disgusted. "It looks like you showed her, didn't you, Sam? I thought you'd changed, but you haven't. You're the same bully you always were. You don't care about anyone except yourself!"

Samantha gasped, the harsh words erasing the last wisps of rage circulating through her bloodstream. "You don't mean that, Mandy. You're the only person left on this planet that I know."

Amanda laughed, the hollow sound resounding through the quiet room. "That doesn't mean that we're friends, Sam," she said and walked out of the room, the horde of prying eyes and ears parting for her to pass.

"Thank you," said a hushed voice behind Samantha. Samantha turned to confront the battered face of the remaining fighter.

"Leave me alone," Samantha said, sliding her hand into her pocket and fingering the red paper hand.

The woman reached out and grasped Samantha's shoulder with bony fingers attached to busted knuckles. "Wait, hear me out, I want to tell you something to repay you. You don't have anything to lose."

Samantha thought for a moment and nodded.

*   *   *

His hands were handcuffed behind his back, his feet tied together in a random mess of knots. She could tell, even in the dim light of the elementary school's storage basement, that he was tall, muscular and unmarked by pox scars or open sores.

Samantha stood staring, her mouth gaping wide open, until Kate, the woman who had survived the scuffle, spoke.

"I found him hiding down here this afternoon, about an hour or so after *Exodus* lifted off. I conked him on the head with that shovel," she said, pointing to a dirt-caked shovel on the concrete floor of the dank room, "and then cuffed and tied him."

"Okay," Samantha said, struggling to absorb the details into her muddy mind. "What about the fight upstairs? What was that all about?"

Kate sighed, squatting down and picking chunks of coagulated earth from the tip of the metal shovel and rubbing the soil between her fingers. "She walked in just as I finished tying him up. I told her 'let's just keep this between us', but she wouldn't listen. She said she was going to trade him for food and other stuff."

Bile burned the back of Samantha's throat. The man, bound and shackled, was the most precious resource left on Earth; a living commodity to be traded and used. She spared another look in the man's direction, his head held high, pride and fear lurking in the murky depths of his gray eyes.

He reminded her of a tiger she had seen on a fifth-grade field trip to the zoo, caged and subdued, but with a feral ferocity concealed behind his tame, meek demeanor.

She shivered, rubbing her hands against her upper arms for warmth.

"Then what happened?" Samantha prodded.

"I told her we could split whatever we could get for trading time with him. I'm almost fifty years old. I've buried two sons and lost a daughter in the riots. I can't have children. But I know there are plenty of women left on this planet who're willing to give me anything I want in exchange for a night or two with this guy."

Samantha buried her hands in her pockets, caressing the construction paper cut-out. What would she do for an opportunity at motherhood?

She wasn't sure she was ready to face the darkness within her.

"And the dead lady had a different plan?"

Kate barked out a harsh laugh. "No, she thought it was a great plan. But she didn't want me for a partner. She said she had a twin sister in one of the classrooms, and she wasn't interested in a three-way-split. I tried to get her with the shovel, the same way I took him down," she said, gesturing toward the man, "but she was quick and took off running to get her sister before I could stop her. I caught up to her in the hallway outside the room you were in, and things went south from there."

Samantha crouched down next to Kate. "So why are you telling me all of this?"

Kate stopped chipping dirt off the tool. "I can't do this by myself. I proved that upstairs. If it weren't for you, I would probably be dead. I need a partner, somebody strong."

Samantha fell silent, going over the choices in her head. Reaching a decision, she yanked the shovel off the ground and hopped to her feet in one smooth motion, swinging the shovel executioner-style through the air in a powerful arc. The sharp side of the shovel's head sliced half-way through Kate's neck.

Blood spurted out of the partially decapitated head, pouring down Kate's body and collecting in a macabre pool on the concrete. The corpse dropped to the dirt, twitched for a few seconds, and remained still.

Samantha dropped the makeshift weapon to the ground, the clattering noise jarring her to reality, spurring her to quick action. She fished through the pockets of Kate's pants and coat until she found keys, then hurried to the corner where the man watched with a stunned expression. Tiny droplets of blood blemished his otherwise perfect complexion.

"Can I trust you?" she asked, hesitating to remove the handcuffs from the large man. She had no doubt he could easily overpower her. "I want to help you."

His measured gaze bore into hers. Finally, he nodded.

"Say it out loud. Tell me I can trust you," she demanded, fitting the key into the small lock of the metal cuffs.

"You can trust me. You have my word."

With a deft flick of her wrist, she freed him.

*   *   *

"Where're we headed?" he asked as they took a break from their brisk pace, their position concealed in a thick nest of trees and bushes that had survived the rampant fires.

Samantha lifted the water bottle to her mouth and took a long drink, then handed it to the man. They had been walking, jogging and running for hours. Her body ached with fatigue, her muscles tight and tired.

"My house is a mile or so away. If we stay off the main road, we should be safe. Most people around here are at the shelter, so we shouldn't run into anybody."

"Okay," he agreed, handing the water bottle back to her. "Why are you doing this? Why did you let me go?"

She looked away from him, toward the direction of her house. "It was the right thing to do."

He chewed over her words, then accepted her statement. "I couldn't believe that I escaped quarantine to be captured by an old woman. It was pretty embarrassing," he chuckled, a low, genuine rumble.

"I'll bet," Samantha bantered, at ease in the man's presence. "A big guy like you taken down by little ol' Kate? Good thing your buddies weren't around to see it."

She regretted the words the minute she spoke them, the easy camaraderie stifled by unpleasant memories. For a moment she let herself forget the devastating aftermath of The Fevers.

He broke the awkward silence with a crooked smile, putting a large, gentle hand on her shoulder. "Hey, don't worry about it. I know what you meant." He dropped his hand to his side. "Anyway, we should start walking. The sooner we get to your place, the better I'll feel."

Samantha returned his smile, falling into step beside him, as they resumed traveling. "How did you do it?" she asked, overwhelmed with curiosity.

"What?" he asked, swatting away a tree branch blocking their path. "Get off *Exodus*? I hid underneath a heap of dead bodies. They threw them into a burn pit before the ship took off. I waited until I heard the shuttle leave, then I crawled out."

Samantha shivered with revulsion. "That's the grossest thing I've ever heard. And I've heard a lot of stuff since The Fevers spread."

He shrugged. "You gotta do what you gotta do. I refused to spend the rest of my life a prisoner or a guinea pig for some science experiment. Once they realized that I was immune to The Fevers, I would never be free."

She thought back to when she punched the woman in the classroom, then to when she killed Kate in the basement. She did what she had to do. She couldn't fault him for doing the same.

"What's your name, anyway?" she asked, realizing they had never introduced themselves. "I'm Samantha. Samantha Yeager."

He stopped and held out his right hand. "Nice to meet you, Samantha. I'm Kevin Johnson."

She frowned. "Kind of a generic name for the last living guy on Earth," she muttered, stupidly disappointed.

He laughed. "What did you expect?"

"I don't know," she replied, gripping his extended hand in a firm shake. Then she took the lead, trail-blazing a path to her childhood home. "Adam, or something biblical, I guess."

She reached into her pocket for the paper hand and fiddled with the worn creases.

His warm, callused hand was more comforting than the paper one.

*   *   *

They locked themselves in the basement of the old Victorian the Yeager family had owned for generations. Samantha was comforted by the smell of her things and the photographs of her family hanging crookedly on the hallway walls.

"How long do you think we'll have to stay holed up in here?" Kevin asked.

Samantha looked around the sparse room, grateful she left a couple of jugs of water and her mother's jarred preserves behind. A twelve-gauge shotgun and a box of shells rested on an otherwise empty metal shelf. She hadn't declared them as part of her trade agreement for passage aboard *Exodus*.

Maybe she always knew she would never escape Earth. She marveled at the contradiction between herself and Kevin. She had pawned off everything of value in a post-apocalyptic nightmare for a chance to leave the diseased and broken world behind; Kevin risked life and limb to remain on Earth.

"I don't know. Until we figure out a better plan, I guess." Her heart skipped a beat when she heard light footsteps shuffle across the floor above them.

"Shhhh," Kevin sounded, crossing his index finger over his lips.

Samantha nodded, and stood still. Moments later, someone tried to open the hatch to the basement. She reached over and slid the shotgun off the shelf. She checked the barrel, making sure it was loaded, then lifted it to her shoulder.

"Sammy?" a scared voice called out from upstairs. "Are you down there?"

Samantha lowered the gun. "Mandy?" she cried out. "Is that you?"

"Yes, yes, it's me. Open up."

She handed Kevin the gun and walked to the stairs to unlock the door. He shook his head, his brow furrowed. "What if she isn't alone?" he mouthed.

Samantha paused. "Who's with you?" she asked loudly, her voice echoing through the empty cellar.

"Nobody! Come on, Sammy. I'm all alone up here! Let me in!"

Convinced, Samantha unlocked the hatch door and Amanda climbed down the stairs. "Thank God I found you. I felt so bad after..." her voice trailed off when she spied Kevin standing in the room, clutching a loaded gun. "Oh my goodness, Sammy. You've got a man down here!"

"Relax, Mandy," Samantha murmured, wrapping her arms around her friend's large frame. "I'm glad that you found me, too. How did you know where to look?"

"Ummm, I couldn't find you anywhere and I figured you went home. Halfway here I thought that maybe I should turn around and go back to the shelter, but I wanted you to know you're my friend, and I shouldn't have said what I said back in the classroom. I don't want to be alone, either." Amanda's gazed was still fixed on Kevin.

"It's okay, Mandy. It was quite a shock." She pulled out of her friend's embrace, and made introductions. "Kevin, this is Mandy. We went to school together. Mandy, this is Kevin. Don't ask how we met. It's a long story and I'll tell you all about it some other time."

Kevin and Amanda nodded hellos, each taking silent inventory of the other. Finally, the mood relaxed, and the three sat down in a circle on the floor and shared a jar of wild strawberry jam.

*   *   *

The business end of the shotgun barrel nudged Samantha out of a sound sleep. She opened her eyes and saw Kevin next to her, unconscious, with a large gash at his hairline. Amanda was above her, pressing the weapon into her side.

"Get up, Sammy. We're going outside."

"What's going on, Mandy? What are you doing?" Samantha rose to a seated position, then rolled onto her knees and stood. "We're friends."

Amanda shook her head in disagreement, her frizzy, dull, brown hair dancing wildly with the motion. "You're just so lucky, Samantha Yeager. You found the only man left on Earth and you're going to keep him all to yourself. What did you expect me to do? Sit around and watch him fall for you? Pretend that I'm asleep while he makes love to you and puts a baby inside of you? You always get *everything* you want, and I get the leftovers!" She poked Samantha in the stomach, hard. "Now get up the stairs!"

Samantha did as instructed and climbed the wooden stairs attached to the wall of the basement. She scooted out the hatch with Amanda and the shotgun hot on her heels.

"Don't even think about running, Sammy, or I'll make this painful. Just do as you're told and it'll all be over quick. Put your hands up and walk out the back door to the old wishing well."

The well was in the backyard, shaded by a giant black walnut tree. It had been partially filled years ago, when she was a child, but there was still enough room left to hold a body.

Samantha lifted her hands above her head and walked at a slow, sedate pace until they reached the stone circumference of the well.

Amanda peered down the barrel of the gun. "Jump inside."

Samantha looked down into the dark, damp hollow and cringed. She had always been terrified of tight spaces, and Amanda was well aware of her claustrophobia. Her vision narrowed and her breath came in shallow, gulping gasps as she envisioned herself entombed in the well.

The shotgun slammed into her shoulder, knocking her backward. "Go!" Amanda screamed, shoving her harder with the weapon.

Samantha was too terrified to cry. She climbed into the decrepit hole, her body shaking and convulsing with terror. "Please, Mandy, please don't do this," she pleaded.

She was hanging on the stone rim, her fingers gripping the perimeter. Amanda brought down the bottom of the gun's handle onto the exposed digits, crushing them, until Samantha lost hold and fell ten feet to the bottom of the abandoned water source.

She looked up, the glare of the sun obscuring her view until Amanda's hulking frame blocked out the rays and shadowed the well. Samantha closed her eyes as Amanda shouldered the gun and took aim, imagining the burning bite of the bullet as it passed through her brain.

She counted down the final seconds of her life.

One, two, three.

She held her breath, choked with fright.

Four, five, six.

Images of her mom, dad, and brothers floated across her mind. She pulled the red paper hand out of her pocket and clutched it between her shaking hands, taking a small measure of comfort from a third-grader's art project.

Seven, eight, nine.

She grinded her teeth, expecting a loud boom followed by nothing.

Ten.

She was still alive.

Samantha opened her eyes and saw Kevin holding the shotgun down to her. She grasped the barrel and held on while he lifted her out of the well.

Amanda was in a crumpled heap on the dead and yellow lawn, her thick neck twisted at an unnatural angel. Samantha watched as Kevin scooped up Amanda and tossed her into the well, then glanced down at the wrinkled and torn paper cutout in her hand. She dropped the red memento into the dark hole and watched as it drifted down to rest over Amanda's heart.

"Thank you," she said, regaining some of her composure.

"I said you could trust me," he smiled.

THE VERY LAST ONE

LANCE LOOPER

A few months after Avery's mom and sister disappeared; her dad showed her a satellite photo of the United States. He actually showed her two photos. One was taken before the crisis started and the other a few months later. The photos showed the continent in total darkness and timestamps at the bottom of both said they had been taken at three a.m. Eastern Standard Time. The first one showed hundreds of tiny pinpoints of light, with large clusters of these pinpoints where the big cities were. The second photograph had only a single tiny string of pinpoints right down the center, cutting the country in almost two equal halves. The little stars of light were sporadic, with just a few places where there were clusters.

"It's a highway," her dad told her as she looked at the screen. "There're people there and that's where we need to be." His tone was gentle but resolute.

By then all of their neighbors were gone; some disappeared with Avery's mom and Jackie, but others had packed up and left trying to run away from whatever was happening. Her dad didn't believe that was possible and wanted to stay put. He'd never mentioned leaving until he showed her those pictures.

They left their house in Illinois and marched west for nearly three weeks until they came to the place the lights were supposed to be. When they got there, it looked just as desolate and abandoned as everything else on their journey.

"Dad," she said as they walked onto a freeway and headed south. The pavement was growing thick with grass but if you looked close you could see the white stripes under the growth.

"Yes, sweetheart?" he asked.

"Where are we?"

"Good question, Ave," he said as he stopped and pulled off his backpack. "But I'll tell you." From the front pocket of his backpack he pulled out the folded satellite picture. "I think, Avery, that when I saw all these lights over here," his index finger traced the line of pinpoints. "And thought about us way over here," his finger moved to the blackness over Illinois, "that was the first time I realized just how lonely we were.

"I guess that's what it took to convince me that we needed to be around other people," he said. "Though from the looks of things we'll have to walk a little bit longer."

So they walked the rest of the day until they came to a line of tractor-trailers lined up along the shoulder of the highway. Nobody was around, but it was clear people had been there recently. They decided to pitch their tent a good distance away from the trucks; close enough for them to see if anyone showed up, but far enough away so they wouldn't cause any alarm.

Avery was asleep when she heard the first rumblings of people. The noise was so alien to her it took several minutes to figure out they were voices. She jammed her dad's sleeping back with her foot but it was empty. She tentatively unzipped the tent, just far enough so she could peek through. A group of people were gathered at the rear of one of the opened trailers. All along the line of trucks, the doors of the trailers were being shoved open and people were streaming out. Lights went on all along the highway and in just a few minutes the street that was pitch black when Avery had gone to sleep was lit up like a carnival. She spotted her dad with a group of men near the first trailer and relief washed over her.

The men were gathered around her dad, the way men always did, and she could tell by the way his hands were moving that he was deep into some baseball story. Avery knew the routine like a poem and though she couldn't hear him, she was certain that his southern accent was shining through. Anytime he talked about baseball, he slipped back into that drawl where the emphasis is always on the first syllable of a word. Behind. Outfield. Sumbitch.

The men were gathered around him, soaking in every word, and if this had been three years earlier the group would probably be passing around his World Series ring by now. Avery's mother hated the way he'd take it off and hand it to anybody who asked. In restaurants, at the movies, in the hardware store, it didn't matter. He wore it everywhere and loved it when people noticed. He'd tell

Avery and her mom that the ring could be replaced or that he might just win another one some day, but that might be the only chance he'd ever have to be nice to that person.

The first few days at the encampment along the highway were spent talking to the people, finding out how long they'd been there and listening to everyone's theories about what happened on The Tenth. That was the day Avery's mom took her and her little sister for a walk, October 10th. Avery was thirteen at the time and her sister Jackie was only four.

That day was a little windy and looked like rain, but Avery's mother wanted to go for a walk. The three of them hadn't gone very far when Avery noticed her shoe had come untied. She let go of Jackie's hand and bent down to tie it, and noticed that all at once an awful, metallic smell filled the air. It was like she could taste whatever was in the air. It reminded her of the time when she was six and her friend dared her to put a handful of pennies in her mouth.

She tied her shoe in a double knot and looked up, but her mother and Jackie were gone. She stood up and looked around, down the street, and then back toward their house, but they were nowhere to be seen. Her dad was at home by himself and didn't notice anything out of the ordinary, not even the metal smell.

That's where Avery was on The Tenth, but she didn't like thinking about it if she could help it. She left the theories to others, and like her dad, didn't see much point in trying to figure it out. She knew her mom and Jackie weren't coming back. She wasn't sure why she knew, she just did.

What they learned in those first few days was that gathering along the highway was more or less an accident. The people left in the towns along the highway started making their way in that direction. And the more people came, the more people just kept showing up. It seemed to work pretty good because people seemed to have what they needed. There were big community gardens and wells had been dug where these communities cropped up along the route.

Pretty soon they told Avery's dad about their idea to organize and consolidate everyone in one area. The more people and resources they have in one spot, they said, the better it'd be for everyone. But to make that happen, someone would have to go talk to each of these communities in person and everyone was scared to go. They couldn't be sure everyone was friendly and were afraid of how they'd react to a stranger showing up.

But, they said, if someone were willing to go whom everyone already knew, that would probably increase the likelihood they would cooperate. And since Avery's dad was a celebrity, they could be reasonably sure they'd recognize him and even welcome him. Plus, if he were traveling with Avery, any perceived threat would be further mitigated.

So Avery helped her dad pack their gear and they hit the road for what would be a very long and interesting existence walking up and down the overgrown highway. They would be meeting the people who made up the last and largest neighborhood on Earth.

Not very long ago Interstate 35 had been just another sorry stretch of road; a loathsome, deadly highway that bisected the United States damn near down the middle and connected the northernmost tip of Minnesota with the southern tip of Texas.

It took almost an entire year for Avery and her dad to cover the entire distance the first time. On that trip he would tell her about the cities that used to populate the route. In Oklahoma he told her about how a crazy man blew up a building and killed a bunch of kids. In San Antonio he told her about Davey Crocket and the Alamo. Avery couldn't understand how someone could be both a mountain man and a congressman, but then she was just sixteen and there was plenty she didn't understand.

During that first trip, they met with every village south of where they first arrived at the highway. Everyone was friendly and welcoming and they treated Avery's dad like a movie star. They listened as he told them about the people they'd met and about the idea to gather everyone together in one place. It was clear from the start that this idea was not going to be popular, so before too long they stopped bringing it up altogether. But they continued their travels, trading tips on growing different crops or how to build a system to catch rainwater.

When they finally got back to their original encampment, they didn't stay long. Avery's dad decided it was important for all of these little enclaves to know what the others were doing and that the two of them could fill that need by staying on the road full time and keeping tabs on how all of these little communities were doing. If there were droughts in Texas, then they would know and could arrange for carriages to ship water from the north. It was a service welcomed by everyone along the highway and people even wrangled and broke wild horses for Avery and her dad to ride so they didn't have to cover so much distance on foot.

Avery named her horse Jack because it reminded her of her sister. Jack was brown and white and had a star shaped marking on his muzzle.

As they made their way up and down I-35 on these ambassadorial trips, Avery's dad would marvel at how such an unremarkable landmark could now be the center of the world. Having seen both ends over the course of the past couple of years, Avery shared her dad's amusement. She could speak with authority about how both points were wickedly desolate, one buried in snow and the other in dust. And how the more than 1,500 miles in between didn't change all that much. There were no purple mountains majesty and the fruited planes were neglected and reclaimed by nature.

Today they were due in St. Paul, where the northern-most outpost was cloistered. It was January and the cold was biting as Avery dismounted Jack. Besides the icy wind it was eerily quiet. Even for this particular outpost, which was typically the least populated of all their stops, it was unusual that someone wasn't out and about. Usually there were even people waiting for them. But there was just the wind to greet them today.

Avery followed her dad toward an outbuilding that served as the encampment's main shelter. He was moving a little more cautious than Avery was comfortable with and it made her nervous to see him uneasy. He was about forty feet in front of her when he tilted his nose into the air and took a long drag from the biting wind.

"Smell that?" he asked, turning back to Avery. Then something flashed in his eyes and he held up his hand, signaling Avery to stay put. She watched him walk toward the side of the outbuilding and look around the corner. When he cleared the turn, he tumbled backward in the snow, scrambling from whatever it was he'd found.

He sat in the snow for a second, looking toward the wall. "My God."

"What is it, Daddy?" Avery piped up.

"Stay there, sweetheart."

She knew if ever there was a time to obey, this was it. But she couldn't. Her feet shuffled forward almost without her knowing and she peered around the corner. Against the wall of the outbuilding were the bodies of eleven people. They were sitting up, lined up neatly next to each other. Had it been springtime, they might have even looked alive. But the snowdrifts covered most of their lower halves and their faces were frozen in terror. Their eyes and mouths were open and there was a woman on the end who had tipped over. Avery could see that her hands and feet were tied with rope.

All at once the smell hit Avery and she came close to passing out.

"Ave," her dad said, running towards her. "I told you to stay put." But she could tell he wasn't mad at her. "Get Jack," he said. "We're leaving."

The two of them mounted their horses and thundered away from the encampment. It took all Avery had to keep up with her father and he showed no signs of slowing down. Here in the north, the encampments were farther between and Avery knew it was at least two days' ride to the next one. She wondered if her dad meant to run all the way there.

Then she was seized with fear when she realized what he was doing. For some reason, maybe it was the cold or maybe because she was so tired, but it was only now she realized that what happened to those people had to have been done by other people. Then she understood the urgency and raked Jack with the heels of her feet, getting him to give her that little bit extra she always knew he had in his tank.

They got to the next encampment just before noon. It was also eerily quiet and Avery could tell her dad was rattled.

"Stay as close to me as possible," he said. "If anything happens, take Jack and ride west. Stay as far away from the highway as possible."

There was no snow on the ground here, but it was just as cold. There were a line of tractor-trailers that had become the standard communal shelter for these outposts and they were all shut up and looked abandoned. Avery watched her dad smash one of the locks with a hammer and push the door open. She didn't have to see this time; the way he dropped the hammer and bowed his head said they'd been too late.

"Jesus," he said. It might have been the closest to tears she'd ever seen him. Even when her mom and Jackie disappeared, he was stoic. That scared Avery even more than having killers on the loose.

"We can make it to Harris in just a couple of hours," she said, hoping to stoke whatever optimism he had left.

"Avery, you don't understand. We were through here, what, a month ago? And I can't tell for sure of course, but this didn't just happen. It might have been weeks."

"What does that mean?" she asked.

"People are doing this, and you and I are probably the only ones that know it's happening. If we're this far behind whoever they are, there might not be anybody left to save."

Avery couldn't fight back the tears that came this time. The thought of losing everyone again was too much. She sat down on the cold, snowy grass and cried. He sat down and hugged her.

"Daddy," she said.

"Yes?"

"There's someone sitting in the car over there."

He stood up and turned toward the junk cars. Sitting behind the wheel of an antique pick-up was the hulking silhouette of a man. Avery was frozen in place and couldn't muster a sound when he moved toward the car. The door of the truck swung open but the man at the wheel didn't try to get out.

"Hey!" her dad yelled. His tone was perfectly even, neither threatening nor alarmed. "Who are you?" he yelled again. And with that the man stepped down from the cab of the truck and started running toward one of the outbuildings. Her dad bolted after him and was on him before he could get very far. He grabbed him by both shoulders and dragged him to the ground. As the man rolled over, he swung wildly at her father, connecting a solid blow to the side of his face. Avery's blood ran cold when her dad crumpled in a heap beside the man. The man's arm fell to his side, and from his hand, the hand he'd hit her dad with, a rock dropped to the ground.

He shoved her dad's limp body off him and it came to rest in an impossibly awkward position, doubled over at the waist. Avery watched the man stand up and start towards her. Her mind raced but she couldn't get the message to her body.

"Do you know what you are?" the man screamed at her. "Do you know what we are?"

His voice, deep and grating, was the wake-up call her legs needed. She spun around and sprinted to the highway, jumping over the short cement barrier. She stopped just long enough to look back and saw him chasing her. She crossed the highway, jumped the barrier on the other side, and ran into the field of tall coastal grass. She ran with everything she had and could have gone even longer but she spotted a rock outcropping and thought it might make a good place to hide. She veered left toward the rocks but as soon as she did, she realized it was a bad plan. The rock outcropping was the only thing you could see in the vast expanse of chest-high grass and that made it the most obvious hiding place. She'd be found out there for sure. She snuck a look behind her and he wasn't there, so she decided to continue to the rock. At least from the top she would be able to see the entire field and tell if he was still chasing her.

She was running so fast she had to brace herself from smacking into the sheer rock face. She was drawing deep, raspy breaths and looked at the stone facade to see where she could start her ascent. Finding a suitable first foothold, she made it to the top in just a few graceful movements, despite the burning in her chest.

At the top she sat down and her breathing eased. Surveying the field, she could see no trace of the man but could clearly see the path of trampled grass she left. She thought about how easy it would be for him to just lie down in the grass and disappear. She needed to get off this rock as soon as possible, but she needed to sit and catch her breath. She went to slide her backpack off and froze when she remembered it wasn't there. Her heart sank.

There was no way she'd make it very far without her pack. When the sun goes down it would get close to freezing and she wouldn't last until morning. She looked toward the encampment, the tractor-trailers were tiny white squares on the horizon, and wondered if he'd gone back.

She would have to go back; there was no way around it. But she would wait until dark. In the meantime, she had to get off this rock and find a place to stay put for a few hours.

She climbed down and sat in the grass a few hundred yards away. While waiting for dark, she had plenty of time, too much time maybe, to think about what had happened today. She held no hope that her dad was alive. The way he fell when the man hit him told her that. And even if he did survive the blow, could there be any doubt that the man who did it was the same as who had been killing everyone? Just one man had killed all those people?

She knew the odds were good that by now her dad was lying in the tractor-trailer with the rest of the bodies. And if the killer had gone back to the encampment, their backpacks might not be there. But as she hid in the grass, she realized that she wasn't going back just to retrieve the backpacks, she had to make sure her father was truly dead.

There was no moon and no stars, and the plains looked like an ocean of black. She could make out the rock outcropping silhouetted against the horizon, but the encampment blended in with the rest of the landscape. She walked slowly, listening intently to the grass swaying in the breeze, listening for anything that didn't ring true. It took longer than she expected to get back to the highway; she must have run farther, faster, and longer during her escape this afternoon than she thought. When she got to the concrete barrier, she sat against it, training her eyes in the direction she'd come. She couldn't be sure, but nothing looked amiss in the darkness.

She peeked over the barrier towards the encampment. Their backpacks were right where they'd left them. Without considering it, she bounded over the barrier and across the highway. She squatted behind the second barrier and scanned the encampment - nothing. She sat on the barrier and swung her legs over, touching her feet down quietly on the other side. She went to the backpacks and knelt down next her father's. She opened a side compartment and pulled out a box of matches and a flashlight. Then she reached in another pocket and pulled out a six inch boning knife, unsheathing it and checking the edge of the blade. Her dad kept a sharp edge.

She slid the knife into her pants and tried to hoist the backpack onto her shoulder. Something tugged at the pack, then somewhere in the darkness a bell erupted. It clanged like an old-fashioned dinner bell. She examined the backpack and noticed a length of fishing line had been tied to it. The other end disappeared into the darkness. She gave it a little tug and the bell clanged again.

He was on her before she knew it, tackling her from behind as they crashed to the ground. His momentum carried him off her, long enough for her to check that the knife was still in her pants as she took off running. She looked back just as he was getting to his feet but she was fast and she could easily outrun him. When she turned back around, she ran straight into the tractor-trailer, face first, knocking herself cold.

When she came to, she was sitting in a chair.

Despite it being impossibly dark, she could tell she was inside. Her hands were bound behind her and her feet were tied to the chair. Some kind of cord, probably the same fishing line that was used to booby trap the backpack, bit into her wrists. She shifted slightly and let out a wince and a moan.

A match ignited in the darkness, for an instant throwing a splash of light on a man's face. It was just a flash, but she got a good look. She knew him. Not by name, but he was from one of the settlements along the highway. The match settled into its flame and he held it between them.

"You know what I am?" he croaked. "I'm the last person in the whole wide world!"

She tried loosening the bindings on her hands. It didn't give any, but she could tell her hands were only tied together, not tied to the chair. And she could feel the handle of the boning knife rubbing on her side. He didn't know she had it or he would have taken it.

"The last person anywhere!" he was practically cackling. She watched the match burn, the flame shaking in his hand, working its way towards his index finger and thumb. She wondered how long before he would blow it out. The flame worked its way down the blackening stem and he just watched her, ignoring the match even when it exhausted its fuel and extinguished itself between the pads of his fingers.

In the darkness, she went to work. She quietly pulled her arms to her side and was able to retrieve the knife. As carefully and quickly as she could, she spun the blade around in her hand and worked it between her wrists. The line snapped easily and silently when the blade's edge made contact.

The room was again bathed in the light of a newly lit match, but Avery's hands were back behind her back and she was sure he wasn't wise to her escape plan.

"You ever think what it would be like to be the only one?" he asked. "I woke up one morning and thought to myself, 'self, good buddy, most of the work's been done for you. Might as well finish the job.'"

The match flickered and danced as he spat each word. It seemed to Avery that there was something sane left in this man, but that it was fading as fast as the match.

"I started at one end, the way you and your dad do. I was only a day or two behind you and I worked very fast. It's amazing the things you can get people to do when they think they've already lived through the worst this world has to offer! Get them all in one spot and the rest is easy." The flame was again snuffed out between his fingers and if he felt it, he hid it well.

Avery went to work on her feet and again the line surrendered easily to the knife. Her hands went back behind her back just as another match threw another flash of light onto her and her captor.

"Did you know that you can make cyanide using apple seeds?"

"You killed my father," she said, though it seemed like a reflex, like the words had been working this whole time to come out whether she wanted them to or not.

"I killed everyone!" he yelled. Then he scooted closer and held the match nearer to his face. "But not you." His voice softened and the words hung in the air, waiting for Avery to register their meaning. That is if the ramblings of a madman could mean anything. "We'll have to start over, me and you."

"There are others," Avery said. "The settlements weren't the only places people went."

The match went out and this time he hissed a little at the burn. "Have you seen any others?" he asked in the darkness. She heard him shuffle closer. "There are no others."

"Then do you know what that makes me?" she asked, again unsure of where the words were coming from.

Another match sparked to life and his face was only inches from hers. She could smell his acrid breath and she had to fight back her gag reflex.

"Tell me," he said, curiously. "What does that make you?"

"The last person!" she yelled as she buried the boning knife in his throat, all the way to the handle. He dropped the match and staggered backwards, then fell to the floor. He struggled with the knife, slipping and sliding in the blood pooling around him. The match ignited a pile of newspapers and the room was bathed in light. His gurgling stopped and in the firelight she could see that most of his blood was spilt on the floor. She left the growing fire blazing as she opened the door and walked out.

They had been in one of the outbuildings and the fire that was consuming it cast the entire encampment in light.

She went and found her father and he was dead, just as she'd thought, though prayed wasn't true. It was hard but she dragged his body to the fire, placing him on the edge. The ground was too hard for a proper burial, so cremation was as good as she could give him.

With tears in her eyes, but a firm jaw, Avery walked to where her and her father's packs were, picked hers up, and slung it onto her shoulders. She also fastened the waist belt the way she did when they were in for a particularly long walk.

With one last glance at the funeral pyre for her dad, she climbed over the barrier onto I-35 and headed south.

48

GREEN WORLD

B.L. BATES

Phase I: Outbreak

Unusual wind and heavy rainfall patterns noted in the northern United States have now been documented in parts of Europe and Asia. -- National Weather Service

Reports from the American Botanical Society announcing the discovery of new plant species have been confirmed. Similar reports from other countries are under investigation. -- American Botanical Society

Central Michigan

Wilma Baxter stood in her field under the hot, Michigan, midday sun, watching as seeds fell from the sky. She caught several in her hand. When the bounty ceased, she closed her hand and walked back to the house. This would be the third time this month seeds had fallen from the sky. God had smiled on her, and she would accept it, not search for a scientific explanation. All the *rainseeds* as she'd dubbed them, grew rapidly and produced more blossoms and fruit than other seeds.

In her kitchen, she sat down to examine the seeds.

Several looked like pumpkin or winter squash. Some were vegetable seeds. The rest were flowers or hay seeds.

She picked up a pumpkin seed and cracked it between her teeth. Warmth spread within her mouth, sending tingles of energy through her. She'd plant these seeds; they'd produce strong plants with magnificent fruit. Grabbing a straw hat, she went back to finish her chores.

Upper Maine

Ben Foreman slammed the window shut and cursed. He'd lost another batch of mutated mosquitoes. The gas should have made them lethargic. When he'd lifted the screen to put them into containers, they'd swarmed out *en masse*.

Even though he'd increased the potency of the gas each time, three batches had gotten out -- so far. If he didn't get some into the shipping container the next time, he'd have to tell Ruth something.

He couldn't admit three batches of mutated mosquitoes had managed to escape.

He shook the jar containing only a fraction of the altered insects. They would have to do. Creating another batch would be too risky.

Wait a minute. He could ship the mosquito eggs to her; yes, that would work.

He scratched the bites he'd gotten after the first batch escaped; he hadn't worn protective gloves. After donning the gloves, he opened the screen and used a glass container to scoop up the mosquito eggs.

When the container had been filled, sealed and put into a mailer with the few live specimens, he sighed with relief. He added the other items and called a local carrier.

The carrier acknowledged his authority call. He lied, telling them the shipment was for his employer, New Generations, a genetics research lab. The carrier told him they'd send out a truck within the hour.

He flopped down into a chair and tried to put the pieces of the puzzle he and Ruth had discovered together so they made sense.

Coastal Maine

Trevor Cashman pushed another grow table into the corridor of *Green World Labs* and turned back into the devastation he called *his* lab.

Flames rushed to meet him.

He slammed the door and pulled the Room Cleanse lever.

The door locked and the light above it flashed red. An alarm blared throughout the corridor and heat sensors came on along the ceiling.

Several figures burst through the door at the end of the corridor; a security guard and two Maintenance personnel. Scientists from other parts of the lab followed at a distance.

Ken Armstrong and Cindy Marshfield from Maintenance wore respirators and thick gloves in addition to their protective oversuit required for all personnel. They waited outside the door until the light flashed green. Armstrong pulled the lever down then unlocked the door.

Smoke billowed out and Marshfield held the others -- especially Trevor -- back while Armstrong investigated.

Those minutes lasted forever for Trevor. Didn't they realize his life's work had just been burned then sterilized by absorption foam? He had to see. What could be taking so long?

Armstrong emerged from the smoke. "The fire's out. The foam should be washed away. You'll need to file a report." He nodded to Marshfield and they left.

Trevor stood in the doorway and flipped the fans in his lab to high.

Within minutes, the smoke and fumes had been drawn into the filter system. A dull haze remained. Blackened husks of the prototype trees lifted burned, broken limbs to a nonexistent god. Beds of flowers and food crops had become fields of ash.

He turned the sprinklers on high.

Rain pelted the grow beds, leaving funnels as dirt left with the foam. Then the sprinklers fizzled and died.

He'd have to hose out the foam and check the sprinkler system.

When the foam was disposed of, he stood before the three foot diameter tree he'd grown in less than four months, and sighed. He'd been so close to finding a stable gene structure, allowing accelerated growth leading to reliable, mature plants.

He put his arms around the blackened trunk and tugged. The damaged roots, unable to maintain their grasp in the life-giving earth, released their hold.

The new growths were already over a foot high.

He turned and rolled the trunk toward the disposal unit.

New growths!

He disposed of the trunk. Then he raced back, falling to his knees where the tree had stood.

Two new shoots reached for the light, growing where the burned tree had stood.

His hands dug into the blackened soil.

New shoots for the grasses and different mosses had already begun to reach toward the surface. All the blackened soil and plant detritus had to be removed, pronto.

Later, as he finished cleaning up the burned debris, something fell into the dirt in front of him. He looked up and gaped as insulation dripped from the ceiling. This must be investigated, now.

Two hours later, he burst into the director, Dr. Stan Jackson's office carrying a box, and stopped short. Three unfamiliar people, one woman and two men, sat at the table with Dr. Jackson.

Dr. Jackson said to those at the table, "This is Trevor Cashman, our leading Accelerated Growth Specialist. Trevor, these are scientists working at our sister facilities."

Trevor grabbed a chair and slumped into it. "There are more facilities like ours?"

Dr. Jackson smiled. "Let me introduce them. Dr. Debi is the director of the African unit." A slender, dark-skinned woman with beaded hair nodded.

"Next to her is Dr. Ted Wagner, running our South American facility." A stout, coffee skinned, bald man glared at Trevor and nodded.

"And, Dr. Hans Szinger heads the European facility." A fair-haired man with brilliant green eyes smiled at Trevor.

"Agents from our Australian and Asian facilities aren't here as those establishments aren't up to speed," Dr. Jackson said.

Trevor felt the blood leave his face. There were five other plants...

"Is something wrong?" Dr. Debi said to Trevor.

Trevor looked at her. "Did you duplicate this facility and its processes exactly?"

Dr. Debi nodded. "To the letter. Why?"

"Because there's a problem, a big problem." He turned to Dr. Jackson. "May I speak to you privately?"

"Anything you can say to me, you can say to us all."

Trevor swallowed. "First the bad news. A fire started in my lab this morning; the sprinkler system failed."

Trevor removed a section of blackened wires from the box he'd brought. "This is what's left of the insulation around the electrical wiring. Most of it has been eaten away."

Before anyone could speak, he took out another blackened mass from the box. "And this is part of the filter system from the storage silos next to my lab."

"Let me see that filter." Dr. Szinger held out his hand.

Trevor gave him the filter.

"It's the wrong size. It's too small."

"It wasn't when it went in, two days ago. It was eaten away," Trevor said.

"What are you saying?" Dr. Jackson squirmed.

"Half of our stored seeds are gone. Some kind of microbe, or bacteria, or whatever, has also been mutated by our genetic alteration process. It's eaten through every polyfilter, poly-joint, and most of the electrical insulation. All the polyfilters and poly-joints have been checked and look like that."

"What else?" Dr. Jackson clenched his fist.

"Half of our mutated seeds and all of the delta variant seeds are gone."

"That's impossible. The deltas have been kept under positive pressure."

"Dr. James, our Climate Specialist, claims these microbes, or whatever, have the ability to affect the air pressure. So, not only have they released the seeds, they've changed the weather patterns to aid in their dispersal." Trevor banged the table.

"It never showed up in the simulations," Dr. Jackson said.

Trevor clenched his teeth to keep from screaming. "Bullshit! I went through the simulations; they showed up in three out of seven. Why wasn't it mentioned?"

Dr. Jackson paled. "We took precautions to avoid this probability."

Trevor gritted his teeth. "It seems they didn't work. If the other facilities are like ours, then they've been releasing seeds and microbes into the atmosphere, too."

"We may be jumping the gun, as you say," Dr. Szinger said. "How long has this been going on?"

Trevor shook his head. "No way to tell."

"There have been no reports of detrimental effects to date," Dr. Szinger said.

Trevor felt light-headed, what was this idiot saying? "Not only has over half a ton of mutated, fast-growing, extremely productive seeds been let loose in a non-monitored environment, but possibly several other types of mutated lower life forms as well. All of these altered forms have the ability to reproduce extremely early and often. To mutate to fit environmental changes, and have an extended life span."

"Trevor, did you have something you wanted to show us about your lab?" Dr. Jackson asked to diffuse Trevor's growing volatility.

Trevor took several deep breaths. "Yes." He took out some digital photos. "The good news. Like I said, an unexpected fire started in my lab. The sprinkler system failed. The area was sealed, the air sucked out and the entire lab was sterilized with foam. Despite all that, new shoots have already started. I had a tech take these." He pushed the photos toward Dr. Jackson.

Dr. Szinger snatched the photos. "My God, we've done it."

"But not according to plan," Dr. Debi said. "We've lost control of the experiment. Unknown are the rate of mutation, their ability to overwhelm local populations, how far the take-over will extend, and a way to control them."

"One could accuse you of helping plants take over the Earth," Dr. Wagner said.

Dr. Jackson clenched both fists. "How can you say that? We've spent our lives trying to return Earth to a stable yet productive environment. Consensus of the genetic organizations granted us the time and resources to try and 'regrow' the Earth back to health. We gave it our best."

"But something's got to be done!" Dr. Wagner pounded the table.

"Do you want us to find a way to kill off the experimental species it's taken us years to produce?" Dr. Jackson said.

Dr. Hans Szinger shook his head. "There's no way to stop the advanced rates of growth and propagation, not without killing off every other plant and probably insect species on the planet."

Dr. Jackson took a deep breath. "Then we've got to get the word out to every genetics lab in the world; to let them know about any 'new' species they find, and to do an in-depth genetic analysis on them. And to send the reports to us."

"What will that gain us?" Dr. Debi asked.

"It will tell the extent and amount of genetic alteration. And hopefully, it will buy us time to find a way to control the plants' rapid expansion."

If they can be controlled, Trevor thought but kept silent.

Northern California

Ruth Adams debated whether or not to call Ben. She didn't want to nag, but she needed more information. Besides, he'd piqued her curiosity by his reports of Maine's weather. Similar patterns had begun here, in northern California.

Her curiosity aroused, she decided to call her Aunt Wilma in Michigan.

"Aunt Wilma?"

"Ruth. How good to hear from you. Did your brothers call?"

A sick sensation hit Ruth's stomach. "No, why? Is everything okay?"

"Right as rain," Wilma giggled. "They're working here and are doing fine."

Her voice lowered. "Ruth, seeds have been falling from Heaven. And they grow fast and bountiful."

Had Aunt Wilma finally lost it? "I called to check on the weather you're having out there. Anything strange?"

"It's been raining a lot, and the wind's acting funny."

"Funny how?"

"Picking stuff up and putting it down somewhere else, without harming it."

Confirmation. "And you're doing okay? I miss the old farm."

"You'll always have a place here. And things are doing better than fine."

"Okay, I just wanted to check. Bye." Ruth replaced the receiver.

She'd made a map of the weather patterns. Weather forecasts on the Internet worked okay, but talking to a person felt better. Weather similar to Maine and now Michigan and here had shown up in Europe, Africa, and now, South America.

She picked up the telephone and punched Ben's number.

"Hello?" Ben said.

"It's Ruth. Two things. First, is the weather there still the same?"

"If anything, it's gotten more unpredictable. Short bursts of heavy rain and unusual wind patterns."

"It's started here as well. And I called Wilma; she's noticed the same rain and wind patterns.

Ruth took a breath. "Did you get the samples out?"

"The results were as we feared. I express mailed the samples of insects and their eggs; they should be there late tomorrow."

She felt the blood drain from her face. "You're sure about the locations of the insects you gathered?"

"Right near the holes in the exhaust system. There was some kind of mold or fungus growing around the holes; the insects were feeding on it. Ruth, the fungus moved when I touched it."

"And nothing happened on the ride back, right?"

"It's less than an hour. Nothing happened."

Ruth held her breath until her head stopped spinning. It could be worse than she'd imagined. "Tell me what you did."

"I collected enough of the gas to fill the chamber twice. And I hatched some of the insects inside the gas-filled chamber. I sent those."

"I couldn't find examples of the insects that hatched in any of the books. Their mutation rate must have gone through the roof. All the insects were green."

"You took pictures?"

"Of course; even some of the growth around the holes near the exhaust."

"Can you Email me the photos?"

"Sure, let me know if you come up with anything. Take care."

The dial tone buzzed in her ear. She sat, looking at the telephone receiver for a long time.

Phase II: Expansion
Excessive amounts of mosquitoes and black flies have been noted in many areas of the country. The high amounts of precipitation, humidity, and temperatures could account for the increase. -- National Weather Service
The Urban Planning Association (UPA) and Urban Transit Authorities (UTA) have issued a report concerning the 'take-over' of plants, most classified as weeds, in some major US cities. These plants have rooted through our roadways and into buildings, and into the water and sewage systems. Normal extermination measures have proven ineffective. -- UPA and UTA survey

Central Michigan
Wilma mowed, for the second time this week, the hay in the field. The other seeds she'd planted from the *rainseeds* had practically taken over the fields. Three truckloads of produce had already been brought into town and sold.

Some of the hay had been fed to her own cows and goats. And the wheat auns had fed her chickens. These *rainseeds* would grow anywhere, and practically matured overnight.

Her years of piety and devotion had finally paid off. She'd say an extra prayer of thanks tonight.

But before she went inside, she'd have to gather another load of eggs, and milk the cows and goats for the third time today. Bless God and Her bounty.

Upper Maine
Ben applied more moisturizer to his arms and chest. No matter how much he used, his skin still felt scaly and rough. True, he'd spent more time outside lately, but that explained his tan, not the condition of his skin.

He sat near the open window, catching the last of the sun's rays. Unfiltered sunlight felt good; he couldn't get enough.

Later, he got up to water his plants.

Greenery covered every flat surface in his living room and bedroom. More pots filled the other rooms. The plants comforted him and brought a sense of peace.

The telephone rang.

"This is Ruth. Turn on your TV, there's a special broadcast!"

Ben reached over and turned on the television, pushing tendrils of ivy off the screen.

A commentator gestured to a destroyed building behind him. *"According to the landlord, intrusive plant life is responsible for the collapse of this apartment building. Tenants have raised a cry that substandard materials were used. An investigation is underway. Watch our special at seven."*

The mass of rubble showed plant stalks and tendrils woven through the building's outer walls; through brick and concrete.

"Ruth, did it say why the building collapsed?" Ben asked.

"A tenant said another tenant didn't like plants and tried to fumigate her apartment. Obviously the plants didn't like it and fought back."

"That's not funny, Ruth."

"It wasn't meant to be."

Ben felt the vibration as the plants moved to see the screen. He turned the TV off, not wanting to upset *his* plants.

"What should we do?" Ben said.

"Take good care of our charges and let the unbelievers reap what they've sown."

"Okay. Take care."

"You, too."

Ben replaced the receiver. What if the plants wanted things to return to a time before man gained dominance? No, that was a ridiculous thought.

At least, he hoped it was.

Coastal Maine

"You can't prove the plants that caused the destruction in the city came from our seeds," Dr. Jackson stated.

"So, give me another plausible explanation," Dr. Ted Wagner said.

"I can't," Dr. Jackson sighed and shook his head.

"And none of the experiments to control or eradicate these growths has born fruit?" Dr. Una Debi asked.

Dr. Jackson turned to the African geneticist. "Every time we find a solution, the plants mutate, making the solution unviable."

"Could be a form of intelligence," she mumbled. I've heard reports that insects have also been affected."

"If there have been mutations in these populations, we don't have the facilities to investigate."

Dr. Debi tapped a pen. "We're checking out the theory that a mutated form of chlorophyll is responsible for the insect mutations."

Dr. Jackson frowned. "Chlorophyll isn't a part of an insect's make-up. Neither animals, birds, fish nor insects have the correct cellular structure to utilize it."

"This mutated chlorophyll is different. It can thrive in cells other than plants. We've found mutated chloroplasts in insect cells," Dr. Debi said.

"But, these insects would be green." Dr. Jackson's frown deepened.

"There have been reports of green insects for weeks now. And the analysis of these insects reveals chloroplasts in their cells." Dr. Debi pushed a report to Dr. Jackson.

"In addition," Dr. Debi continued, "our scientists have determined the size of the Sahara desert has shrunken by ten percent. The mutated vegetation has been thriving upon the desert sands. So, not only have the escaped mutated organisms begun altering the climate, but the characteristics of the Earth's surface, and other organisms as well. Where will it go from here?"

Dr. Jackson bit his bottom lip. "If we only knew."

Phase III: Mutation

Worldwide reports have surfaced concerning a new malnutrition malady. Thousands of people are found to be malnourished, despite consuming large meals. Physicians, observing the food isn't being digested properly, are investigating a strain of new bacteria as the cause. -- World News report

Worldwide reports of numerous animal 'litters' being born to species normally birthing individual offspring, have been super-ceded by accounts of both domesticated and wild -- animals, birds, and fish; being born with streaks or spots of green. --AP Wire Service

Central Michigan

Wilma sat on a stool and leaned against the wall, taking deep breaths. She'd never seen anything like this.

Molly, her favorite and oldest cow, had given birth to four calves, all streaked green. The old girl looked fit, healthy, and unperturbed.

A little extra bounty was a good thing, but now things seemed headed toward the unrestrained. Goats, green and white, had to be given away, as they'd overrun her stable. Her milk contract brought her milk to several nearby states. But she was only one person, and had been forced to hire her good-for-nothing nephews to help on the farm. Though, truth be told, they'd started working after being here for a while, the outdoor life seemed to have a positive effect on them.

The extra workload hadn't done her any harm either. She felt better than she had in years, and was eating more and sleeping less.

Wilma threw feed into the goat pen.

So many of the newborn goats had come out a pale green color. The chickens had started being born green earlier. Even the new-born cows had turned green before the goats. Gosh-darn, stubborn goats.

She hadn't left the farm for months and didn't feel the need. Everything she needed was here. Praise God. She had food, water, fuel; both wood and excrement, and the plants outside to protect her.

What more did she need?

Nothing.

Coastal Maine

Trevor sat in the meeting feeling apprehensive. Rumors of shutting down *Green World Labs* and removing Dr. Jackson had run rampant.

"Your attempt to revolutionize the propagation habits of plants has managed to affect the entire planet," Dr. Ted Wagner said.

Dr. Jackson gritted his teeth. "I resent you stating we planned this. And, we've tried as hard as anyone else to stop the aggressive growth of the plants and other organisms, once we became aware of the problem."

"What do you intend to do to stop these processes?" Dr. Wagner asked.

"Nothing we've tried has worked. I'm open to suggestions."

Dr. Wagner sighed. "There have been reports of green human babies."

"The green coloring is due to a type of chlorophyll being absorbed from the plants ingested," Dr. Jackson said. "By those who can ingest them."

"Cities all over the world report plants encroaching into their transit, water and sewage systems, rendering them inoperable; all attempts to eradicate them failing. Yet you tell me nothing can be done," Dr. Wagner said.

"Suggest something."

Dr. Wagner sighed. "If I could, I would. How long do you think we have?"

Dr. Jackson looked startled. "Before what?"

"Before the Homo sapiens species is lost. Unsubstantiated reports claim the mutated chlorophyll alters human DNA."

Dr. Jackson stared. "Chloroplasts can't affect DNA."

Dr. Wagner slid a report toward him. "Not according to this."

Upper Maine

"Ruth. I communicated with the green dogs. They can converse over distances. They said they know where the children are, and will show you. There are some cases of fungus among the changing children. It has to be treated; it can cause either death or madness.

But *you've* got to go. The children were scared by some unchanged adults and won't trust just anyone."

"I understand, Ben. Where and when can I meet with the green canines?"

"Right now. One's waiting outside."

Ruth hung up and stared at her green skin. She felt sure it had been another color once. Shaking her head, she went outside to meet her escort.

The cool night air felt refreshing. Streaks of red and yellow from the setting sun illuminated the sky. Something touched her root-encrusted leg. She looked down; a large green coyote nuzzled her. She squatted down and offered her hand.

The coyote sniffed, then put its paw into her hand. She sniffed the paw. Smells and feelings of woodlands, cool streams, and brisk winds caressed her nostrils. She put the paw down, smiling.

The coyote loped off.

She followed, her gait uneven but steady.

At the opening to the sewers, she shut off the flashlight. Three girls, four boys, and two toddlers hid in the now useless sewers. All had green skin.

Ruth squatted at the edge of the crumbling tube and waited.

A boy and girl approached. "How did you find us?" the boy asked.

"I asked the coyote to guide me to you. You and especially the babies must be checked for fungus infections. They can harm you."

"Who sent you?" the girl asked.

"A friend from the east. He's farther along than I am and understands more."

"You're one of us?" the boy said.

"Yes." She turned the flashlight on and illuminated her green arm. "Some grown-ups can change. And it's not just skin."

"What else?" the boy asked.

She took a penknife from her pocket and cut her forearm.

The blood ran green.

Phase IV: Stability
Most of the world's cities lay in ruins, caused by the unstoppable plant growth. Bridges, buildings, dams, and other structures of concrete, brick, and wood have crumbled under the insidious assault of these Trifid-like beings. They've invaded our deserts making them green, our seas giving 'aqua' a new meaning, and even our artic areas, creating green penguins. Will our sky remain blue? -- AP wire Service

Microscopic algae-like organisms in the atmosphere have increased its density and trapped heat. The warming of the atmosphere has shrunken the ice caps, raising the water level worldwide. Coastlines have changed as land is lost. As the Earth's overall temperature and that of the oceans rises, more changes are forecast. -- National Weather Service

The decimation of the human population has been attributed to: the numerous chlorophyll-based microbes in the atmosphere that have clogged human lungs, resulting in asphyxiation; and the inability of unchanged humans to digest any type of the new food crops and mutated animal food stocks, causing starvation. -- World News Report

Central Michigan
Wilma trekked out to check the 'junk pile'. She'd pulled out her unneeded electrical fixtures, and driven her truck, tractor and other automotive machinery to a place her farm had made ready. She dumped the useless apparatus onto the cleared field.

Now days later, the pile of metal and electrical equipment had been covered by a variety of plant life. Flowers in vibrant colors bloomed from the plants absorption of the metals and other non-organic substances.

She'd put up a windmill and some solar panels to keep being self-sufficient. Her microwave still worked and so did her computer, though with a sporadic Internet.

The animals had helped plow the fields and gather the crops. All the animals left on the farm had some green. The others had died. Their inability to adapt had killed them.

Wilma knew chlorophyll had developed its rightful place in the world. God had decreed it. She looked over her fields.

Reds, oranges, yellows and some blues and purples abounded in flowers, fruits and vegetables. Color hadn't been lost from the world because green dominated. Green showcased the other colors. God had commanded this, it should be accepted.

She shook her head and went into her vine-covered house, grabbing some berries from a bush as she entered.

Coastal Maine

Trevor spread the flesh colored make-up over his pale green arms. He could no longer stand eating the canned and preserved crap the others inside *Green World Labs* called food. Not when one could go outside and feast from Nature's bounty. And the filtered air smelled stale and felt oppressive. He needed to breathe real air.

Marilyn came in and he handed her the concealing cream.

She re-covered her face and arms. "I got the results from the intelligence tests."

"And they showed the plants have something like a 'hive mentality'." Trevor tried to gauge her reaction.

She stared at him, open-mouthed. "You knew."

"It makes sense. Accelerated plant growth taking over all terrains. Chlorophyll mutating to become part of every organism. Plants altering Earth's climate to that of an earlier age. Intelligence is behind it, but a collective intelligence. Or, we may have 'woken up' an inner dormant planetary life force."

"You're amazing. I'd been trying to think of a way to tell you about what's happening, and you're already there." Marilyn hugged him.

"That's what love does, it brings out intelligence."

"That's not what it brought out last night."

"With love, you can have both." He released her and sat down on the bed. "Let me read your report."

She handed it to him.

"I had an analysis done of the chloroplasts responsible for the mutations in higher organisms," she told him.

"And?" Trevor skimmed her report.

"A large percentage of existing organisms won't make the change. Unable to accommodate the chloroplasts, they'll probably starve, or their lungs will cease functioning."

"How large a percentage?"

"Over eighty percent."

Trevor's head shot up. "You sure?"

She shrugged. "No, the theories I've proposed are based on existing data. Our sample size is small and we're not sure the chlorophyll won't mutate again."

"But...?"

"Unchanged organisms can't digest the new food crops, nor breathe the organism-filled air. And, reports have come in concerning the former *cities*." She looked at her hands. "Larger plants have grown out of the decaying human matter. Some of the smaller cities have already disappeared under the rapid and uncontrolled plant growth. Sea level has risen due to the rise in temperature and the melting ice. Deserts and other wastelands have shrunken in size under plant infringement. Weather patterns have changed so weather forecasting has become hit or miss. The world has changed and survivors will have to change with it."

"After the meeting, why don't we leave and set out on our own? We can take some supplies -- tents, tools, communication devices, whatever. But I'd feel better if we became more a part of what's happening out there. I don't want to watch it all go by. We can join an existing community, living closer to the Earth and its rhythms."

Marilyn smiled. "I like that idea."

Upper Maine

Ben stared at the picture Ruth had mailed.

Ruth stood among giant sunflowers, smiling, with a green canine at her side. A basket of large fruit and vegetables lay beside them. Ruth *stood* among the sunflowers. She'd been wheelchair bound since the accident five years ago in the defunct California genetics lab. He read the accompanying letter.

Ben, I've accepted the new order. Like you I find peace surrounded by plants. And the plants have accepted me. You may not be able to make it out in the attached photo, but I've 'grown' braces for my legs. Or rather, braces have grown around my legs. I have to drink more water and get as much sun as possible, but I've even been able to jog around outside. It feels wonderful. Let me know how you're doing. Love, Ruth.

Ben stared at the picture.

Thin, light brown lines ran around Ruth's legs; her crushed leg bones had been supplemented by fibrous plant growths. Ben took the picture and lay down on his bed in the plant-filled room. He considered the new world.

He cracked a green walnut and shared it with a splotched squirrel that had come to sit on his windowsill. As the rodent jumped to a tree branch and disappeared into the tree, he smiled.

Life was good on this new, green world.

Central Michigan

Wilma opened the letter from her niece. Mail only came once a week now and still didn't amount to much. Inside the envelope, there was a short letter and an old-fashioned photograph with white edges.

The photograph showed Ruth standing among a group of children; all had green skin. A splotched green canine lay at their feet.

The letter read:

Aunt Wilma, My acceptance of the new plants has allowed me to walk again. If you look closely at the photo, you can see thin roots growing up and into my legs. Their support allows me to walk. Four of the children pictured with me are staying at my home. Their parents died during the change, so my house finally has the children it was meant to. Hope everything's fine with you. Your niece, Ruth.

Wilma pressed the photograph against her breast as a single tear slid down her cheek. "The Earth abides and the Lord provides."

* * *

The world has a much smaller population. Its lands, air, and waters, are less polluted; the microbes and bacteria present in all three media ingested pollution and excreted inert carbon compounds. The microbes and bacteria in the atmosphere caused some of the satellites to fail, but ways would be found to communicate around the world again. Several television and radio stations still broadcast over the airways, but news seemed limited to scientists exchanging data. Few seemed to want, or need, to listen to inane programs, though music was still in demand.

Most national governments have fallen. Smaller territorial societies have sprung up. Little currency, including gold, is used, and bartering is the transaction method of preference. Small and mid-sized communities are thriving with various technological devices still in use. The failing of many satellites makes world-wide communication difficult. -- World News Report

Human population is less than one-tenth of one percent of its total before the release of the mutated organisms. An uneasy stability has been reached with about eighty percent of the land-masses now 'green'. While humanoid life still exists, the genus Homo sapiens has fallen by the wayside, allowing Homo Chlorophyllus to emerge. It may take years for the entire old race to die; in the mean time, we of the new race will care for our home planet in the way we were originally meant to. – Green World Society

The Earth revolved about its sun -- thriving under its 'second chance'. No wars, little pollution, and minimal famine marred its journey. Though there's still a way to go, for now, the planet traveled in peace.

"Men go and come, but earth abides." -- From Earth Abides, by George R. Stewart

ASHEN SKIES

MARC WIGGINS & ANTHONY GIANGREGORIO

Blackness, implacable and pure, buried the night and land. Unseen above was the cause; perennial, boundless and something akin to clouds. These obese features--bloated with dust and debris kicked up from a long silenced Earth -- were motionless and lazy from their burden. They were always there, shapeless, lifeless and forever.

The turning of seasons was a distant memory and each day drifted into the next with little variation, except for a dirtier shade of gray when it rained. On those occasions, the sludge of their heavy guts fell to the earth and stained it with a filthy ink. Whether that happened with a downpour of rage or a depressed drizzle, the accusation was the same. All landscapes had been destroyed, thrusting their fiery waste into every layer of the sky and deforming it into a clotted cesspool. As if angry, the expanse would spit the poison back down onto the land.

The Earth was in too poor of shape to really care. Its bounty was once of cities, farmlands, beaches, country sides, deserts and jungles. Now, all that previous diversity was gone and all of it was reduced to the same identity: gray, sluggish, broken and scattered. There were some remnants of life, likely on borrowed time and feeding on itself or the precious few and hard-to-find remains. The soil was impotent to growth, and the food chain was well underway to a flat line. With each transpiring day, there were fewer and fewer to claim a hold on life, or what passed as one.

There was no longer anyone who looked up into the heavens in wonder or contemplation. The moon and stars were a distant notion and the sun could only penetrate far enough to create a diffuse distinction between the grayness of day and utter blackness of night. Any temptation to look up was gone as there was no horizon. The sky looked much the same as the land. The only real difference was at one's footsteps, which marked a limited range of vision; one that held gray shapes and defunct angles from the scoured carcass of the past. Quickly beyond that was a dismal gray, a mist that promised little more in wait for those who bothered to go into it.

However, on this night, there was a man who gazed up into the immeasurable depths. Rather, he snatched quick glances in that altitude of blackness and his thoughts were a bastardized echo of himself before it all happened.

He was once a priest in a former life, a compassionate and learned man. His counsel and teachings were now a luxury never welcomed by others. The truths and aspirations he had taught them, held no ground in the realities of today. They haven't in a long time. His foundation; God, prophesies, promises, tenets and warnings, were now discarded in favor of brutal axioms that must be observed to undertake another day's survival. This world he inherited was not one for the meek.

These ruminations of his were ancient and forgotten, only now revisited due to a matter of luck or curse, depending on how he framed it. One of the houses he rummaged through that day produced a fifth of Jack Daniels. Not coated in dust and appearing new with an unbroken seal, he found the bottle tucked far into the dark corners of a high kitchen cabinet and undiscovered by scores of past scavengers. A rare find but still the only prize awarded to him by the number of homes he picked through that day.

This evening's meal would be drawn from his own meager provisions. He decided upon a can of stringed beans, leaving only two others in his knap sack, one consisting of spaghetti sauce and the other a future surprise, its label long devoured by rats and its bare surface coated in a thin rust. However, its shape was intact and without bulge. He decided to trust the mystery can and included it in his supplies. Not a concern tonight, the eventual outcome of his judgment would come within his belly another time.

He was taking a chance as it was, but he really didn't care. Since he could remember, he never really cared. His continued existence was more out of stubborn habit than desire. Tonight, he was sharing his expired and tasteless dinner with a stranger, a scraggly and anorexic woman whose tired age could have been anywhere between twenty-five and fifty. He'd met her only hours before and he had decided she was harmless after she acquiesced to his terms for his shelter and company. Therefore, he felt comfortable to break the seal of his found treasure and welcome an artificial reality which unearthed memories and notions from his useless past. The woman simply sat alongside him and next to a dying fire while he drained the small bottle. He never offered her so much as a sip. That wasn't part of the deal and she sat without comment.

His senses dulled with each swallow and he supposed she could have taken advantage but she never did. Perhaps she didn't care either. She had eaten tonight like he did and that was lucky for any night. Her inaction certainly wasn't from any sense of gratitude or loyalty, for that he was sure. Again, he didn't care and she only sat there.

While he drank, he recounted the day's events that led to this moment. How he was no longer a solitary figure but now a party of two, however temporary that might be.

He had come across the wordless shell of a woman hiding in a bedroom of the last house he rummaged through that day. Their greeting was nothing more than a lock of eyes, hers frightened, his impassive. Their introduction spanned barely a moment before he simply stepped out of the room and left her as if she wasn't there. That was his safest and preferred etiquette and she should have considered herself lucky. Others would have raped her or more likely eaten her. Or both.

The woman was either brave, stupid or very desperate. After leaving the house, the former priest noted her following him a good distance behind while he set out to find a spot to camp for the night, one that was hidden away from chance of discovery. Most days he didn't encounter others and on those times he did, he would slip away before detection and ensure a good distance before easing back into his solitary routine. Most of those he encountered were obvious threats or possible ones. He rarely took chances. However, he was an experienced wanderer and the glances he shot back in her direction were not so much at her, but in search of hidden marauders who might have been using her as bait or cover. But all telltale signs of others were absent and he decided it was only she who followed.

His path was uncomplicated, almost inviting her to track him. Two figures, a good distance apart, traversed a dusty and lifeless wasteland. They meandered between the deteriorating tract of homes and a field of brutally chopped stumps, where trees were long ago taken down and consumed for campfires during those first seasons of starving hell and disease. His destination was much further down towards a gully of rocks that would hide tonight's camp from the nearby road. The sky above was no less gray and desolate than the landscape but the shade was slipping and carrying both entities into black. There wasn't much time before that would happen.

Along his slow trek through the cemetery of tree stumps, he gathered the best the picked over land had to offer. Twigs and other small flammable objects slowly accumulated in his satchel, giving an allowance of perhaps an hour of fire. No matter, that was enough to boil and sanitize his canned meal. The most important thing was to have the fire where no one else could see it.

He reached his desired location, one between an opening of two massive boulders, and he made camp. His small fire was already established with the opened tin set to cooking when she finally came within speaking distance. No words were shared. Rather, she stopped and placed her hand on the rock's edge to balance her tired body. Their eyes connected, his having the advantage. A wordless agreement was formed, one he had made before.

She tentatively walked over and sat beside him along the fire he stoked, the opened can not yet reaching a boil. She was a pathetic creature, bony, fragile and desolate. Her caked filth and battered clothes matched the color of the earth. The priest looked at her blankly and then down at her crotch.

She understood and moved to rest her hand on his squatting knee. Foreplay was not part of the deal and before her hand connected with him, he leaned over and brought her down, not brutally so. He pushed up the tattered remnants of her dress to reveal her bargain. With no panties to pull away, he worked to shove his pants down to his knees.

His hardness grew without pleasure and he mounted her. Her legs spread wider to receive him and swayed lethargically to his thrusting motions. His head was alongside hers and he faced the ash-covered dirt. It billowed into confused plumes with each of his exhales and he tightened his lips to draw in air while he collected her payment. His build-up was quick, with no more than a handful of gyrations before the conclusion. The timing was good since that was all he had energy for. There was no thrill or sensuality to it as his seed drained into her. This was merely a business transaction, a matter of payment for his food, and any beauty possibly drawn from it was nonexistent since any real human bond was dangerous and burdensome. Had he still held any Catholic rationalizations, any ultimate outcome of this kind would be an introduction of another soul who had no more to look forward to than either of them. Most likely much less, but that would have been her problem, provided she had the humanity to raise a child in this world. Most likely she didn't. He'd seen too many picked over bones of infants within the ashes of discarded campsites to believe she would. However, such advanced thoughts did not enter his mind as he made a few more thrusts in an attempt to collect a pleasure that was never really there for the taking.

He let out a final sigh next to her head, kicking up a slightly more excited plume of dust. He never allowed his body to ease and collapse onto hers. Instead, he grunted and pulled away.

Back on his knees, he fastened his pants while she simply sat up to a squat and allowed her filthy dress to fall back between her knees.

They were again as they were a few moments before, sitting next to each other along the fire. Small, heated bubbles marked outlines of old stringed beans skimming the surface of the can. Both mutely studied the progression of the boil before he decided it was ready. He took a tin from his knap sack and divided up the contents, giving her the heated can and favoring a larger portion for himself.

They ate in silence. Used to near starvation, he was still better fed and had eaten more slowly than she. While limply chewing, he studied her actions in the corner of his eye. She skimmed her fingers around the inside of the can to scrounge the remains with cat like precision. Only after she repeated the small circumference several times, she was satisfied and tossed the can into the fire. There wasn't any elegance to her motions, but there was a quality about them he found interesting. Unlike participants in past deals, she had chosen to stay after she had eaten. She settled in to sit with legs gathered to her chest and arms wrapped around her knees. The pathetic fire did little to ward off the cold.

But really, he wasn't surprised at her continued presence and he was impassive. Though as diligent as she was in scraping up every bit of his meal, his actions were quicker than hers in licking his plate clean. When done, he placed the tin aside and looked into the dwindling fire.

The gray beyond was all but exhausted and blackness was quickly closing in and shrinking their universe. He threw in the rest of the twigs and the flames limply grew in thanks. She sat motionless and he considered her for another moment.

No conclusions were drawn other than she was nothing to worry about. He pulled out his bottle and broke the seal. The first sip was harsh to his dull tongue and he flinched at the foreign experience. His second was a gulp and more welcoming. She appeared to ignore him while a warm burning crept from his stomach to his spine. Upon the third hit, his mind softened to the glow.

Strange and foreign thoughts formed, ones filled with ghostly memories of a life that had abandoned him along his aimless trail. It started with flashes of simple things: his favorite burger joint, faces of lost friends, the green and freshly cut lawn of his church, driving his car and switching radio stations, popping in a DVD to watch... all simple pleasures.

The fourth drink gave a more vivid quality to those memories but his fifth laid the groundwork for more dangerous and bleak thoughts. The sixth ensured their delivery. He remembered who he used to be.

He once held a congregation of good people in a small Midwestern town, all of them hard working and honest. He was a man of faith who helped and mentored them. He had sustained the *saved* while bringing many others into the fold.

His seventh swig brought back circumstances of the various people he had helped; healing damaged marriages, eulogizing the departed, counseling the youth, lending a hand to small farmers, bringing humor and perspective to hard situations.

His eighth gulp marked the slow demise to that illusion, the *event* and spiral afterwards. His mind turned to a myriad of scenes to the disintegration of his small and noble community, scenes similar to those everywhere else. How they were initially successful in gathering together and sustaining an existence with him as a spiritual leader. And then the following season where stocks had dwindled and an epidemic of cholera took away so many, and finally the dying resolve of mutual neighbors.

His ninth drink outlined his crisis of faith. His followers were lost and had turned their backs to his pleas and leadership. Relationships were destroyed and paths were chosen. Some holed up and protected what they had left, while others took to murder, stealing and rape.

His final downing from the bottle was cut short by the fact that he had reached its bottom. It was enough for him to revisit his dead heart. All that he had believed in wasn't only gone but had revealed the ugliness within all good things. It wasn't supposed to happen that way. What had happened to the Book of Revelations? There was supposed to be an antichrist and a prophesized time line to salvation for the believers. None of that had happened. Instead, there was this senseless and drawn out horror.

He attempted a final tilt of the bottle but only teasing drops came his way. He threw it into the fire.

He had nearly forgotten the woman and looked at her. She sat there as before. Perhaps more tightly huddled into herself to fight off the cold. Nightfall was complete and engulfed them with the black nothingness of a closing casket. The only crack of light on that closing lid was from the fire between them and it was nearly dead. Soon, that too would extinguish and even their hands held to their face would be invisible to them.

His only conclusion was as before, to simply forget and not think about anything beyond his immediate needs. He looked back into the fire and noted the anemic glow of dying embers. Taking advantage of the fading light, he reached for his knap sack and pulled out two thin blankets. He huddled underneath them but the warmness of his drink wasn't enough and he realized the cold. As on cue, he heard a soft scuffling towards him. The woman tentatively searched for the edge of his blankets. She pulled it away and scooted in, her body forming a cradle he could cup. He relinquished some more of his covers and shifted into her. His chest gathered the warmth of her back and his knees dug into the back fold of her legs.

He could hear, as well as feel, the rhythm of her breathing. It was neither relaxed nor alert; it merely functioned to the commands of her body that didn't know any better than to continue its existence. His arm found itself across her side and he soon fell asleep.

*   *   *

A dirty hand over his mouth snapped the priest from his dreams of a better life. His first instinct was to cry out, but with the dirty and crust-covered hand over his mouth, that was impossible. The fire was dead now and there was barely any light to see by. A break in the ashen clouds allowed the smallest amount of light to penetrate and with that light; he saw a ragged and nearly toothless face leering over him.

He'd seen enough of the attacker's kind to know a cannibal when he was no more than two inches from his face.

The cannibal smelled like two day old dung mixed with bad cheese from lack of bathing, one of the most prevalent problems with a cannie. The man wasn't wearing clothing, but instead had a simple loin cloth wrapped around his privates. His left hand was over the priest's mouth and his right held a small carving knife.

The priest's eyes went wide at the sight of the dull knife reflecting whatever ambiance was about. He knew that knife was about to be plunged into his chest, where the cannie would then feed on his organs like he was a Christmas banquet.

But the priest wasn't ready to die just yet and he kicked out with his feet, pushing back on the cannie. The blanket was tossed aside to fall into the dirt and the priest idly noticed the woman was gone. He had a passing thought that she had abandoned him and that this had all been staged from the beginning, but then any thoughts of plans and plots was lost on him as he fought for his life. The knife came down, but the priest used his right arm to block the blow. But the arm wielded by the cannie was strong and the blade all but touched his shirt, but pierced the skin beneath to draw blood.

The pain was sharp but he couldn't cry out with the fetid hand still on his mouth. He sucked air through his nose like a bellows; the odor coming off the hand trapping his mouth overwhelming. Despite his predicament, he had to wonder if the cannie wiped his ass with that bare hand, and it was now on his face!

The priest bucked his hips and spun around, breaking the cannie's grip as the knife fell away to clatter between a couple of head-sized boulders a few feet away.

The priest leaned forward, his arms wide and ready to grapple with his attacker.

There was no right or wrong here, only two enemies battling; the winner allowed to live while the loser would die.

The cannie gibbered like a fool, and the priest recognized the madness immediately. It had to do with eating the brains of another human being. Man was not meant to feed on man and there was now a new disease running rampant from cannie to cannie.

The priest could see this cannibal had the disease and that made things only more perilous. The cannie wouldn't think rationally, his actions without reason; he would only attack like an animal, wanting nothing more than to feed on the priest's carcass.

The cannie howled like a wolf and came at him again, the two wrapping their arms around one another. The priest kicked up with his left knee and felt the solid impact of bone to testicles. But the cannie, lost in madness, barely grunted, though a syrupy yellow and red ooze now slid down his inner thighs.

At least the priest could take solace in knowing whether he lived or died this night, the cannie would never spread his seed again. Both men grunted and breathed heavily as they fought to get the upper hand over the other. Though once a man of God, the priest was no victim. Before the skies darkened, he had wrestled and boxed, spending many a day in the gym exercising. Though he was vastly out of shape and weak from malnourishment, his instincts came back to him and he pummeled the cannie in the kidneys and lower torso, trying to get the man to release him.

But for each blow he landed, he received one of his own, and then he felt one blow impact his stomach which caused him to taste bile and see bright lights that weren't there.

He fell back to land on the dusty ground as a puff of ash floated around him. The cannie ignored him at first, and the priest didn't know what his attacker was doing. That is until the cannie lunged for the fallen knife and spun back with a maniacal gleam in his eyes while waving the retrieved blade back and forth.

The priest was winded and his side ached as he saw twirling lights flashing across his vision. As the cannie grew closer, he prepared himself for the end, knowing he wasn't going to be able to escape this time.

The cannie stepped forward, his mouth partly open to show the few teeth he had left. Brown and yellow, they looked as if they hadn't seen a toothbrush long before the event happened.

The priest set his jaw and stared at his intended killer defiantly. If he was going to die, then he would do so like a man, not cowering and begging for his life.

But as the cannie leaned over and raised his arm holding the knife, his deranged mind already imagining cutting up the priest, a shadow came up behind him and brought a head-sized rock down onto the top of his head.

The cannie's head seemed to disappear in a spray of blood and bone, the rock replacing the head. The weight of the rock was so much that it had actually caved in the skull, sending brains and blood squirting out the sides like someone had stepped on a water balloon full of pudding.

The body stood immobile over the priest, the rock for a head seeming to stare at him accusingly as dark red plasma shot out from under it. Then, like a fallen tree, the corpse toppled over. The priest dove to the side as the body landed in a puff of dust, and the bloody rock rolling a few feet to come to a stop. The jagged stump of a neck still spurted crimson, the ash soaking it up to make a red slurry.

The priest looked back to where the cannie had been standing to see the rock-wielding shadow morph into the woman.

She stood over him, not saying a word, their eyes connecting like before when she first met him.

"I thought you left," he said simply.

"No, the food was good," was her simple reply.

"Fair enough," he said as he came to his feet, wavering slightly as blood rushed to his head.

Without a glance to the dead cannie, he gathered what he considered his belongings and tossed them over his shoulder. The woman carried the blankets, doing her best to shake them free of dust and ash. But she knew, as did he, that the ash could never be truly removed. It was in everything, and it was a part of them, of their lives.

When he was ready, he cast her a look that she returned. Only this time there was a hint of a smile on her face, as there was on his.

He reached out his right hand to her, the woman taking it without thought, as the two weary survivors headed off, leaving the fouled campsite behind. They would move down the trail a bit and find a new place to spend the rest of the night.

As the ash gray sky doused the world in darkness, the two souls that were now one moved on for something better.

WE'RE NOT IN KANSAS ANYMORE

G.R.MOSCA

My name is Gunnery Sergeant Spencer Newman. All around me is a white-sanded desert as far as the eye can see. White sand that finds its way into everything: the engine, the cab of our Humvee, in our desert boots, our ears, eyes and any other cavity that's open to the elements. We call it salt because it's in everything we eat. We call it "Irit" because it is a pariah. It poisons our cuts and abrasions causing endless infection and sores, it's in the axle grease, it jams our weapons and invades our engines, gumming up the carburetor and slowing down our convoy.

Time is something we have little of. The longer we stay in the desert; out in the open; the faster our food spoils and the faster they will find us. It's my responsibility to ensure this convoy reaches its destination. Food is all we have to sustain what's left of our society and if we fail, humanity dwindles by just a few more souls until the day when nothing is left.

Not even the memories of who we were and what we were able to accomplish will matter when we're all dead and gone.

I'm in position, manning my M2 shock-mounted turret gun. I sight through the scope scanning the horizon in a semi-circular pattern. It's nearly evening but my night-vision lens basks everything I view in a bright, green glow. I love my weapon, my job and my people. It is up to my weapon and me to get this food through. We're fifty miles outside of our target area. Home. It should take us no longer than another day to slog through the mire of sand and ensure the convoy is keeping up with us.

My Humvee rides point. No one likes point but I love it. I get the first action, the first kill. I draw first blood and woe unto them that cross my path. The radio crackles, position Charlie Alpha is picking up spots to the west on our horizon. Charlie Alpha is the rear guard, Tail-end Charlie. They pick up a lot of action but they're more vulnerable than we are because it takes longer to redeploy to cover our rear.

My best friend is the gunner for Charlie Alpha. His name is Cristos but we call him J.C. because he's so damn lucky. Last year we were making an end run back to base when insurgents surrounded us and we had a running battle for forty minutes.

In the middle of this, the Humvee J.C. was riding in flipped over and killed the driver; another good guy named Daggert. Even with the Humvee flipped, J.C. still held off two-dozen insurgents. How? His M2 is facing the right direction when the Humvee flips and he's in the sand shooting his weapon upside down. He deserved a Silver Star for sure but he was happier with extra rations and a steak back at base. He still talks about that steak. It might have been one of the last one's there. We haven't seen good beef in years.

The word over the radio is sun-flares. What that means is the setting sun is reflecting off of something in the distance. It could be a can of beans someone threw off a truck six months ago or it could be the reflection off a riflescope or sand goggles. Either way, it's nothing or we're in for a fight. Insurgents have always been tough. When they aren't sending suicide bombers into the cities, they're trying to disrupt our supply chain or steal our food. My driver picks up his radio mike and asks for confirmation. Each of our detachment replies in order: no visual confirmation. I scan the horizon real slow now with night-vision off. I want to see the real world and catch any stray reflection.

The horizon is blood red, the sun sending out its final rays of the day. They're focused like a laser beam, bright enough to blind. I still see nothing but I take my time and scan to my east, then to my west and finally behind me. Nothing still; start again, breath through my nose, nice and gentle, keep the scope steady. A few minutes left then we'll be in the shadow world of twilight. The radio crackles: LT Drake confirms sun-flares at bearing one-two-five degrees south-by-southeast. He's taking a detail to investigate. We wait patiently for a report. Thirty seconds. One minute goes by, then another soon turning into three minutes. Too damn long. I pick up the mike and click twice, our code for report. I wait ten seconds and click again. Minutes moving quickly past us, I think the longer his silence, the more trouble he's in. I double-click again. No response. I decide to break silence. Request a quick-response team; meanwhile order the convoy to move forward double-quick with remaining units on high alert.

I'm moving quickly to the coordinates last called in by LT Drake. Two units, Spiccola's and Cristos', accompany me. The three of us are kicking up a plume of sand behind our Humvees. Time moves on. We maintain constant radio chatter reporting our positions and observations. Spiccola reports flares to our right, the three of us simultaneously veer off into the direction of his report. We soon stop in unison. What we see sends chills up our collective spines. Drake's detachment is in smoking ruins. Six men are staked out on the sand, throats slashed, bodies eviscerated. We look around and see nothing. No tracks, no enemy. I look up and notice a flock of birds. Hawks, twenty or more are circling our area to feed on the entrails and blood. The first real meal they may have gotten in a while.

"Stay sharp," I whisper into my microphone. We circle – like circling the wagons in a cowboy western. "Stay close men." No sooner do I say this than I hear the crack of a rifle and a hole the size of a quarter opens up in the armor plating two inches from my head. A sand storm advances from two hundred yards to our left. We face it in unison. The storm becomes a horde. They advance on horseback and on foot, wailing and waving scimitars and rifles, throwing grenades, stopping to kneel and fire RPG's and semiautomatic fire. I see a crater open up right before Spiccola's Humvee rushes into it. The Humvee does a forward flip but lands back on all four wheels. Spiccola's gunner looks rattled but okay. He lays down deadly suppressing fire. As if on command we all fire into the horde with devastating effect. I look through my scope and see an insurgent holding a pole; I follow its line and find myself looking eye-to-eye with LT Drake's head. I squeeze the triggers of my gun and the insurgent's body vaporizes. I get on the microphone: "No quarter."

The firefight lasts only a few minutes more with deadly effectiveness. We have confronted our enemy and he is obliterated. We stop our vehicles in a tight circle to regroup and search for any Intel. I see an insurgent twitching in pain; I walk over and assess his wounds. He has a hole through his chest; I grind the heel of my desert boot into it. He screams and faints. I smile.

The radio crackles: "May day, repeat, may day. We are in the shit. Recon support at Vector Seven, Charlie."

I look at my guys, and realize this was a distraction from the main event. "Food convoy in danger." We hop into our vehicles and make dust towards the coordinates.

It is full dark and we turn our searchlights on. White sand is reflected back at us as far as the eye can see. We make for Vector Seven Charlie with all haste. I grit my teeth hoping we're in time. The radio crackles: "Group Nine reporting. Hostiles are gone for now. Over."

I pick up the mike: "Report current position. Over."

"Five-by-five by the wayside. Over." More code. I know just where they are. Hunkered down and tucked in for the night.

"See you in five. Repeat. See you in five." The three of us make a beeline for the convoy's position. We should be there in no time flat.

* * *

We arrive at the five-by-five. Tensions are running high but spirits are good. Groups of workers and military personnel are chowing down, cleaning armaments, and checking vehicles. An active perimeter greets us within fifty feet of the convoy: arc lights and alarms. We're waved through almost immediately.

We find a place to settle in for the night; we need to relax. The six of us break out rations and I take out the tags for Drake and his company. They're still warm from the firefight and some are covered with blood and bits of gore. I'll have to write up the report and send letters to their loved ones and families; six families. Just looking at the tags makes all of us angry and I feel a surge of adrenaline rush through my body. Must relax, daybreak will be here soon enough.

I pick up the tags and balance them in the palm of my hand, feeling the weight of them. I see a flashing image of Drake's head on a pike and the rebel's body vaporizing seconds later.

Cristos, Spiccola, Manson, Hobson, the other "Runners" take turns talking about our friends, our fallen comrades. In this quiet moment; hours before dawn; we honor our friends by bringing them back to life in our minds, our hearts. For a few brief moments they're alive again, laughing, smiling, full of life.

A life that only hours ago left them forever.

Hobson suddenly remembers that Drake had been at the World Trade Center. That's why he joined up. Then we talk about how the world went to shit. It started with the strange weather: global warming. Flooding where it had never rained, droughts where it had always rained, heat waves in the far north and cold snaps at the equator. Then it got really strange: tornadoes tearing through city centers, floods in ancient European cities, snow in India. We all remembered when the Koreans and Chinese tested their first high-altitude warheads. Nothing was the same after that; farmland became desert, icy tundra turned to verdant pasturelands, oceans rose and the landscape changed forever. It took years but the changes became irreversible and unchangeable.

Cristos smiles and says, "We ain't in Kansas anymore, Sarge."

We laugh.

I notice a young woman appear from between two convoy trucks, materializing fifty feet from where I'm sitting. I notice her because she's wearing a long, white, hooded robe with leather sandals on delicate feet. The other men continue talking but her youth and natural beauty mesmerizes me. Her eyes are the most iridescent blue I have ever seen. Our eyes lock from across the distance and at once it's as if we're inches from one another.

I can see a small scar on her left cheek, a tear beginning to coalesce in the corner of her eye. I begin to wonder who she is and why she has appeared here. Her presence seems so foreign in this harsh desert, this critical mission. Something seems wrong. I study her more closely; my eyebrows knit together.

Her mouth curls into a slight smile and then she explodes in a violent burst of light and sound. Flames shoot upwards on the spot where just moments ago she stood. By reflex my men and I fall to the ground and we cover our heads. Others aren't so lucky. Thousands of pieces of metal shrapnel fly in all directions, cutting mercilessly and effortlessly through canvas, steel and flesh. The area is immediately filled with screams and explosions. We slowly pick ourselves up off the sandy floor and look around. Behind us, the side of my Humvee is stippled with hundreds of tiny metal crucifixes.

Cristos turns to me with the saddest look I have ever seen on his face. "We ain't in Kansas anymore, are we Sarge."

* * *

It is an hour before dawn. Our convoy is stirring back to life after a fitful rest. I tell my "Runners" to warm up the Humvees and check their ammo and rations; we'll be home soon. The last leg of our journey takes the convoy on to the *Yellow Brick Road* and home.

Meanwhile, I unfold my map onto the hood of my Humvee and study its lines: where we are, where we've come from, where it will end. It's been two weeks since we left the northern fields rich with oil and abundant with food and produce. We were once a verdant and fertile land, now we're cursed. We're forced to travel great distances and suffer great peril and loss in a land whose blessings have been stolen through a cruel twist of nature and man's ignorance and greed.

A meadowlark lands on my map. It's a beautifully fragile creature with an iridescent yellow breast and small black eyes. It pecks absently for a moment at the map creases and sings its song. It stops, looks up and suddenly takes flight towards the east. I follow its flight and notice the orange sliver of a rising sun. Its rays barely crest the horizon, as if it's still more night than dawn.

I gently grasp the edges of the map and fold it back into its case.

* * *

I cannot shake the feeling of foreboding even though we're so close to home. Once we hit the *Yellow Brick Road* it should only take us a matter of hours before we're embraced by the safety of our compound. Yet I can't stop seeing those blue eyes that signal death and flames. It will haunt me for a long time to come.

END OF DAYS

* * *

The sun rises higher on the horizon, casting shadows across the dunes like long fingers inching across the solitary landscape.

"Sarge, you gotta come see this. You ain't gonna believe this shit."

The voice is Manson's and there's an edge of panic lurking under his voice. I've served with Manson for years and he's no one's fool. He's a battle-hardened veteran of more food runs than I can count and it is not like him to become unnerved; especially this close to home; but I can sense his awe, his fear, his outright disbelief at whatever it is he's seeing.

I look out past the perimeter to the desert slowly illuminated by the rising sun and see nothing unusual. I glance over to Manson and he points back at the landscape. I look harder at the desert floor, trying to figure out what I'm missing, trying to decipher the shadows within the softly undulating landscape. I hear Cristos let out a resigned sigh, and then Spiccola mumbles a curse under his breath. The sun mounts higher above the horizon and suddenly I see it as well.

We're surrounded by a hundred white-hooded figures still some distance away from us but they're slowly advancing on our position. We've heard of this phenomenon; they're called the "Sisters of Mercy" and we were nearly devastated by just one of them last night. They're women and small children who quietly bring death and fear upon our doorstep. They are the ultimate horror of war brought into sharp focus: innocents who will sacrifice their lives for an ideology in which they fervently and unquestioningly believe; even if they don't understand the cause for which they sacrifice.

I curse under my breath then turn to my men, "Get ready to roll."

I spot the convoy commander; he nods with an understanding look. We "Runners" will need to punch a hole through this tightening circle then act as forward guard for what lies beyond the horizon. The convoy will have to be quick and nimble or we'll be buried here in the sand or vaporized in a burst of flames and crucifixes.

85

* * *

We're jetting towards the *Yellow Brick Road* but first we must pass through the deadly Sisters. As we advance, we check our weapons. I check my automatic weapon for sand that can cause jams. We cannot afford any mishaps or problems.

I hear a pop to my left; like someone just lit a firecracker very close to my ear; I see a burst of flames a hundred feet ahead of me. Crucifixes barely reach our position and I gaze at the Rorschach-pattern of blood splatter left behind. I wonder if the Sisters are setting off their body charges or if proximity sensors are detonating them. We careen ever closer towards the *Road*.

Our caravan is spewing sand behind us in great clouds, creating a miniature sandstorm our convoy can use for cover as they follow closely behind us. We're setting a brutal speed and I fear we may lose them, however our captain is an experienced soldier and this isn't his first mission with us.

We continue on.

The rising sun is making it difficult to see beyond a hundred feet. The glare intensifies as it reflects off the sand. Then we see a ribbon of golden glass snaking in the distance towards home: The *Yellow Brick Road*. It was once a country road but when fields turned to desert, the intense heat coming off the asphalt turned the sand to a golden glass; our ticket home.

Another pop to my right and then another closer to our left flank. Metal crucifixes are slamming into the sides of the Humvees, barely missing my men and me. Another pop happens so close to Cristos' vehicle that a long, slender arm of a "Sister" slams against the windshield before falling beneath the vehicle. I grasp my weapon and aim, squeezing off short bursts of fire into a group of four angels; children from what I can tell. They burst into flames before my eyes as we drive through their position. I can feel the heat of the blast; moments later their small body parts splatter to the ground. It looks like we're through the worst of it with no casualties; we're almost on the road with our convoy following closely behind us.

I notice a dust cloud in front of us and I'm trying to decide if it's a sandstorm or something else. I call my point vehicle; Manson is keying his mike but I'm having trouble understanding him. I look through my scope at his Humvee and I see Manson clutching his throat, trying desperately to staunch the blood jetting out onto his flak jacket. I think what a damn shame; he's a good man, a good soldier. Through my scope I can see the small metallic arm of a crucifix sticking out of Manson's throat. He turns towards my vehicle and I see the confused and frightened expression on his face. He sinks down to the platform of his Humvee and out of sight.

I focus past Manson's vehicle and I now see the storm is an army of insurgents advancing quickly on our position. They lie between us and home.

The *Yellow Brick Road* has stopped glistening and I look to my left. The sun has disappeared and in its place are a number of massive tornado funnels heading straight towards all of us. Either God is being kind to our mission or this is the cruelest joke about to be foisted upon all of us. The tornados gather strength and speed and they move ever closer in an undulating path of wind, sand and destruction.

I pick up my mike and radio the convoy commander to stay close and move fast; we are heading home. My men are reporting in now as we gather speed and close our formation. We swarm across the desert floor as the atmosphere charges with bolts of lightning and the sky darkens to an artificial midnight. We can barely make out the funnel clouds but they are moving away from us and towards our enemies. Soon we see men and horses flung through the air as if they were toys. We move faster still past the storm until we see the horizon brighten to a rose color. We lay on more speed, the caravan traveling now as one single entity hellbent for the safety of our base.

* * *

We can see the base, and as we pass the sign for Junction City, I hear Spiccola's voice over the field radio: "Hey, Sarge, looks like this is Kansas after all."

Fort Riley beckons to us as the gates open and MP's fan out to escort us back to our compound. I think of the old days when we were the breadbasket of the world. I think of my youth spent in the verdant fields and hills of this great state, then I think of that September morning when everything changed, and I found myself in the Middle East when the troubles started.

Terror and war were our daily bread and no corner of this planet was spared. It was when we had gone too far that the planet decided to shake us off of it like a dog that has fleas. When I returned from Iraq, I couldn't tell the difference between there and here. The weather patterns had changed: extreme storms, wildfires, dust bowls, hurricanes; this became our new reality; still it wasn't enough to unite mankind or to persuade us to change our ways. We behaved badly and things got worse in proportion.

The future didn't die on September 11th with the collective screams and outrage of a nation united by tragedy. It died quietly behind the closed doors of politicians whose self-interest transcended their commitment to their country and its people. It died with the continued abuse and neglect to our Mother Earth. It died because of the ignorance and selfishness of mankind. Now we truck food in from the great northern reaches of Canada, an area that was once desolate but which is now fecund and fertile.

Our terrorists come from our own cities and towns, not from some backwater village on the other side of the world. And still the planet shakes continue to shake us off; little by little.

I absently look at the open gate beckoning us back into its temporary safety, while out of the corner of my eye I see an ambulance corpsman lift a body bag from Manson's Humvee.

Where did we go wrong?

We are back in Kansas but we're not in Kansas anymore. I unconsciously click my heels three times and whisper silently to myself: "There's no place like home, there's no place like home, there's no place like home."

RAT

PERRY P. PERKINS

*H*ow *Ironic.*

It was not the great atomic bombs of the nineteen-fifties, the ones that led countless millions of American children to huddle fearfully, and futilely, beneath their school desks during "war drills," nor was it the horror of nuclear conflagration, whose vivid terror was the bastard child of modern science and the Hollywood screenwriters of the nineteen-eighties and nineties. Not even the doom-filled sermons of pollution, and global warming, and over-population that brayed from a thousand cable channels and a million paranoia blogs that ushered in the twenty-first century.

No, the end of the world, at least the world that millions of middle-class, tax-paying, overweight Joe Americans had known, came with celebration, and star-gazing, and the pop of countless champagne corks.

A planet-wide party to celebrate a chunk of space flotsam that burned through the night sky on what the scientists assured us was the last spin of a journey that had begun with the big-bang and would end in a matter of days as the weary traveler finally plunged into the Earth's sun, causing sun flares that would arc through millions of miles of space and a light-show the like of which might never be seen by man again.

And, in fact, it wouldn't.

The unnamed comet and its train skimmed the Earth's atmosphere at 11:47 pm on October 14, 2008, causing an aurora borealis visible to the entire Western hemisphere, which ohhed and ahhed even as the corks popped and she brought death with the brief passing of her glowing tail.

If you flipped your radio dial fast enough, you might hear her theme song...

"Oh, say can you see..."

"...it's the end of the world as we know it..."

...and everybody danced the last dance.

*   *   *

The Trail - Zigzagging its way from Mexico to Canada through California, Oregon and Washington. The 2,650-mile Pacific Crest Trail boasts the greatest elevation changes of any of America's National Scenic Trails. Over the past decade the PCT has become a favorite target of thru-hikers, hearty souls who attempt to hike or ride an entire long-distance trail in one "season."

Most thru-hikers complete the 2,650 trail miles in five to six months that means averaging twenty or more miles a day

Less than half finish.

Diary entry October 10, 2008.

Happy birthday to me! On October 10, 1987, my mother named me Horatio Nolan Smith.

She named me Horatio for Horatio Alger, a writer who knew what it was to fall and get back up, and dedicate oneself to redemption. (Her words, not mine!)

She named me Smith for the soldier that she knew and loved for one night, and who died a few weeks later in the sands of Baghdad.

I'm not sure where Nolan came into the picture.

When I was nineteen, I walked into the woods as a boy, a backpack on my shoulders and a map in my hand, determined to find out what the world meant to me.

My trail friends named me Rat. Not a great name, but it was that or "Hor," so I went with Rat. Six months later I came out of the woods a man, and found that the world had ended.

*   *   *

Rat woke, as he did every morning for the past four months. The first brush of dawn was painting the mountain peaks in shades of pink and pearl. He lay still for a while, comfortably warm in his sleeping bag and watched the faint breath of the forest ripple across the green nylon wall of his tent.

Outside, he could hear the waves lapping gently against the shore of Scout Lake while starlings sang in the pines.

He felt better this morning; the stomach cramps were gone, as was the aching thirst of the last three days. Putting a hand to his neck, he could feel that the swelling there had subsided as well.

Whatever he had eaten, or, more likely, drunk, along the trail that had left him folded over and puking, seemed to have finally passed through his system. It had left him a little shaky but finally, after days and forcing down water and reconstituted chicken broth, he was actually feeling hungry for solid food again.

Just a bad dose of beaver-fever, he thought, though the symptoms didn't exactly match what he'd read of the water-borne Giardia virus. Whatever it was, he was grateful it was gone and he was eager for a hot breakfast and the chance to, finally, put some more miles behind him. It would be a slow day, he knew; his legs still felt weak and his lightweight backpack wasn't looking particularly light. Still, he'd make it an easy goal, just the ten miles to Olallie Lake, where his next resupply box would be waiting for him. Ten miles was less than half of his daily average, but right now it was probably the best he could hope for.

Some fresh food, a chance to talk to other people, maybe even his first 'legal' beer...it's amazing what could sound like heaven after 2000 miles on the trail.

And, even if he didn't make Olallie tonight, he still had barley adequate, and not particularly appetizing, amount of provisions in his pack. A couple of packets of instant grits, one of instant oatmeal, but no more freeze-dried packets of lasagna or shepherd's pie...even the chicken bullion, which had been all he'd been able to choke down for the last few days, was now depleted.

And that, Rat thought, wrinkling his nose, *is just fine by me. If I never see another cup of instant chicken broth, I think I'll die a happy man.*

No, there was no danger of starving before reaching his awaiting supplies, but it had been a close thing, much closer than he had planned for, damned giardia, and not only that, but he was several days behind, days he would have to make up if he wanted to reach Canada before snow blocked the passes in Washington.

Also, there was Ma.

Ma would be getting worried by now.

Rat grimaced again, reaching for the zipper of his bag.

No, knowing Ma, she was already frantic and working herself toward a full-moose panic, convinced that he was dying a slow and horrible death beneath a rockslide, or was being digested even more slowly in the belly of some wild animal. Just two of the many probable ends he would have on this silly, dangerous adventure, as she had warned him many times...*not that he ever listened to his poor mother who, God knows had given her life to keep him safe and healthy, and now this was the thanks she got for all her sacrifices...*

Rat was still grinning as he slipped out of the tent into the cool morning air.

After taking care of business, he pulled the small mesh bag that contained his kitchen from a pocket of his pack. Setting up the tiny, three-legged frame beneath his titanium pot, he lit a white cube of solid fuel beneath it, grimacing at the stink as it was engulfed in a blanket of blue flame that would soon have water boiling for his ritual breakfast of instant oatmeal and instant coffee.

In a few more days he would reach Timberline lodge and, as he leaned back against the sodden moss of the tree that sheltered his tent, he envisioned sinking into a soft, padded chair in front of the stone fireplace, pouring heavy cream into a mug full of fresh brewed coffee while waiting for a platter of steaming huckleberry pancakes, glistening breakfast sausages, and a mountain of scrambled eggs.

Rat's belly growled in protest and, with a sigh, he dug a plastic spoon from his pack.

* * *

The forest was deep and dark, a soft drizzling rain creating rainbows along the tree line.

Rat, however, was in no mood to appreciate beauty. Wet and cold, despite having layered on all the clothing he had--some of them grown decidedly funky--and pulling his rain suit on over the top, he was still weak from his bout of beaver-fever. For the first few miles he'd tried to avoid the deepest holes and long-step over the rivers of mud that flowed down the steepest sections of the trail. Now he simply slopped through the mud-holes, head down and arms swinging to the rhythm of his stride.

He grumbled as he went.

This was his fourth day with neither his GPS nor digital camera working. Both had crapped out his first night at Scout Lake, and though he'd packed two extra sets of batteries, neither device gave so much as a flicker when powered on.

The GPS was a matter of convenience, but not really a necessity. The trail was clearly marked and he had maps in his pack. The failure of the camera, however, was nothing short of a disaster. This might be a once-in-a-lifetime trip, and there would now be a huge black hole of the center of the slide-show he hoped to put together.

The biggest loss to his album, however, would not be of campsites, and elk, and sunset vistas, but of never having snapped a shot of the comet as it passed through the pristine skies over the Obsidian Falls lava fields south of Jefferson Park. He had spent weeks planning his route to catch the comet over the moonscape-like fields, longs days humping extra miles to make it to the site on time...all for nothing.

Besides, it was just plain galling.

He'd counted and recounted every ounce, discarding luxury after luxury to maintain his pack weight, only to find he'd been hauling six dead batteries all the way from the High Sierras. Rat ground his teeth as a wet pine branch slapped him in the face, speckling his glasses with pitch and water.

He stopped a moment to dry his specs and catch his breath.

"Well," he grunted, eyeing the dripping woods ahead with a baleful eye, "if it was easy, everyone would do it!"

This was his mantra whenever the trail started to get him down.

If it was easy, everyone would do it.

He wasn't sure if it really helped all that much, but you had to have *something* to hang on to out here.

Reaching into his pocket, he pulled out a baggie of semi-smoked trout, the last of three fish that he'd taken from the lake that morning. It wasn't as good as jerky, but the jerky had run out south of Three-Fingered Jack, and there'd be no more until he reached the camp store at Olallie Lake.

Prob'ly not even then, he thought, *they're gonna want an arm and a leg for a couple of ounces of that stale shoe leather they call jerky.*

He still had a few bucks in his pocket, but his low-income upbringing balked at the thought of paying forty-dollars a pound for beef jerky, especially when he could pull trout from the numerous lakes for free.

He licked the last of the smoky fish from his fingers. He was still hungry.

That was another fact of trail life, you were pretty much hungry all the time.

A hiker simply couldn't carry enough food to make up for the number of calories he burned each day, and so, except for a couple of memorable food orgies during town breaks, he'd slowly been starving for almost four months.

It was amazing how many of his thoughts of the future, the great questions of life, and even daydreams of sex had fallen by the wayside since starting from the Southern Terminus at the Mexico border in April, all replaced with unending fantasies of deep dish pizza, mushroom cheese burgers, and the Cornels extra-crispy chicken.

Rat tried to force away the mesmeric images of food, reminding himself that he'd reach the store in just ten more miles. Ten more miles and they would at least have candy-bars and microwave burritos. He was hiking slow, his already scant reserves depleted...ten more miles...just ten more miles.

Then five...

Then two...

The rain returned in full roaring abandon by the time he staggered into the Olallie Lake Campground at dusk.

It was deserted.

Rat collapsed beneath the covered porch of the store and watched the rain bouncing off the silvery surface of the lake. Somewhere behind that dense layer of clouds was Mt. Jefferson, but he wouldn't see it tonight. Finally, he slipped off his pack and rose with a groan, to see if he could roust someone in the camp.

None of the cabins seemed occupied and, though there was a huge Suburban parked in front of the camp hosts RV, no lights shone through the covered windows and no one answered the door.

Later, as he walked between the quiet cabins, Rat's nose twitched. There was a smell in the campground, low and heavy like fog. It had been there since he arrived, but only now registered. It was the smell of something dead; something large and dead.

It happened on the trail sometimes, though not often in campgrounds. Once, coming down from the Sierra Nevada's at twilight, he found the flyblown corpse of a black bear lying in the trail. It had been 97 degrees that day and he'd hiked an extra mile and set up camp in the dark to escape the sick-sweet aroma of decay.

This wasn't as bad as the bear had been, but it was similar, maybe newer...hinting that worse was yet to come.

Whatever it was, it was nearby, and the stench of it lingered over the campground. Why the hell hadn't someone cleaned...whatever it was...up? For that matter, why hadn't anyone cleaned the campground, period? Two of the trashcans he passed on his way back to the store were overturned. Raccoons, and maybe even coyotes, had spread the contents all over the grounds. As he stepped over the ant-infested remains of someone's chicken dinner, a candy bar wrapper and assorted garbage rustled past in the evening breeze.

Whoever the camp hosts were, they were doing a lousy job.

Down by the lake, where the fresh mountain breeze came over the water, the smell dissipated.

Stumbling back to the covered porch, he pulled his penlight from his belt and then cursed; he'd forgotten it was dead as well. Rat spent a couple of minutes facing the darkening lake and cursing roundly at the top of his lungs: cursing the rain, the campground, and the Pacific Crest Trail in general. Then, in direct violation of the sign over the porch, he yanked his sleeping bag and pad from his pack and laid them out in front of the door before crawling in to shiver himself warm.

When someone finally got around to opening the place up, he was determined to be the first one to know about it.

As he settled in, Rat wondered if the store had been closed all day, and, if so, how many hikers had been forced to press on towards Timberline Lodge without their resupply boxes or even the small luxury of a candy bar or ice-cream sandwich.

He furrowed his brow, trying to remember how many hikers had passed him on the trail today...God knew he'd been hiking slow enough. In fact, how many hikers had come past Scout Lake during his three-day sick spell...had any?

That can't be right, he thought, yawning cavernously, as he cinched the hood of his bag down around his ears, *I must have seen someone in the last week...*

Pulling a dog-eared copy of *The Fellowship of the Rings* from his pack, Rat settled in to read for a while from his favorite novel. It was his ritual. How many campfires has flickered and ebbed as he turned these pages, how many too-long days of humping along the trail had ended with Frodo Baggins' adventures?

The road led ever on and on.

Exhausted, Rat was asleep before his mind could take a closer look at these questions, the tattered paperback slipping from his fingers.

He wouldn't stir again until the sun climbed over the high ridge of the Cascades the next morning.

Fangorn forest would have to wait another day.

*   *   *

It was one of those perfect mountain mornings that leaves a hiker wondering if he's awake or still dreaming; as he rubs sleep from his eyes and squints into a robin's egg blue sky.

Rat winced as he sat up, the porch creaking wearily beneath him. He rubbed his neck to loosen a kink and reached for his glasses where he'd left them the night before, protected within one of his boots. It was a tip he'd read on another hiker's blog before starting out on the PCT and it hadn't failed him yet. He hadn't lost, or God forbid, broken his glasses once in the last fifteen hundred miles.

The internet was the invaluable goldmine for the thorough-hiker. A thousand journals posted online, replete with hints, tips, and tricks for not only surviving, but *enjoying* a season on the Pacific Crest Trail. Rat had read them all, and gleaned the wisdom of them for his own adventure.

A thin fog lay over Olallie Lake as crows heralded the day with rusty calls. The store was still locked, and certainly no one had woken him to enter.

Frowning, Rat peered through the dusty glass of the door window, but detected no movement within. What he could see, however, was two thin rows of canned and dried goods, a small freezer, and a cash-register laden counter beyond. Behind that sat several shelves and, on the middle one, was a cardboard box sealed with bright yellow packing tape, the same tape his mother had brought home for him from her job at the post office.

His resupply box had arrived at Olallie, and sat there waiting, as he did, for someone to unlock the door. His stomach growled, thinking of the pop-tarts and Mars bars that were packed, amid the rest of his gear, inside that box. The clock on the store wall read 4:00.

That's weird, he thought, *the sun's too high to be four in the morning or four at night.*

Then he noticed that the second-hand was frozen at fifteen after. Apparently the camp's batteries had failed as well.

Pulling on his boots, Rat left his pack leaning against the door, and hiked up the trail to the Camp-host's site. There was still no sign of movement within or without the big RV and, after knocking on the door and waiting several minutes, he began to worry.

Something wasn't right here. Sure, the weather hadn't been the greatest the last few weeks, but that wouldn't keep Oregon fisherman away from Olallie Lake, nor would it shut down the campground, whose business depended on renting cabins and selling supplies to the folks who trolled the lake in search of lunker trout. Rat had spent enough time bobbing about the surface of the lake over the years, often in the pouring rain, to know that this wasn't about the weather.

Had there been a fire warning? None of the campsites seemed to be occupied, but the host's vehicle was still sitting parked in front of their trailer. Of course, the hosts could have had more than one vehicle but still, shouldn't someone have left a sign, or at least a note, letting folks know that the area had been abandoned?

But, again, it had been raining solidly for three days, he thought, *and off and on for the last two weeks. Fires seemed unlikely and while an unusually wet summer --even for Oregon-- might have kept a few of the campers away, the hosts should still he here.*

Besides, if there was a fire warning, why were the skies clear? Rat sniffed the air and turned three-hundred sixty degrees; the sky was clear and blue, and free of smoke.

Maybe they'd had two rigs, and they took the other one.

Still, they should have posted something, to let folks know that they'd left.

"Hey..." he shouted, pounding on the door, "anyone in there? Anyone home?"

No answer.

Rat walked back to the store and flopped down on the porch.

The lake was a calm, blue blanket, occasionally broken by the spreading rings of rising trout. Low hanging clouds still hid Mt. Jefferson beyond, so no pictures even if the damned camera had been working. The only sound was the soft whisper of the wind over the water. A handful of canoes bobbed at the end of the wooden pier.

Grimacing and stretching, Rat fished a tiny lantern and a fuel canister from the bottom of his pack. These had been his emergency back-up lights and had, thus far, been untouched. Setting the lantern on the table, he lit the single mantel to wash the porch with a soft white light. He would have preferred a good, bright two-burner lantern, but the pack had been heavy enough without the extra burden.

Item by item, he emptied the lightweight pack and inventoried his gear. Most of the main pouch was taken up with his sleeping bag, clothes and rain gear. The pack also contained the sadly deflated bag that held his food supply and he set this aside.

One of the last items purchased before starting from Campo had been a water purifier that, with a strict regimen of boiling the water from the nearby creek, should have kept his unfortunate intestinal incident from occurring. Still, believing that safe was a lot better than sorry, Rat had added an extra roll of biodegradable toilet paper to the pack as well, which had turned out to be a very good idea. A compact first aid kit was nestled in the outside pouch for quick and easy access.

Lastly, his once new, now battered, ultra light tent was strapped to the bottom of the pack, along with a thin foam sleeping-pad.

With almost two-thirds of the trail behind him, there wasn't much to inventory; most mornings he could tell just by the weight of the pack if something was missing.

By two o'clock, the rumbling in his stomach and the silence of the campground led Rat to break a window in the store's door and unlatch the lock.

Feeling some guilt as a burglar, he let himself into the store and lifted his resupply box from the shelf.

"What am I supposed to do, starve?" he consoled himself, "Where in the hell are the camp hosts?"

A rank smell accosted his nose as he stepped toward the counter. Sitting next to the cash register was what appeared to be the remains of a chicken-salad sandwich and a glass of milk. The latter had curdled and grown gray-green with mold, the former was...moving.

Rat swallowed hard and looked away. The smell of decaying meat was sickening but familiar. Hadn't the campground smelled like that, albeit not as eye-wateringly strong, the night before?

Trying not to look at the maggots that were feasting on the re-mains of the sandwich, Rat used a magazine to scoop the whole mess in a trash can, which, holding his breath, he carried outside.

How long must that food have sat there to go that bad? he wondered. *Who cares? Get in, get done, and get out, before some-one comes along, yelling about that damned broken window.*

He set the box on the porch and slit the tape with his pocket knife. Inside were six packets of dehydrated Mountain House dinners, fresh underwear and socks, a set of maps for the next section of the trail, and several sets of batteries.

The batteries, much to Rat's frustration, proved to be as worthless as the ones he'd already packed. The GPS, the camera, and his flashlight, each refused to return to life, and finally, with a teeth-grinding curse, he returned them to his pack. Batteries from the store shelves didn't work either.

Duracell was going to get an earful from him when he got back home.

Rat stared reproachfully at his pile of electronic gear scattered across the counter in front of him.

"What are the odds," he asked to no one in particular, "that the camera, flashlight and GPS would all crap out at the same time?" For that matter, what were the odds that the batteries on the shelves wouldn't work any better than those he'd packed six months ago, back home? Things were getting seriously weird.

The power in the store was out also. He'd flipped the light switch by the door, but the bulbs had remained dead. Resting a hand on the door of the freezer, Rat felt no hum of power, and the puddle of water on the floor gave mute testimony to the fact that everything inside was melting.

The microwave was just as dead, so there were no burritos or Hot-Pockets to be enjoyed, but Rat feasted on a couple of cans of cold ravioli and three, somewhat soft, ice cream sandwiches from the freezer.

His first duty was to his stomach and, after, filling himself on canned pasta and sugary treats, he could figure out what to do next. Taking a pad of paper from the drawer beneath the cash resister, he wrote a quick note explaining his situation.

Sorry about the window. Arrived on September 12...no one was here. I needed my resupply box. Took $12.98 in supplies. Happy to pay for food and damages. Please contact me at... he then wrote out his address, phone number and email.

Sitting on the wood floor, after stripping and changing into fresh underwear and socks, Rat repacked his gear, adding several packages of Ramen noodles, a couple of cans of Beef-A-Roni, and a handful of candy bars from the stores shelves. The store didn't carry the fuel blocks he used for his stove, but there were several in his supply box. The rest of the camping gear that lined the shelves was stuff he didn't need or already had.

After eating his fill, he dumped the empty containers in the garbage can and pasted his note over the keyboard of the cash register.

Then, after he patched the broken window with cardboard and a roll of duct tape he'd found in the back of the store, Rat repacked his bag, closed the door behind him, and started back up the trail.

Cinching up his pack straps, Rat popped the half of a Snickers bar in his mouth and wondered, not for the last time, *Where the hell is everyone?*

The trail from Olallie to Timothy Lake was flat, forested and easy hiking. Rat crossed Highway 26, looking for traffic both ways and finding none, before camping the night at Frog Lake. The camp was every bit as deserted as Olallie had been.

Rat fought back the tiny fingers of panic that were beginning to tickle around the edges of his mind, as he pitched his tent. He feasted on lukewarm ravioli before bedding down to read about Frodo and the hobbits meeting Elrond. After ten minutes of staring unseeingly at the same page, his brain tripping over confused questions for which he had no answers, he gave up, banked his fire, and fell into a thin, troubled sleep.

Tomorrow he would reach Timberline Lodge and find out what the heck was going on.

It was now almost a week since he'd seen another person.

*　　*　　*

Rat broke camp early the next morning after a quick breakfast of cold Pop-Tarts and water. He skipped the coffee and hiked back to the trail at a quick, not quite frantic, pace. He'd slept poorly, and his eyes felt like they were filled with sand; a small headache pulsed at the base of his skull.

Caffeine withdrawal, he wondered, *or something else?*

He had just crossed Highway 35 at Barlow Pass, which was equally as deserted as 26 had been the night before, and started up the steep grade toward the timberline. Rounding a sharp oxbow in the trail, he caught sight of something on the trail ahead, something orange.

Rat slowed his pace, wiping moisture from his glasses as he moved closer.

The body, or what was left of it, had been laying face up on the trail for at least a couple of days; he could see that much by the collection of dirt and pine-needles scattered across the front of the blaze-orange parka and sodden jeans. Two huge hiking books, their toes pointed up into the rain, faced him and he could see that the mud had been washed from the sides of the trail by the weather. The man's head was arched back over the pack that lay beneath him, his Adam's apple protruding horribly from the angle of his neck.

From where he stood, Rat couldn't see the corpse's face, but one hand lay palm up in the mud, the fingers like gray, withered sticks.

He blinked, thinking for a moment that he must be dreaming.

Sure, that's it, I'm still back in my tent at Frog Lake, or maybe I'm still sick and haven't even gotten to Olallie yet. I'm sick and this is some bizarre dream brought on by giardia.

Somewhere overhead a crow cawed angrily and water dripped from the brim of his hat, bringing a shiver as it inched its way beneath his jacket and down his chest. His calves began to quiver from the strain of standing lock-kneed on the uphill grade.

He blinked again, and the gray hand was still there. A drop of rain fell from the curled pinky into the palm. It was the deadest-looking hand Rat had ever seen.

I'm not dreaming, he thought. *I'm really standing here, wide awake and looking at a dead-guy laying on the trail not a mile out from Timberline Lodge.*

"I'm awake," he said aloud, and the sound of his own voice breaking the awful stillness made him jump. He swallowed hard and forced himself to take another step, then another, edging his way around the body until he could see the dead man's face.

The next thing Rat knew he was on his hands and knees, retching into the bushes, the remains of his breakfast a steaming mess six inches from his face. He heaved again, and all that came up was a thin stream of saliva; the third one was dry.

He stayed like that a while, resting on trembling arms, trying to force away the hundreds of tiny black spots that swam before his eyes, and taking huge gasps of cold, clear air into his lungs.

The man's face...

He felt another cramp rip through his abs and forced it down before he heaved again.

Once, when Rat had been a second-grader at Rockwood Elementary School, his class had spent a day carving faces into apples and then drying them to make shrunken heads for Halloween. A pretty sick craft project for a little kid, but he'd thought it was cool at the time.

The face of the dead hiker looked like those shriveled, brown apples that had come from the oven in Mrs. Jones classroom. It looked just like them.

Mummified was the word. The man's face was a thin, dry stretch of skin across the cheekbones, eyes sunken and *mercifully* closed. His gaping mouth was a puckered horror, thin lips pulled back from shockingly white teeth. Suddenly Rat knew, he *knew*, that if he looked into that mouth, the dead man's tongue would be a dry and brittle bit of shoe leather against the roof of the mouth.

He didn't look.

...those shriveled, brown apples...

Rat bit his lip, trying not to think of the sweet, overripe cider smell that had wafted from the oven, knowing if he did, he was going to keep heaving until something in his belly tore loose.

Finally his gorge subsided and he rose shakily to his feet.

What was going on?

The hiker's body couldn't have been lying there long enough to dry out into the shriveled husk it was now, nor would it have, under the nearly ceaseless rains. Someone must have dumped the body there.

But who?

Why?

....and with a pack still on its back, for God's sake?

Besides, it didn't look like it had been dragged and dumped. The mummy-hiker looked, for all the world, as if he'd just stopped, mid-stride, and fallen backwards into the mud.

I should check to see if he has a wallet, or any ID, Rat thought, which he followed quickly with, *I don't care if he has diamonds in his pockets and gold bars in his pack, I ain't touching that thing... no way!*

The Lodge was only a little further up the trail, he would have to double-time it and find someone who could send for the authorities. Rat wanted desperately to rinse the bitter taste of bile from his mouth, but he knew that any water he drank while still in sight of the corpse would come right back up.

Time for water later.

Before he left, he forced himself to walk back to the body and, trying his best not to look into the dead face, he removed his own pack. Pulling his poncho up and over his head, he laid it across the corpse, covering everything from the knees up. He felt like he should say something before just going off and leaving the hiker lying in the middle of the trail.

Instead, he reshouldered his pack, cinched down the straps, and started back up the trail at a healthy pace.

* * *

By the time he reached the summit, Rat was bent over and gasping for air, one hand pressed against a deep stitch in his side. The view was breathtaking, both of Mt. Hood above and the lodge below. But Rat barely noticed the pristine beauty of the mountain; his eyes were filled with the wondrous sight of electric lights blazing from the windows of Timberline and the view of cars scattered about the parking lot. There would be people in the lodge who would go to retrieve the dead hiker, a phone to call Ma, maybe even a hot meal and a soft bed.

He scrambled down a steep path of the loose shale, always keeping the lodge in sight; not quite in a panic, but not willing to lose direct contact with his personal Mecca, either. His eyes stayed fixed on the lodge, on the great wooden front doors, on the life-size bronze deer in the entryway.

It was at the foot of the parking lot, which he had made it to, miraculously, without slipping and tumbling down the trail, that he slowed to a stop.

It was too quiet.

So quiet he could feel the pressure of the silence against his eardrums. The lights still burned in the windows, cars of every make and model still scattered about the parking lot, but he didn't see a single person; and he now realized he hadn't seen anyone, absolutely no movement whatsoever the entire time he was coming down the trail from the summit.

The deer statue stepped from the doorway and walked slowly away from him and into the tree line, its black tail flicking slowly but showing no sign of alarm.

Suddenly, Rat knew the truth. He wouldn't find any help at Timberline, because there was no one there.

No one alive, anyway.

The lodge is full of mummies.

Something in Rat's head slipped a gear, and the world went gray for a while. A fog seemed to roll over his eyes and he went away a bit. The ship sailed on but without his hand at the tiller, one might say.

Horatio can't come to the phone right now, please leave a message at the sound of the beep.

When the fog at last lifted, he found himself in the driver's seat of a red Toyota pickup, parked near the front of the Lodge. Rat shook his head, clearing away the last tendrils and wisps, and looked around. Several cars sat with their driver's doors open, apparently he'd tried each of them in turn until coming across one with the keys still in the ignition; the key that his fingers were closed on now.

Had he gone into the lodge?

The lodge is full of mummies.

He was pretty sure he had, but it was hazy. It was mid-morning when the fog had rolled in, and the sun was heading for the far horizon now. How much time had he been away, four hours? Six? He could only remember thinking, *I have to get home.*

A broken record, played over and over, a thirty-three vinyl turning at forty-five.

IhavetogethomeIhavetogethomeIhavetogethomeIhavetogetho meIhavetogethomeIhaveto...

Rat depressed the clutch and turned the key.

Nothing.

Not even a click from the starter. It's dead as... Rat didn't finish that thought.

It didn't make sense that the battery would be drained after just a couple of days, maybe a week at most, of sitting in the parking lot. But then again, what had made any sense since he'd crawled into his tent, sweating and shivering, at Scout Lake?

Nothing.

He got out of the truck, closing the door this time, and walked back to the Lodge. The front door stood partway open, which answered one of his questions. The woman lying on the floor just inside the doorway answered a second. Her face was another dried apple under a wealth of blousy blond hair; another mummy.

There were more, he knew; uniformed mummies scattered about hallways and kitchens, a nattily dressed mummy wearing a tuxedo shirt and suspenders lying behind the bar, probably dozens more tucked safely into their beds throughout the lodge. The massive clock above the fireplace was still ticking, but every watch, on every desiccated wrist had stopped at precisely the same time.

The same time that the battery operated clock in the Olallie Lake store had stopped; probably the precise moment that his camera, flashlight, and GPS had all given up the ghost, as well.

Four o'clock in the morning on September the Sixteenth, Two-Thousand and Eight.

The morning of the comet.

*   *   *

Evening was a spreading purple bruise in the eastern sky when Rat hiked to the edge of the parking lot and quickly set up his tent on a narrow swath of grass behind the hedge.

Hundreds of soft, warm beds waited a hundred yards away, but he could have no more brought himself to sleep in that mausoleum, than he could have sprouted wings and flown home. No, by the look of things, he'd be sleeping in his tent a lot from now on, and walking for the foreseeable future.

He'd found a stack of newspaper that had been delivered to the lodge on September fifteenth, the front page filled with a blazing, full-color photo of Hemmingway's Comet passing Saturn. Seventy-two point font heralded, **Welcome To Earth!**

Ouch.

Nothing in the paper had so much as whispered about any plagues or viral outbreaks anywhere in the world, certainly nothing in the United States. Just the typical partisan squawk-talk at the various levels of government, a minor war here and there, and pages and pages of the latest and greatest gizmos and gadgets at absolutely, positively, the lowest prices you would ever find anywhere.

And, of course, several related stories on the comet.

The one piece Rat found even mildly amusing was a condescending little article about a group of Arizona spiritualist who had burned their compound to the ground before walking into the desert to await the end of the world and the return of the Messiah. Strangely, the paper didn't mention which *messiah* in particular but the writer made it clear that the world would probably be a better place if the group stayed in the desert, Messiah or no Messiah.

On any other day, Rat might have grinned to think of who had gotten the last laugh on *that* particular joke.

Electrical power seemed to be unaffected, as the lights were evidence, and a television set in the Lodge bar had caught Rat's attention. He found the remote in a drawer beneath the cash register and turned it on. The screen filled with snow, and he scrolled up the dial station by station…snow…snow…snow…

He began to suspect that the cable was down as well when the screen filled with the MSNBC News desk. Rat's breath caught in his throat and he toggled the volume higher; when the reader reached sixty-eight, he realized it wasn't the television; it was the newsroom that had no sound. Faintly, he could hear a monotonous beeping, like a telephone receiver left off the cradle too long, somewhere in the background, maybe even in another room.

All three news positions were empty; Rat could see the tops of the chairs behind the desk.

After several minutes of watching, hoping someone would walk into view, or say something off screen, the empty newsroom started to give him the creeps and he thumbed the up arrow on the remote.

Blasting static filled the room and Rat leapt from his chair with a curse, his heart trip-hammering in his chest as he jabbed the mute button with his thumb. As his pulse returned to normal, he started channel-surfing again, after a dozen more dead stations, he found another in operation, and it was worse than MSNBC.

The camera was skewed slightly to the left so the stage and podium were off center, as was the American flag that hung in the background. At the center of the podium was the presidential seal; and when he thumbed off the mute, the room again filled with that tomb-like quiet. Rat stared at the screen for a long time, his hands limp like pale dead birds in his lap, then he slowly lowered his head to the bar and began to weep.

The camera angle was skewed to the left, but not quite far enough to cut from view a single black wingtip shoe. Above that were several inches of black sock and the cuff of a pair of suit pants; the rest of the body was hidden from view.

The bottom of the screen glowed with the message, *Live from the Whitehouse...*

* * *

Rat was certain there must be any number of laws prohibiting campfires on the Lodge property but, as it seemed unlikely anyone would be showing up to give him a ticket, he gathered an armload from the storage shed behind the parking lot, gathered some kindling from a nearby grove, and set to making camp. At first, he tried kicking together some rocks to create a fire circle, then gave up and simply built his fire in a parking space adjacent to the hedge.

If he'd thought that an illegal fire might bring the authorities, or in fact, anyone at all, he might have simply torched the lodge and then stepped back and awaited arrest.

Once the fire was crackling merrily, he walked back to the lodge porch and gathered an assortment of goods he'd taken from inside. He still had one or two of the freeze-dried meals he'd gotten at Olallie, but the thought of another *just add boiling water* meal made him want to gag. In the cavernous kitchen he'd found a frying pan, a couple of dishes, a fork, and a walk-in cooler. After months of trail food, the bounty of the walk-in refrigerator was nearly as overwhelming as the news--or lack of it--he'd found on the television.

Hundreds of pounds of fresh meat, green vegetables, milk, butter...enough food to feed him for months, if the power stayed on and he didn't go crazy. He'd stood a while, the cool air frosting his breath, transfixed at the bounty. After weeks of reconstituted protein and carbs, and almost no fats...it wasn't deciding what to eat that left him paralyzed, but what *not* to eat.

Surely there was also a freezer on the premises, which would hold even more food, and pantries stocked with canned and dry goods. Eggs, cheese, fresh bread...

Finally, he took a thick New York steak, several russet potatoes, and a pound or so of fresh green beans. Before he'd left the lodge, he went behind the counter of the bar and grabbed a six-pack of expensive beer, the kind in the green bottles.

Setting up his kitchen beside the fire, Rat wondered why he wasn't freaking out. Why wasn't he screaming and crying, or cursing God?

Because I'm in shock, he thought, slicing potatoes into thin rounds with his pocketknife, *I've taken on more than my brain can handle, so it's put all of my emotions on hold for now. That's why I'm so calm, and why I can sit here and eat a steak dinner when everyone I knew is likely dead, and everyone in Timberline certainly is. It's all dammed up between my ears right now, but I've hit the mute button.*

Also, there was the fact that he'd just spent three months living a very solitary existence. Days would go by, once an entire week, without seeing another hiker or reaching a resupply town. The few times he came to populated areas, it had felt strangely uncomfortable to be around so many people. It was in his nature to be solitary, he'd always been the guy on the edge of the crowd, watching, or more likely locked in his room along with a book. Perhaps the possibility of being alone in the world hadn't come crashing down on him yet, because it was going to take some time to determine how he felt about it. Maybe there was no dam to...

That, and I'm starving.

What'll happen when that dam finally breaks? he wondered, then shuddered the thought away and turned to cooking.

What'll happen when that dam finally breaks? It had been Ma's voice, asking.

The meat turned out a little overdone, but not bad, given his lack of experience with pan-frying forty-dollar steaks over a camp-fire. The potatoes, which he cooked with a cube of butter, were a little black around the edges and the beans were undercooked. Also, he forgot to get salt or any spices while plundering the kitchen.

But hunger is the best sauce--another Ma-ism-- and he devoured everything with gusto, washing it down with cold draughts of smooth, imported beer. The dirty cutlery and pan he simply dropped into a dumpster beside the woodshed.

The moon was rising though a break in the clouds behind the lodge when he finished, and he sat for a while, watching the embers of the fire and belching contentedly thanks to a full stomach.

Wiggling into his sleeping bag, he found he was wide-awake, and more than a little fearful of a long sleepless night; visions of dead hikers, and that single black wingtip from the news station danced in his head until morning. A soft wind in the fir trees seemed mournful, like the faint cry of a lost child and he feared, that too, would keep him from sleeping.

But the exhausting day, both physically and emotionally, coupled with his orgy of fresh food and beer, had him snoring soon enough.

It was almost like any other night on the trail...almost.

*   *   *

When Rat opened his eyes, the first thing he realized was that he felt pretty good. His stomach had a bloated, contented feel to it, a feeling he hadn't woken to in a long time. Also, he was able to lay in his bag for a few minutes and savor the feeling. Freeze-dried dinners had a tendency to launch one from their tent at dawn, scrambling for their camp-shovel and toilet-paper. In fact, after several weeks of that diet, Rat had learned to dig his cat holes the night before; there'd never been an accident, but there had been some near misses.

The second thing he realized was that it was not, in fact, first light. The sun was up in all its glory and he realized he had slept late again.

He lay for a while, listening to the morning, hoping to catch the hum of a far off automobile or even a plane flying over.

Nothing.

With a sigh, he finally pulled himself from his bag, fished around for his glasses, and pulled on his boots.

The third thing he was aware of, a few minutes later, was that with his morning absolutions done, he was starving again. He remembered hearing Ma talk about how this was one of the differences between Americans and Brits, how they dealt with stress.

The Brits, they start to panic and they drink tea... she'd said. *Us Americans tho', we start getting' stressed and we head for the nearest Burger King. That's why Brit's are healthier than American's, but us Yankees are happier than them Brits. Tea ain't no good for nerves...nothing calms nerves like a super-size helpin' of salt and grease!*

Rat also seemed to remember that they were munching on a take-out pizza at the time.

With that thought firmly in his mind, Rat proceeded to the lodge kitchen, trying not to look at the occasional withered form laying in the hallway or leaning against a wall. Safely behind the wide, swinging doors, he began gathering the makings of a monstrous breakfast.

Soon, he had half a dozen eggs scrambled with milk and simmering over a low flame in a lake of browning butter. To this, he added generous handfuls of shredded cheese, along with some chopped onions, peppers, and mushrooms he had found in the cooler beneath the salad bar. The veggies were just starting to dry out, but they served just fine for a breakfast scramble.

A vat-sized tureen was half-full of cold coffee and Rat drained a quart of the tar-black liquid into a saucepan and heated it along with his breakfast, adding a big slug of cream to cut the bitterness. Still craving fresh food, he added a half a cantaloupe and half a honeydew melon to the platter he was using for a plate, and the sat down on a folding chair at a small table in the corner of the kitchen to stuff himself.

Like his sleeping arrangements the night before, he could have chosen a more comfortable chair and a linen draped table in the dining area, but, even though it seemed to be mummy-free, the vast room was quite and empty as a tomb.

A small CD player rested on a shelf above the table and Rat was pleasantly surprised to find it held a copy of *Journey's Greatest Hits*. He attacked the mountain of eggs as the first steely rifts *Only the Young* echoed off the tile walls, and was half-way through *Any Way You Want It*, before his groaning stomach made him slow down. Three quarters of the scramble and all of the fruit was gone by the time Steve Perry was wailing about *Lovin', Touchin', and Squeezin'* and Rat pushed himself away from the table with a sigh of pleasure.

He poured the rest of the coffee into an oversized mug and braced himself to begin exploration of the rest of the Lodge.

Rat's first stop was the gift-shop. The doors were closed, but not locked, and he found a light switch after a moment of groping along the wall. Most of the shelves held little of interest. Coffee mugs, key-chains, about a hundred different postcards, nothing that you wouldn't find on the shelves of any hotel shop in the world.

Towards the back were racks of clothes, and these *did* interest him.

His current ensemble was decidedly funky; stiff with sweat and dirt and starting to unravel at most of the seams. Everything on the racks had the name of the lodge, a picture of the lodge, or both on it, but they were clean and, unless someone showed up to open the cash register...it seemed they were also free.

Rat picked out two tan t-shirts, a long-sleeve denim shirt, a fleece vest with a hood, and a lightweight windbreaker. The last probably wouldn't replace the battered rain jacket that was stuffed down in his pack, but it would keep him warm and it didn't stink. He also grabbed a pair of hiking shorts and promised himself he'd get some new jeans in Welches or Sandys later.

Finally, he added two pairs of thin nylon swim trunks to his stack in lieu of underwear.

The clothes were heavy and bulky, unlike the ultra-light clothes he'd been used to wearing, but the hike was over, he realized, glancing around the shop for anything else that might be of use.

His Pacific Crest Trail adventure had ended when he'd found the dead hiker's body on his way up the mountain, and the chances of him ever finishing the Washington to Canada stretch looked pretty slim. Not that his hiking days were behind him, by any means. Unless he could get a car started, and after his failure in the parking lot, he tended to doubt he would, he had a long walk home. Highway 26 would take him nearly the entire way, through Sandy to Gresham and from there to Rockwood.

With a bit of luck he might be home in less than two weeks.

Is Ma there waiting for me? he wondered. *Is anyone there still alive?*

Rat closed his eyes and squeezed that thought, along with several tailing behind it, back into its box. Plenty of time to take them out and play with them later, but for now he had to just keep doing what he'd been doing for months.

He had to pack up and keep walking.

THE LUNATICS BLOODLETTING

ALVA J. ROBERTS

The frigid wind blew chunks of snow and ice across the street. It was a balmy twenty-two degrees Fahrenheit, a beautiful June morning in southern California.

"The freaks are at it again," David said, his voice full of undisguised disgust.

"Better call the captain. He'll want to get the boys here in case they riot again," Ben Johnson said. He understood how David felt. The Cult of Luna was full of odd balls and zealots, dressed in long silver robes. How could anyone revere a rock drifting somewhere in outer space?

Ben wasn't sure he would have worshiped or cursed the mythical goddess Luna had he believed in her. The moon had saved the Earth from total annihilation, sacrificing itself when a rogue planet entered the solar system. But without the moon to regulate the tides, weather, and Earth's rotation, the planet was dying a slow death. Sometimes Ben wished the rogue planet had just struck them and put them out of their misery.

"Move along!" Ben shouted, walking towards the group, holding his rifle. "There're no public demonstrations allowed in the refugee camps."

"It's our right as American citizens to practice our religion!" one of them shouted.

Ben sighed. No orders had come from DC in almost three months, and in all likelihood, there was no America left. It didn't matter anyway, martial law had been declared a few days after the moon was knocked from orbit.

"You have the right to do as you're told. No demonstrations that could lead to civil unrest. Now clear out!" Ben shouted.

He hoped they would listen. If they were still outside when Captain Henderson arrived, there would be hell to pay. And the members of the fanatical moon cult would be the ones paying. Henderson was the highest ranking officer in the camp. For all intents and purposes that made him king of Refugee Camp 45893, and he hated anything that hinted at being a threat to his power.

Ben heard angry mutters from the group. The leader of their procession walked toward him. He was a small man; dwarfed by his heavy winter coat and the shimmering silver robes he wore over them.

"The great goddess Luna sacrificed herself for us, her only children. We gather to pray for her return and an end to the winter, my child. We have no desire to riot," the priest said. The cultist went silent and still as a group of soldiers entered the area, Captain Henderson leading them. Ben swallowed hard. There was no telling what would happen when the captain's volatile temper mixed with the fanatical zeal of the cultist.

It was a recipe for disaster.

"Private Johnson, fall into rank," Henderson ordered. Ben scurried to do as commanded.

"We only wish to perform our religious rites in peace," the priest said to the captain.

"The way you peacefully performed your rites last week? Three people died." Henderson's voice held a hard edge.

There was a loud crack of a gun being fired and Henderson fell to the ground in a spray of blood. The priest dropped to the ground in a ball, his hands covering his head.

Ben and the rest of the platoon opened fire, the sound of their assault rifles cutting through the crisp, cold air. The cultist dropped like flies.

A few members of the religious group returned fire with the hunting rifles they carried for protection, but with little effect.

It was a massacre.

Ben was breathing hard when the shooting stopped. It was the first combat he'd ever seen and he hoped to God it would be the last; he felt a little sick to his stomach.

Silver clad bodies lay piled on top of one another. Steam rose from the rapidly growing pool of blood beneath the heap of shattered flesh.

The body closest to Ben was a young woman, a girl really, maybe sixteen years old. Her blonde hair wafted in the breeze. Her dead eyes stared at Ben, accusing and cold.

"Jesus," Ben whispered, staring at the dead bodies. Death was a common occurrence in the refugee camps, but Ben had never been the instrument of it.

"Hell, yeah! We got them bastards good!" David yelled.

Ben spun, smashing the butt of his rifle into David's leering face. There was a satisfying crunch as David's teeth flew through the clearing, blending in with the snow when they landed.

"Take him to the brig!" Henderson yelled, climbing to his feet. The captain held a hand to his shoulder as he stood, bright crimson fluid flowing between his fingers.

Ben felt something thick and hard crash into the small of his back. Pain shot up through his kidneys and he dropped to his knees. Something else struck him across the temple. His vision blurred and his head throbbed in time to the beating of his heart. He felt someone take his rifle and bind his hands.

Then the world went black.

*   *   *

"Come on," a voice whispered in the dark.

"What about the soldier?" the priest's voice from earlier asked.

"You go. It's the summer solstice, and Luna will need all her servants. I'll take care of the butcher. He will not live to see the glory of Luna's bloodletting."

Ben rolled over, coming fully awake. He couldn't see a thing. The prison was the darkest place he had ever been, twenty feet underground with no windows. The priest must have been locked up in the same cell. Space in the brig was growing scarce, and the tiny, single occupant cells each housed two prisoners.

He drew in a deep breath, sliding from his bed with all the stealth he could muster. His back throbbed and his head felt like it was full of cotton, making his movements awkward and clumsy. He drew up against the wall nearest him and listened. He heard the scurry of the priest's feet, and the sound of voices greeting him in the hall. Then, he heard a different set of feet draw closer to him.

116

The man was standing right over Ben's pallet. There was the soft swoosh of steel being drawn from leather. A nervous sweat rolled down Ben's face and he wondered if the man could hear the thundering of his heart. Ben needed to move soon, or else his attacker would find out he wasn't sleeping on the pallet.

Ben threw his arms wide, as if getting ready to give someone hug, and lunged forward. His left arm slammed into someone as he ran. He wrapped himself around the man, tackling him to the ground.

The knife darted outward in the darkness, scoring Ben's forearm. Ben wrestled for the blade, curling his whole body around the attacker's arm. Ben felt the coppery taste of blood as he bit into the man's hand.

"Damn it!" his assailant shouted, dropping the blade.

Ben's elbow darted upward, cracking into his attacker's nose. He felt cartilage shatter beneath the blow. Ben twisted around, his hands clamped around the man's neck.

He kicked and struggled, clawing at Ben's hands. Ben brought his knee up into the man's sternum and counted to two hundred before he let the man's limp body go.

Ben trembled as a wave of nausea passed through him.

Dear God, he'd just killed a man with his bare hands.

"It was me or him," he whispered, the old saying having little effect on his guilt.

The cult was going to have a *bloodletting*. If the peaceful cultists had turned militant, then Ben needed to find out what they were up to before it was too late.

Ben's hands ran across the floor, searching for the lost blade. He wasn't about to leave the cell bare handed. He'd gotten lucky the first time, but Ben hated gambling.

Something sharp nicked his thumb and he put the injured digit in his mouth. The blade was just an old kitchen knife, twice as long as Ben's palm and as wide as three fingers, but its worn wooden handle felt good against his palm.

Ben crept to the wall and ran his hands along it. Without his sight, he felt practically helpless. He felt the stone door frame, and then his fingers ran over empty air. He stepped through the open doorway.

"You take care of him?" a voice asked.

Ben grunted an affirmative.

"Come on then, we need to get to Hob's Clearing before midnight. The others escorted the priest."

The beam of a flashlight flicked on, illuminating the way out of the prison. Ben followed close behind the man. Where were the guards? A sticky pool of blood coating the hall in front of them answered Ben's question.

The guards were dead.

The blade of Ben's knife shook in his white-knuckled grip. He had to do it, he didn't want to, but he had to.

Ben grabbed the man's shoulder and thrust the knife into the small of his back. The man screamed in pain and Ben could feel hot blood gush over his hand. Ben stabbed again, this time the blade piercing the man's heart.

The body hit the concrete floor with a thud. The flashlight fell to the ground with a crack and its light went out. Ben was glad he couldn't see the man he had killed. His hands continued to shake as he searched the body. He started to feel sick again and stopped for a moment, gagging.

His questing fingers found the butt of a revolver tucked into the dead man's waist band. He felt the cylinder. It was loaded; he had six shots. He hoped he would never need them.

He had to get to the captain, tell him what was happening. Ben rushed out of the building. Captain Henderson should be in his quarters.

He stopped dead in his tracks when the icy wind struck him, freezing his sweat to his forehead. His coat was inside somewhere, taken when he was locked up. Snowflakes were starting to fall from the sky, floating gently to the ground.

"Who goes there?" a commanding voice asked.

Ben could see the silhouette of two guards making their rounds.

"Private Ben Johnson. I need to see the captain."

"How'd you get out of your cell? Don't move!" one of them snapped.

"Hey, he has a gun!"

Ben dove to the side just as a bullet tore through the air where he was standing. Snow caked his body as he stood up. He ran for the edge of the camp.

Almost twenty thousand men and women lived in the camp, and their foot traffic had condensed the snow, making it easy for Ben to see the perimeter.

More shots rang out in the crisp, cold air. Fire lanced through his shoulder as a bullet tore through his tender flesh, going in his back and coming out his front. His hand grasped the wound but he didn't slow down.

If he stopped, he knew they would kill him.

Ben was out of the camp's cleared area. The snow was deeper here, past his knees. He struggled forward, leaning against a tree to catch his breath. The guards wouldn't leave the camp, not in the middle of the freezing night, not for a deserter. Not during a storm.

A *deserter*.

The word echoed in Ben's mind as a horrible throbbing pain in his shoulder sent tendrils of fire shooting through his body. The internal heat was a sharp contrast to the chill of the eternal winter's air. He needed to bandage his wound and find a coat. But he couldn't go back into the camp; the punishment for deserting was death.

Hob's clearing. There would be people there and he might be able to get a coat. He stuck the revolver in the waist band of his uniform.

Ben stumbled through the drifting snow, his breath blowing out in front of him. The wind was picking up and the snow was falling harder, turning into a full scale blizzard.

As he ran, he debated taking his shirt off. The long-sleeved, button up shirt was soaked clear through with water from the slush and snow from when he'd fell. But now it was beginning to freeze, forming a layer of ice around his chest and back that scraped his skin raw as he ran. Ben decided to keep it on; he couldn't stomach the idea of the falling snow landing on his bare chest and back.

Hob's Clearing wasn't far. Just before the rogue planet hit the moon, when no one was sure if it would hit the Earth or not, a man by the name of Malcolm Hob went out into the middle of a freeway and set off a homemade bomb.

It was all over the news. Everyone in the world saw and heard Hob as he made his speech about sacrificing himself as an offering for the goddess Luna. Less than five minutes after the bomb went off, the rogue planet struck the moon and was deflected away from the Earth.

Luna's great miracle. It was no surprise that the goddess' cult would choose that location for their ceremony.

Orange light flickered ahead of Ben. A fire. Warmth!

Ben rushed forward; down into the hollow left by Hob's bomb, the cult of Luna had built a bonfire. Men and women stood around the blaze, passing thick, clay jugs back and forth, drinking from them. A dais was raised next to the fire. Drums pounded out a steady beat, and many of the cultists began to dance, a gyrating twirling movement.

Ben started to make his way down the slope, already feeling the warmth of the fire. He stopped again when he saw the dancers tearing their clothes off. He watched, dumbstruck, as the men and women began fondling each other's most intimate areas. Snow still fell from the sky, making the entire valley look like some perverse snow globe.

Ben shook his head, let them have their orgy. It was far from the *bloodletting* the other cult members had spoken of. Ben slid down the last few feet of the slope.

He reached down and picked up a discarded coat on the edge of the clearing, his ice-caked shirt replacing it on the pile. The dry warmth of the coat was a welcome reprieve from the storm. He inched closer to the fire, feeling pinpricks all over his body as its heat warmed his flesh. The valley was sheltered from the worst of the storm.

The smell wafting from the jugs told Ben that somehow they contained whiskey. The smell of marijuana and burning tobacco filled the air. They must have spent hundreds of thousands of dollars on the party favors. Most drugs had become scarce as the endless winter went on. A pack of cigarettes sold for a thousand dollars back at the camp. Ben heard it was worse up the coast in the other camps, where they were killing each other over canned vegetables.

The drumming grew to a crescendo. Priests ascended the dais. They wore silver robes that reflected the fire light and shimmered as the moon once had. The snow gusted past the men.

Ben craned his neck upward to see better. He was standing right next to the stage.

They walked across the platform in a long line, with a single man in front who wore a ceremonial headdress. The headdress was made of bones tied with black leather strips. What could only be the skull of a child decorated the front.

"My children! It is the Solstice! On this day of light it was foretold that the great goddess Luna would return! As it was at her departure, so must it be now. Luna left when the holy blood of Malcolm Hob was offered to her! So now, we make a new offering!"

Two men walked to the center of the dais. Between them they carried a squirming cloth bundle that they dropped unceremoniously. A girl rolled out of the black cloth.

She couldn't have been more than sixteen or seventeen. Blonde hair swept down over her shoulders, the only covering on her naked body. The girl stumbled to her feet, shivering. Her hands covered her nakedness and sought to protect her from the snow's fury.

"We shall give the great goddess one who is pure. When the sun vanquishes the blanket of night we shall go forth and sow death among the non-believers. And when the blood runs like rivers through the streets, then shall Luna return!" The priest's arms spread wide, as a table rose from the dais behind him. The table was stacked high with guns. Ben could see every type of firearm he could think of, from handguns to a rocket launcher.

He swallowed hard. They were going to do it, they were going to kill the girl and attack the camp. He couldn't believe it.

So many people would die if they did. There were only a hundred soldiers in the camp and there had to be at least that many people around the bonfire. If you added in the element of surprise, the Cult of Luna stood a real chance of wiping out all of Camp 45893.

Ben pulled his revolver out, trying to think. He was just one man. If he tried to stop them he would *probably* die, but if he did nothing, then the girl *would* die.

The head priest pulled a long knife from the folds of his silver robe. The snow swirled around him, lifting his robe behind him. The girl looked dazed and helpless, her eyes pleading for mercy.

The crowd around Ben cheered and screamed. Those participating in the orgy grew frenzied, their pace quickening. Their skin was turning blue, and the fanatical cultists would soon have frostbite or worse.

Ben took a deep, calming breath. It was now or never.

Ben pulled the revolver up in one smooth motion and pulled the trigger. The gun shot reverberated off the walls of the valley, echoing back at Ben, as the bullet smashed into the head priest's chest. Blood sprayed outward, painting the naked teenager bright red. It was a perfect shot, right through the man's heart.

The cult erupted in chaos. Men and women screamed in panic and tried to run out of the valley. The snow plunged down on the squirming men and women, caking their bodies in white. The ice covered walls of the valley made the uncontrolled, chaotic escape impossible. The leaders of the pack slid into those behind them and were trampled.

Ben felt sick to his stomach. He joined the army because they got all the best rations. But now he had killed again. The guilt accompanying the action was unimaginable and overwhelming.

Ben ignored the feelings raging inside of him. He could contemplate what he'd done later. Right now he needed to save the girl.

He ran forward, taking the steps to the dais two at a time. The other priests blocked his path, standing shoulder to shoulder. Ben could see the table of weapons right behind them. If he gave the men a moment to turn around, they would be armed to the teeth.

"Stand aside!" Ben screamed.

"You may not have..." a priest began.

His commands were cut short by the gun in Ben's hands. The bullet tore through the man's left knee, splinters of bone and flesh flying through the air.

"That was your only warning! Move!" Ben snapped.

The silver clad men practically dove off the platform to do his bidding. The injured priest rolled after them, moaning in pain and leaving a bloody trail leading off the stage.

"What's your name?" Ben asked the girl as he reached down to pick up the black cloth she'd been wrapped in, placing it around her shoulders.

"Sara," the girl answered in a tear-soaked voice.

"It's going to be okay, Sara. Just stay close to me and keep down," Ben told her in a calm voice.

Ben grabbed the rocket launcher from the table. There was one way he was sure he could get the captain's attention back at the camp. He fired the weapon at the empty space in the center of the valley. A second later, fire blossomed high into the air. The camp wasn't too far away, the sentries should be able to hear and see the explosion easily.

Ben grabbed an M16 from the mass of weapons and took a position in the middle of the stage. No one else was going to come near the table.

The cult was in a state of pandemonium, running in every direction. Whenever anyone tried to get on the stage, Ben peppered the ground with bullets.

It wasn't long before Captain Henderson and the rest of the regiment arrived. They took up positions along the entire rim of the valley and began firing.

Ben pulled Sara to the ground, covering her with his body as he watched in horrible fascination. The cultists were torn apart, in some cases literally. Ben ducked his head, not wanting to see the slaughter.

In just a few minutes, the gunfire stopped. Ben looked up. Not a single member of the cult was standing. Thick rivers of blood ran down the sides of the valley, collecting at the bottom of the slope in gruesome pools that were already cooling in the frigid temperature.

Ben staggered to his feet, swaying as he surveyed the carnage. The soldiers had stopped the men from leaving the valley, but Luna's prophecy had come to pass.

This night, there had been a *bloodletting*.

THE LAST ROUND

JOSEPH & ANTHONY GIANGREGORIO

In a devastated neighborhood in the middle of the United States, filled with the refuse of a dying civilization, resides a man who believes he is the only person left alive on the Earth.

Greg Thomas hunkered down in the bomb shelter buried in his backyard. He was fifty-five years old and a war veteran who knew, or you could say had a hunch, of when the world would come to an end by either a few warheads or some other calamity. He didn't know exactly *how,* but he was sure pretty sure of *when.*

It all started a few months ago when a small country in the middle of Asia decided to launch a retaliatory strike against a neighboring country in response to a perceived threat. After that, everything went downhill fast as other countries defended themselves, and the world was snuffed out like a spent cigarette.

Not that it mattered anymore, and in many ways, Greg wanted to forget, knowing the understanding as to the reason for what happened would not bode well for his well being.

But he was still alive, and that was because he had seen the future in a dream. But he was no fool and had kept his dream to himself, knowing no one would believe him, and all the while stockpiling supplies and getting his bomb shelter built in secret under the guise of remodeling his home.

His shelter was equipped with a toilet, a cot, an AM/FM radio, cans of food that would hold somebody over for months if not years, depending on how he wanted to ration it, and bottled water complete with a filtration system and water purifying system to recycle his waste water to drink again. Yes sir, he spared no expense on his shelter. It was state-of-the-art in every conceivable way.

But because of it, he lost his wife of twenty-two years, as she was thinking he was having one of his 'the world is going to end' days. She had hoped and prayed he would eventually stop, but when he didn't, she finally left him. Now, six months later, Greg was starting to run out of food. He hadn't been outside since then, sealing the hatch at the top of the shelter when the first rumble shook the ground, and had only seen the world through a view port, similar to a periscope on a submarine, situated on the top of the bomb shelter.

So far it wasn't safe out there and he had stayed inside.

*   *   *

A month and a half later, Greg had finally eaten the last can of baked beans and was down to one of his last bottles of fresh water. He still had some recycled water but even that was low and would only give him a few extra days.

Peering through his periscope, he had yet to spot another human survivor in the area surrounding his backyard. Spinning the periscope, he stopped when he saw his house, or what was left of it. Now it was rubble, shattered boards and beams mixed with cement and insulation. It was as if a giant hand had smashed it to the ground, as were the other homes on his street.

Other than that, he had no idea what the world would have in store for him, though he could only imagine.

In the devastated world outside his bomb shelter, he knew sooner or later he would have to venture forth in search of food and water. But was the air even breathable? He didn't know and wouldn't until he cracked the hatch. If it was poisonous, he would be dead in seconds, and he supposed it wouldn't matter too much anyway, but still, he hadn't lived in a box the size of an average bedroom for half a year to die now. But still, what if it was radioactive out there? He knew a little bit about radiation poisoning to know it wasn't a pleasant way to die.

Taking a swig of water, he decided to give it another three days, then he would head out and begin to forage.

Realizing his options, he decided to face death head-on and risk going outside, not wanting to die like a coward in his home-made tomb.

Three days later.

A battery-operated clock on a shelf near his cot read nine a.m., and he figured now would be a good time as any to go out into his new world.

He went to a small footlocker and opened it, retrieving the rifle he'd stashed there, but no sooner did he pick it up, then he found it soaking wet. Not understanding this, he reached inside and pulled out the three boxes of ammunition for the weapon, and upon opening them, found they were all corroded with rust. They were worthless.

Inspecting the footlocker, he found there was a five gallon jug of water in the corner and this had sprung a leak. Greg shook his head, not remembering even placing the water in with the guns and ammo. That was a stupid thing to do and now his gun and ammo was ruined.

Throwing them back into the footlocker with disgust, he slammed it closed, cursing his carelessness. He had no idea what the world was like up there and to go out there without a firearm seemed foolhardy.

At least he had a knife, an eight inch Bowie knife with a steel hilt. It was better than nothing, but not much use against an opponent with a gun.

But still, he had yet to see another human being through his view port.

Collecting the backpack lying under his cot, he packed it with all the items he needed for his foray into a dead and barren world. He took the remaining food and water as he didn't know if he would return or not. Actually, if he didn't find food, there would be no reason to ever come back to the shelter.

Before leaving, he went to the small desk in the corner of the shelter. Opening the small drawer in the middle of the desk, he took out a silver locket that once belonged to his wife. Inside the small pendant was a picture containing a photo of them together on their honeymoon. Looking at the locket got him thinking that his wife was probably dead, as was everyone else. Pushing the dreadful thoughts down, he placed the locket in his right front pocket.

Walking towards the door, he slowly unlocked it and opened it. A small stairway led up to the outer hatch, and he took the stairs slowly, like man walking from death row to the electric chair.

With a frightened sigh, he reached the hatch and unlocked it, wondering if his first breath of outside air would be his last. As the hatch was unsealed, he couldn't help but close his eyes.

Greg immediately felt a calming wind caress his face and he opened his eyes, relieved to still be alive and to finally feel fresh air on his skin after months of being trapped in the bomb shelter. Waiting another few minutes, he realized there was nothing odd about the atmosphere of the Earth. He could taste something on the air, and though it seemed to be okay to breathe, something deep inside him told him only a few months ago that wouldn't have been the case.

Stepping out onto the dead, yellow lawn of his backyard, he looked out past the closest destroyed homes to see the city beyond, no more than six miles away.

Even after nearly six months, the devastated, smoking city continued to billow plumes of black smoke out over the city's skyline. Where once majestic buildings stood tall, now there was rubble, more than one building looking as if half of it had been sheared away by a gigantic sword. When he was able to pull his eyes away from the horror of witnessing it first hand, he walked to the front of his house to see cars strewn about like a child's discarded playthings. As he looked closer, he saw the desiccated and shattered corpses of human bodies scattered about like forgotten Barbie dolls. After months of being exposed to the elements, the bodies were now nothing but bone wrapped in dried leather with rags for clothing. More than one was missing limbs, and as he stared into the dead and gnarled trees that once lined the sidewalk, so green and full of life, he saw more than one cadaver in the branches, as if a giant had tossed them there and forgotten about them.

Going towards the closest vehicle, he looked inside to see nothing but the brittle remains of what was once a human being, and after looking at the car more closely, he realized this was his neighbors Cadillac, though now the paint was peeling and in some places only bare metal peeked through.

After looking through the car, he found nothing of value, not even keys, so he left it, closing the driver's door out of habit.

He headed out then, walking down the middle of the cracked asphalt that once defined his street, hoping beyond hope he would find someone else alive.

He walked for the next four days, covering neighborhood after neighborhood in search of someone, anyone, still alive. But everywhere he went there was nothing but blasted ruins and death.

He tried riding a bicycle but he ended up carrying it over rubble more than he actually used it, so in the end he discarded it as worthless. It seemed the only way to get around was by using his two feet.

When he had finished off the last of his food from his pack, he tossed the empty fruit cocktail can to the side of the road where it rolled into the gutter. It stopped next to the desiccated remains of a German shepherd, the fur now matted with filth and what looked like dried blood.

This wasn't the first animal he'd found. The smell of rotting carrion filled the air. Dead cats and dogs were prevalent, the carcasses littering the roads and inside destroyed homes, but he found other animal corpses as well. He found a dead horse in a makeshift stable three towns over from his house and another had pigs and a goat. Before the cataclysm, the owners had broken zoning laws, but now it was all for nothing.

With nothing else to do, Greg continued onward, now not only searching for people, but absolutely for food and water, the latter two the most important item on his list of survival. He knew in a matter of days, if he didn't find anything to eat or drink, he would die. And a very painful death it would be, too.

* * *

His body was screaming for food, the pangs filling him like a hundred knives.

Holding his stomach, he moved to the next house on the street. He didn't know how many miles he was from his bomb shelter, and he knew he was lost. Any landmarks were now gone, replaced by piles of rubble. For better or worse, he was committed to his present course.

He stopped at the front door of this particular house. For some reason, this one structure was still standing, only some of the siding blasted away, the rest still intact. Most of the windows were also fine, though the glass was dirty and looked sandblasted.

Staring at the door, he tried the doorknob, but it was locked. A long window went from floor to ceiling to the right of it, and without hesitation, Greg kicked it in with the tip of his work boot, the glass fracturing and then shattering.

He finished off knocking out the glass with his elbow and he soon let himself inside, closing the door behind him out of some unconscious force of habit.

Upon entering the house, he soon caught the scent of stale death in the air. Approaching the kitchen, he saw the refrigerator door was wide open and he smelled the redolence of rotting food, such as a half eaten chicken, sitting on the second shelf, decaying along with other items such as milk and deli meats. But now it was a green science experiment gone horribly wrong, the mold growing at an alarming rate as white and brown maggots squirmed in the remains.

Covering his noise to try and filter out the smell, he quickly searched the rest of the cabinets and pantry. But everywhere he looked he found rotting food and exploded canned goods. Nothing was salvageable. Whatever had caused the blast that had decimated the world had destroyed the food, too.

When he finished searching anything worth checking, he turned to leave the house and try another one. Before he reached the front door, he spotted the pictures hanging on the hallway wall. There three children and grandchildren, all smiling, their faces full of cheer.

Seeing the photos got him thinking that they were all truly dead now. The children were rotting somewhere, their lifeless corpses drying in the sun.

It hit him then, hard and fast, and a wave of nausea rolled over him. He leaned against the wall and thought he was going to faint, but he fought off the dizziness and remained conscious.

He didn't know why, but staring at the dead faces of the family who once lived in this house had finally made it sink in that it was very possible he was the only one left.

And if that was so, then what would be the point of continuing at all?

But then hunger pains filled his insides again, and though he may have wanted to end it all, at the moment his need for food was overwhelming.

Crying softly, he exited the home of lost dreams and trudged on to the next one.

*   *   *

Throwing a large, head-sized, rock through the picture window of another home, three blocks from where he'd found the pictures of the family, he climbed inside and began searching.

Over the course of the day, he'd been lucky enough to find two candy bars and a bag of potato chips. The chips were crushed and were like breadcrumbs and the candy bars had melted into a syrupy goo, but to him they were the best thing he had ever eaten.

Unfortunately, he was now thirstier than ever after consuming them and he had used up the last of his water more than a day ago.

A few times he came across small muddy puddles of water in the gutter or in backyards, but when he tried to drink the water, he had to spit it out. The water had a coppery taste to it, and though it was possible he would be fine, he had a feeling it would kill him faster than a bullet to the head. No sooner did he think this then he saw birds lying a few feet away, each as dead as the other animals he'd found on his journey.

Walking around inside the house, he first entered the kitchen to see if there was at least something to eat, anything.

Tearing it apart from top to bottom, there was nothing worth eating. All the canned food had bulges and rust on them, the dry food nothing but powder.

Boxes of cereal and cookies were now like flour, and though it might be okay to consume, Greg figured whatever could transform food into to dust would probably kill him as fast as the tainted water outside.

That had him thinking about how this could be so. Whatever had happened to destroy the Earth must have changed the actual cellular structure of food and living beings. Underground, he had survived the onslaught, but anyone else hadn't been so lucky.

The house was two levels and he slowly walked up the stairs to the second floor, his footsteps creaking as he pressed on the warped wood. Reaching the landing, he saw half the roof was gone, water damage and dry leaves now collecting in the eaves and corners of the rooms.

He checked each room until he came to what was obviously a baby's room.

As he entered, his breath caught in his throat at the sight that greeted him.

In a crib was the mummified remains of a small infant, no more than four months old.

The small body was nothing but skin and bones now, the meat having rotted and dried to the consistency of beef jerky. There was a pacifier to the right of the shriveled head and in the corner of the crib was a stuffed bear, now covered in mold.

A dusty mobile of circus animals floated over the crib, the plastic animals shifting from the displaced air thanks to Greg's movements.

Greg looked away, not wanting to see the horrific sight any longer. But though he shifted his gaze, there was still more death in the blue and white painted room.

On the floor, directly next to the crib, was the emaciated corpse of a woman. She was wearing a pink jumpsuit; the lower half stained a dark brown thanks to the woman voiding herself upon her death. Her right hand was covering her face, as if she was trying to block out something terrible, and her left was upraised, her gnarled fingers wrapped around the bars of the crib, as if she was trying to reach her baby.

Greg stared for a full two minutes, his throat locked tight. He imagined the terror the woman must have felt when whatever blast wave had ripped through the neighborhood, killing everything and everyone.

When he finally broke from his stupor, he closed the bedroom door and walked down the hallway.

He made it as far as the bathroom before he ran inside, falling to the faded, dirty tiles to vomit into the empty toilet. In reality he could have puked anywhere, but the toilet drew him, the habit of where to do this overwhelming, almost controlling his actions.

As he threw up, he sobbed. He didn't cry for the woman or the baby, for their suffering was over. No, he sobbed for himself, the only witness to a dead world.

When his stomach finished assaulting him, he climbed to his feet and stumbled into the hallway. He soon found himself in a master bedroom and he barely glanced at the dead body of a man lying supine on the bed. He did see the face was haggard, dried and cracked and the hair was all but gone, tufts still lying on the pillow.

Then, for no apparent reason, he went to the bed and pulled the blanket up and over the corpse, hiding it from view.

As he pulled on the blanket at the foot of the bed, something fell off to land on the carpeting. It was a soft thud, but Greg heard it nonetheless, and he went to investigate.

Leaning over, he reached under the bed to where he thought the object had fallen. He pushed aside a set of dusty bunny slippers and a small cigar box and his hand rested on the grip of a handgun. As he pulled the gun out from under the bed, he also grabbed the cigar box. Opening the box, he found mementos of a lost and distant life, photos and keepsakes such as a ring and a movie ticket. Pushing them away, he studied the handgun, cracking it open to see there was one bullet remaining.

He sat on the edge of the bed and stared at the far wall, where pictures of a man, woman and baby smiled back at him.

The family he'd found, now nothing but dust, matched the ones in the pictures.

He didn't know how long he sat on the edge of the bed in a house he didn't know, from a family he had never met, but the sun soon went down and darkness fell.

When he could stay awake no longer, he merely leaned over and closed his eyes, his feet still on the floor. He slept the sleep of the truly exhausted and nightmares plagued him the entire night. Visions of a dead world filled with dead people, as they tried to find him, catch him and kill him, these demons of Hell trying to pull him down into the abyss.

When he awoke the next morning, he could barely open his eyes.

He was so weak from hunger, he could barely move.

As he sat up with a groan and glanced to the covered shape of the corpse, then he spotted the sleeping pill vial on the bedside table, the orange container empty.

Greg knew the man had taken the easy way out and now he knew it was time for him to do the same.

He didn't want to die, but then he really didn't have a choice. He was too weak to continue and there was no food or water anywhere.

In the end, all he had done is delay the inevitable. He was already dead, he just needed to accept it.

He was as dead as the world he now existed in, one of rotting corpses and diseased animal carcasses lying in the gutters of humanity. He chuckled slightly, realizing he was the last man left alive. Hell, back when he was a kid and his father had asked him what he was going to do with his life, the last thing he would have ever imagined he would accomplish was to be the remaining human alive on the Earth.

But he knew it was time to remedy that. He reached into his pocket and pulled out the locket, the one with the small photo of him and his wife. He squeezed it tight, thinking of better times.

Swallowing the dry lump in his throat, his heart beating fast with adrenalin, he cocked the weapon and placed the barrel in his mouth. He tasted gun oil and dust, but he ignored it.

He didn't know if this was the best way to do it, but he'd watched enough movies to figure out it should do the trick.

He sat for ten more minutes with the barrel in his mouth, too scared to pull the trigger. Tears fell from his cheeks to wet the sheets he rested on as he squeezed his eyes shut as hard as he could.

But he couldn't do it. So he sat quietly with the gun in his mouth, knowing sooner or later he would get the courage to finally end it.

For when there was no hope left, there was always death.

* * *

Outside in the street, all was silent, only the paltry wind stirring the debris of newspapers and assorted paper and plastic. The trash rolled across the pavement and beyond like modern day tumbleweeds, flowing across the road until it became trapped in an overgrown bush or shrub.

Time was irrelevant here, the shattered neighborhood of crushed dreams ageless. Shadows grew and shrank as the sun crawled across the sky.

But then, in the midst of the silence, a gunshot cracked, filling the street for barely a second. Then, as fast as it had sounded, it faded to nothing.

Seconds after the echo had dissipated, another sound could be heard.

It was the sound of an engine, or a motor to a large vehicle.

Soon, a crashing could be heard as a large bulldozer forced its way through the wreckage lining the road. The large metal plow cleared a path for the convoy behind it, forcing the wreckage off the road like it was nothing but fallen snow and slush on a winter's night after a snowstorm.

The bulldozer rumbled by the house Greg had entered, then continued onward. Behind it, another vehicle followed. This one was similar to what farmers used to carry cattle to market. It was open in the back, the sides six feet high with metal rails. And on the truck were more than two dozen people, all looking half-starved and haggard, their faces weather beaten; their clothing filthy.

But they were alive, and here and there between their legs, an innocent face peeked through, the children frightened beyond belief, most of them now orphans.

Behind this truck a military vehicle followed, an old jeep brought back into service. There was a soldier in the driver's seat and another in the passenger seat. Both had rifles over their shoulders and handguns on their hips, the snaps undone for a fast draw if necessary.

As the jeep slowed to the middle of the street, the driver stropped. The bulldozer and truck continued onwards and soon were lost from sight around the next bend.

The jeep sat in the road idling and the soldier in the passenger seat raised a bullhorn to his lips.

He called out to the shattered houses around him, alerting anyone hiding within it was safe to come out. He waited for a full minute, and when nothing stirred, he patted the driver's shoulder and the jeep drove on.

As the jeep banked around the corner to follow the cattle truck, the soldier picked up his two-way radio.

"Base, this is Unit 2. No contacts in zone 5. Repeat, no survivors. Continuing on to zone 6, over."

"Roger that, keep looking, over, base out," came back a voice as static filled the air waves.

The jeep drove onward, leaving the wreckage of yet another neighborhood behind, as the soldiers search for more survivors where ever they could find them.

EXTREME PREJUDICE

PASQUALE J. MORRONE

The fire crackled and hissed. It reached skyward with long slender fingers just like in the stories of the old west. The hunter looked up into a sky that was void of stars and a moon, seeing only a burgundy-red glow stretching as far as the eye could see. Sometimes it seemed like it was clearing up, and then he realized it was only his imagination. Only two years had passed since *The War*.

He pulled out some papers from his satchel. One of them had the layout of the land and, the other, a map of when the whole continent used to be a conglomeration of states, whose sole purpose was to stand united. Now, it was merely all thrown in together. He cursed the Ecumenical Council for waiting so long. They should have taken over long before the humans had the chance to destroy everything, and they had everything. At least that's what he was told.

In pulling out several other objects, two small coins fell onto the hard earth. He stared at them for a moment, remembering some of what he had been taught. They were dimes. A monetary symbol the humans once used. He then raised the image of the naked female to eye level. 'Entertainment for Men,' it read. He laughed, but it came out as only a glottal-type sound. He hadn't mastered the language yet, like some had, but he was steadily working hard at it. It was something they all had to do, so they could communicate with the last of a dying race. "Die they will." He whispered in his own tongue, as he once again looked up into the sky.

His leathery hands grasped the weapon. It was of the most high quality eronori blends of metal. It was a metal not found on many planets or even in many galaxies. No matter how many times it was fired, it was always cool to the touch. He gripped the thick stock and hoisted the staff toward the dry timberline. He knew the damage a proton ball, followed by a laser tracer, caused in wounded or dead humans. He was young and, as of yet, he had not experienced the thrill of a kill, only the hunt.

There were times when his dreams came in various stages. They were dreams he had quite often, although he never had any contact with any humans, least likely, the woman of the human race. He found strange the things they wore on their feet. They were small and slender things with spikes at one end. He picked up other various objects he found lying around in places where they once called their homes. The dreams were always very real. They were exactly as he saw it to this day; a vast wasteland of nothingness. It was a place where all things were burned to a cinder. He often saw human skulls with round and staring eyes that sat in dried out sockets.

Behind him, he was almost always moments away from being picked up by The Guardians. In his own language he was now known as a waltuo, and it was the job of The Guardians to round up all those who had become a waltuo for one reason or another. He knew there was no forgiveness. The council had little or no tolerance for those who were not ready to lay down their lives for the cause.

He had no idea when he finally changed his mind. The human race was no longer a threat to him alone. Their enemy was not to be his enemy. At his first chance on leaving without being detected, he stole one of their weapons and quickly learned how to use it effectively. He had killed, and that in itself was a death sentence without a trial before the council.

Yellow cat-like eyes began to grow heavy as his mind roamed from one thought to the next. His head rolled forward and back, and he placed the weapon down next to his hairy body as he leaned against the coolness of a boulder. The flames made his craggy form grotesque, elongating his shadow, making it dance in a waving motion against a backdrop of solid rock. He began to dream. It was then that he would see the woman. Her body, void of clothing, would dance and gyrate in what he now knew was suggestive body language.

Certain parts of the land were still smoldering. He stood by and watched as the craft hovered over the devastation, periodically blasting a group of humans who decided to make a run for it instead of cowering in the shadows. Even if the proton bolt missed its mark and hit only a tree or rock, the tracer would sometimes slice off a leg or arm, or pass directly through one of their bodies. He turned away and studied his own limbs. He would ask himself, "What if that were me?"

He was not told much about them. Only that they were a most dangerous and selfish race, just like all the humans. They build empires and destroy them at will. They wage war for silly reasons and force their will on others. Their minds are sharp, yet devious. They must not be allowed to rebuild.

He saw the female smiling at him. Small hands held her heavy breasts like in the image he had hidden away in his satchel. She turned and, rising slowly to her feet, the dark patch between her legs stood out clearly on her delicate white form. His eyes raced back and forth behind closed lids as he followed her path towards him. Her breasts swung gently back and forth as she bent forward, inches away from his face. Sticking out her tongue, she slid it slowly around her pouting lips, before pulling it back against the roof of her mouth and making a wet clicking sound.

* * *

A young boy made his way through the maze of rock and rubble with what seemed like choreographed steps. Steam rose up from snake-like holes in the ground in places where the earth had been drained of liquid. An old canteen held the last few gulps of water and, in a small satchel, was a few items that could be eaten without cooking. He threw away the dried beef days ago. It was at least something to put in his empty stomach, but made him use up water faster than he dared.

The young man's nostrils burned from breathing in the dry air. Dead things that succumbed to the barren wasteland long ago littered the ground in the form of dried limbs and skulls. Hollowed eye sockets stared at him in silent and mournful gazes. Huge craters that looked like giant woks often held the remains of human and animal alike. The bones of human skeletons still carried the tattered clothing they lived and died in.

There were times when his eyes burned with tears of recollection. Friends he became separated from when the news of the war was first broadcast. His mind's eye saw his own home move farther away as his family drove quickly away to their hideaway; a place filled with provisions just for this very reason. Roadblocks halted their escape for hours as vehicles from around the state made their way to nowhere. Where were they really going? It was a world war after all. Every nation on Earth had waged war on their contiguous countries for one reason or another.

In the days to follow came the strange flying objects. They didn't seem to be concerned with the giant mushroom-shaped clouds that rose up from all around. It was as though they watched and waited for something. It was a while since he saw their flying contraptions. They were triangular shaped and the color and texture of polished stainless steel.

Some of the machines shot bolts of light that exploded on impact with whatever it was they hit. Others shot a laser beam of bright light. They would cut objects in half. There were times when he actually watched whole wooded areas cut down with one long sweeping motion. It was as though they were looking for those hiding in the woods. Once found, they were blasted down with the proton bolts of light.

In the distance, the boy saw a flicking form of light. He stopped and listened while leaning against a burned out stump. His breath came fast and he quickly tried to control the intact of the thin oxygen that was left, as not to become lightheaded. If it was a camp occupied by those beings in the flying machines, he would have to double back and find another place to make his own bed for the night. He almost laughed out loud. Night. It was always night it seemed.

He quickly and quietly checked his remaining ammo. The rifle he carried was simply Neanderthal compared to what those creatures carried. The thought of being captured and possibly eaten by them came to mind.

* * *

The *alien* moved his eyes back and forth behind closed eyelids. What was it the woman wanted to do to him? It never got that far. He would always wake up and lie there for long moments at a time, wondering what would have happened next. He was always left feeling rigid between his legs. It was the same as the *Entertainment for Men* book he often looked at, which in his mind brought on the strange and exotic dreams.

His eyes shot open. He wasn't alone any longer.

The boy stood with his legs shoulder length apart. "Must've been a helluva dream."

The hunter drew his legs up, shielding his groin. His paw-like hand was on his taser, but he held fast. The boy's own weapon was directly in his face. The creature saw that it was of an antiquated variety, but deadly none-the-less.

"Don't move, fucker." The boy moved to one side and kept his eyes riveted to the being who sat before him.

The hunter cursed his drowsiness and stared back into the boy's eyes.

"Now, slowly take your hand away from whatever the hell that is," the boy said, quickly pointing at it with the rifle. "Do it now! I mean it!"

The strange warrior slowly moved his hand from the taser. His thick nose should have alerted him of the boy's presence. How could he have let this happen? He suddenly realized that sleep was as dangerous to him as it was to replenish his strength. His senses were in tune to the woman whose naked body undulated directly in front of him in his dream.

The boy lifted the peculiar weapon and inspected it. A small lever beside the trigger proved to be a release mechanism; the power pack fell quickly into his waiting hand. He stuffed the pack into his shredded jeans, then the taser down the back of his waistband.

"I kill no humans yet," the hunter said.

The boy nodded. "Yet? Oh, yeah, and you know what? You're gonna die a cherry in regards to that very statement, too. How do you like those apples? Huh?"

"No more apples. Destroyed, like all else."

"Yeah, that's right. But I didn't destroy shit. I had a home and a family. I had a beautiful home right here in what used to be Montana." The boy picked up the alien's satchel and dumped it out, the contents spilling onto the dry ground.

"No more weapons," the hunter said. He looked down at the partial magazine. In its fall to the ground it opened to the naked female. He looked back up at the boy.

"A girlie mag?" The boy chuckled a moment. "You gotta be shitin' me. You know, my parents told me I would go blind." When the creature simply stared at him, completely ignorant of the meaning of his words, he threw the papers down. "All right, who are you and what the hell are you doing here? Let's go! I want answers!"

"The parents of you, where they are?" the hunter asked.

The boy looked around for a moment then back at his captive. "What do you care where my parents are? I don't know where they are. We got separated when we came out of the shelter. For all I know, probably dead. Animals like you were chasing and shooting at us."

The hunter stayed put. He looked at the boy in what might have been pity. "Animals are gone, like apples. We come when before bombs are hit on Earth. The animals taken are some small and large. One like me, I little read about. The Guardians did not let me alone to stay, when I go out."

The alien's words bewildered the boy for a moment. They were jumbled and made no sense at times. He stared at the creature, watching as his thick fingers ran down the sides of a hirsute face. It was a face that bore an uncanny resemblance to a large feline; yet, it held another feature, which soon became apparent to him. He squatted and blinked continuously for a moment.

"You're just a kid. You're probably not any older than I am for Christ's sake."

"Christ, the bible to pray. I know some. Some words for praying to the bible I also know about. Guardians and teach...."

You're saying you were here before the war? Is that right? What were you doing?" Were you studying us like in some biology pro-

141

ject?" The boy shook his head. "You know what? To the victor go the spoils. That's an old saying."

"We came for no humans to study. We came for only animals to take."

The boy rolled back on his buttocks, the gun level with his captive's belly. Easing his finger away from the trigger, he gripped the weapon between the stock and lever action, aiming it toward the timberline.

The creature raised its head to stare at the dark-red sky, which was now with the rising of the sun, showing signs of pink.

"One day, I'd like to look up and see blue again, but I know that's really not gonna happen. It's over," the boy said, following the creature's eyes upward.

"Blue color, never again. Blue, like when before no bombs," the hunter replied.

"My parents named me Damian. Damian," the boy repeated, tapping his chest with his finger. "You talk about these, guardians. What did they name you?" He pointed toward his chest again and then to the hunter's. "My name is Damian, and you are?"

"In my tongue my name is called, Tacregit."

"Hell of a moniker," the boy said.

The fire crackled and began to throw small embers. The hunter slowly leaned toward another broken limb and tossed it atop the ashes, and then another on top of that one. The wood caught immediately and began to tickle the air once again with its fiery fingers.

Damian watched his every move, and then once again watched the flames do their little hypnotic dance. The heat radiated up toward his face and he wanted to close his eyes badly, just for a little while. Continuously moving to avoid the hovering crafts had robbed him of a night's sleep, and it was catching up with him rapidly. He was suddenly lying in a soft bed in a fetal position; the covers pulled up under his chin. Seconds passed like hours before his eyes snapped open again.

"No sleeping good when running away. This is how Damian was to catch me when off my guard." Tacregit said, softly.

Damian bolted upright, his breath quickening. "How come you didn't jump me when I was out?"

"Jump on you is to be like war. Run away like you, I was doing. I am in my own language a citizen who be bad. I am waltou. Do bad things in their eyes they see."

Damian looked at Tacregit, dumbfounded. "Why in the hell would you ever want to run away? Your friends are all running this show."

"Prisoners, some of us are. Guar...."

"The Guardians. They aren't parents then. The Guardians are or were guarding you."

"Against the council, my crimes were. Like crimes the humans do, and their council makes them go to prison," Tacregit said, staring into the fire.

"So you're an outlaw. That's what you're trying to tell me. What crimes?" Damian asked.

Tacregit leaned back against the boulder. His eyes sparkled with the tears that soon overflowed down the soft fur of his face. Meanwhile, Damian realized he had let his weapon drop to the hard ground.

If this was an act, he thought, this being that called itself Tacregit, was good at it. He may have been too good.

"The Sredavni attack. We tried to warn on one time of our visit, the humans, but not too good was our tongue for the language," Tacregit said.

Damian stared, his mouth momentarily hanging open. "I don't understand. You say you warned some of our people of an impending attack by, whom?"

"Sredavni," Tacregit repeated, "is what our race is named."

"Who exactly was warned? How?"

"Area number, now it is called in first long ago landing. Archives say of our race that hit something when before they could land. Many races like Earth. Them that made to the ground died. They looked not like I am. One lived for short time, and in human tongue could not say to soldiers about the attack. Tried, but could not say."

"Area number and long ago. I read something about a landing in.... Holy shit! That really was long ago. You're talking about the Roswell Incident; area 51. That was in New Mexico, in the...Hell, the nineteen forties I think," Damian said.

143

"Did not attack," Tacregit said. "Gave ideas instead on making war. I read books of the Sredavni and know this now. They make human destroy human and watch and wait long times. Sredavni have lot of time. They live long."

"What did you mean about the animals?"

"Like in bible to God. The man called Noah, who took animals with boat. When sky is colorless, only the Sredavni and animals will live on."

"They're going to repopulate the Earth, by exterminating humans?"

"Not Earth. Only Sredavni and Earth animals on Neila then."

"Neila?" Damian asked.

"Our planet, far from Alpha Four. Sredavni also bring back all of old animals, when before Earth have a history."

"You're talking pre-historic animals like dinosaurs?"

"Sredavni will leave soon. What is called ozone no longer will be there when the blood sky is gone. Sredavni Council say, no killing all humans will mean they burn all up."

Damian nodded slowly in recognition of Tacregit's words, staring steadily into the fire and wondering how long it would take to die.

By the time their conversation had finished, the sky was more of a pink color. The sun blasting its enormous heat against the dying planet was slowly but surely burning its way through what little atmosphere it had left. The dust was settling. Soon, there would be nothing to stop the luminary giant from turning the Earth into another incinerating fireball.

Not wanting to be alone, and deciding Tacregit didn't want to harm him, Damian took the alien back to his shelter.

Damian never found out what it was that Tacregit had done to alienate himself from his own kind, but the law of Neila was: No Sredavni were to resort to the outlawed crime of cannibalism. Those who were convicted of such a crime were imprisoned and eventually put to death.

In the underground shelter, Damian opened a can of the remaining rations that would eventually run out as the year came to an end. He never got to see his parents again, nor his brothers and sisters. Assuming they were dead, he went on with his life, thanking what was left of the heavens for each morning he was allowed to open his eyes.

The animals that would eventually share the Sredavni world were being put in place, and their cohabiting would ensure the Sredavni a generous supply of meat. But, there was no longer any meat on Earth. It vanished with the destruction of the animals that were not sheltered, as many of the humans were.

Tacregit turned his back to his companion. His stomach rumbled with a hunger that would soon become unbearable. He would have to make a decision. One was to become a vegetarian. The other, to hunt for the last of the remaining humans. If it were the latter, it would of course be done without Damian knowing, or becoming none-the-wiser.

Each evening he would return to the shelter, eating only the scraps Damian had to offer from the meager rations. When the last of the humans had been taken, like the prisoner awaiting death, he would have to ponder over a serious thought with enormous regard.

In the eerie glow of an old oil lamp, Tacregit silently ogled his newfound friend.

The sweet smell of human flesh made his hunger reach yet another notch.

In the end, when there were no longer any scraps, he would have to contemplate his next meal.

ONE MAN'S FINAL ACT

DAVID BERNSTEIN

John Kerns woke up ten minutes to eleven in the a.m. The house was quiet, an eerie stillness he hadn't heard since he was eight and locked in his cousin's basement. He got up from the living room sofa.

"Marion?" he called, as he walked into the kitchen. A pot of boiled eggs had exploded, covering the walls in yellow sludge. The burner was still on, the pot blackened with burnt-on egg. John turned the knob controlling the burner to the *off* position.

"Marion?" he called again, concerned.

John searched the house, checking bathrooms, bedrooms, the dining room and the basement playroom. His wife and family were nowhere to be found.

Checking the garage and finding it lifeless, he went outside. A cool breeze blew, and like the inside of the house, the neighborhood was silent. A few crows cawed from nearby telephone wires, breaking the stillness, adding to the creepiness of the moment.

He stood at the end of his driveway, glancing around at the other houses. A light coating of snow covered the ground. The leafless trees seemed to watch him, their skeletal structure daunting. It was frigid out and John had forgotten his jacket. On his way back to the house, he decided to check the backyard, and when he reached it, he quickly wished he hadn't.

Lying on the hard, snow covered ground, was his wife, Marion, and his two kids, Melissa and Greg. He ran to them, the numbing cold forgotten. Their faces were gaunt, a hue of blue, their lips purple.

John screamed for help, his voice echoing in the distance as if mocked. He attempted to pick up his little girl, but her body broke, a snapping heard under her snowsuit. He held the two pieces of his daughter now kept together only by her garment. She weighed half as much as normal, as if her body was desiccated. John dropped the corpse in horror.

He had to be dreaming.

But he never remembered feeling so cold in a dream. Calmness fell over him like a soothing melody. He began laughing, feeling relieved.

"A damn dream," he said aloud. With the image of his dead family stuck in his head, he walked away from them and into the house, wondering what he was supposed to do until he woke up.

He left the mess in the kitchen, not needing to clean up in a dream. He tried thinking the mess away, but when he opened his eyes, egg was still everywhere.

Knowing he was in a dream was fun. It sucked that his family was dead in it, but he'd see them soon when he woke up. He went to the telephone and tried calling information, but no one picked up.

Damn. He figured he'd get the operator on the line and ask for the President's number and talk to him about the state of the country. He laughed, finding himself tired, so he decided to take a nap. Maybe that would get him up in the real world.

John awoke some time later. The alarm clock was blinking twelve o'clock; the power had failed, coming back on at some point. He got up thinking he'd originally fell asleep on the living room couch. Dreams and reality had him confused.

"Marion," he called. He walked into the kitchen, saw egg was still everywhere. The room began spinning; John had to sit for a moment so he stumbled to a kitchen chair.

Impossible, he thought.

The backyard flashed in his mind as terror seized his chest, feeling like a giant hand was squeezing. John sprang out of the chair and raced to the sliding glass door, then opened it. There, on the lawn, was his wife and kids. He staggered back inside, his mind in a daze.

His head was swirling. He couldn't think straight. What was happening? A jolting ache punched him in the gut and he fell to his knees and puked. He tried getting up, but couldn't. Crawling to the phone, he began hysterically screaming. "Shit. My Wife. Kids. Ugly. Death." He reached the phone, picked it up, and dialed 9-1-1. Like in his dream, the phone continued to ring, no one answering. John hung up and dialed the number for information only to get the same result. He tried his parents' house and got the answering machine. Every call he made either went to a person's voicemail or simply kept ringing.

John slammed the phone down, breaking it, the crack of the plastic casing reminding him of the snap when he lifted his daughter. Anger coursed through his veins as he rose. He began hitting the wall, puncturing holes in the sheetrock, the white powder puffing like smoke. With bloody fists, John ran to the basement stairs, taking two at a time. He slipped, bashed his head on a step and blacked out. His body, as if lifeless, tumbled to the basement floor.

He regained consciousness sometime during the night with a bruised head. He stumbled back to the first floor, and after popping some painkillers, he went next door to his neighbor's house only to find them dead, mummified like his daughter.

He returned home, wanting to take the car out, but it refused to start.

John left on foot, and after searching multiple houses, he sank to his knees. Everyone was dead and none of the cars he came across had started. He wondered what had happened to the neighborhood. Terrorists were of course his first thought, but then why was he alive? Alien attack? Maybe. Anything was within the realm of possibility after what he'd seen. He lay on a stranger's sofa in a house he didn't know and cried himself to sleep.

He awoke the next morning, nightmarish images of dead people flooding his mind. He left the house, walking back to his, and stopped suddenly when he heard a growl. Turning around, he saw a dog, a Doberman pinscher, its teeth bared in a menacing snarl. The dog had cuts all over its body as if it had run through barbed wire. Foam dripped from its maw.

"Easy there, fella," John said, holding his hands out.

The canine began creeping forward.

John spun, ready to run when he saw a squirrel. It stood in the middle of the street, tail arched and its head lowered, as if ready to attack. John took off toward his house and the squirrel turned to follow. He heard the dog bark, its paws scratching against the pavement as it began to chase after him, also.

He ran, pumping his arms hard, knowing he wouldn't make it to his house. He would have to fight the dog. Craning his neck, he saw that the dog was almost on him. His brain said to run, his heart knowing he had a fight on his hands. Turning his head back around, he saw the squirrel charging at him, too.

What the hell was going on?

As the squirrel neared, it lunged onto his jacket. White foam flew from its mouth as it began attacking him; biting and tearing at his jacket. Surprised, almost to the point of laughter, he took hold of the rodent and tossed it to the ground, but not before getting bit. He turned his head in time to see the squirrel jump on the dog's head and go wild. The canine began yelping, using its paws to swat the fuzzy-tailed rodent to the ground. The dog then lunged at its tiny attacker. The agile squirrel dodged the assault, springing onto the Doberman's front leg, to begin savagely biting the limb. The dog chomped down, silencing the pesky critter before devouring it.

John continued running all the way into his open garage. Once inside, he slammed the door shut. He leaned against the garage wall, breathing deeply, his heart racing.

What the hell was going on?

He went upstairs to the bathroom to disinfect the small incision the squirrel had given him. If the damn thing had rabies he was screwed.

As he passed the family pictures hanging on the wall, a pang of grief filled him. He'd been so confused that he hadn't had time to grieve for his lost family. It hit him all at once and he collapsed on the stairs, tears spilling down his cheeks. He sobbed for a long time and eventually drifted off to sleep below the smiling faces of his family.

Later that night, he searched the internet, browsing for anything that might explain what had happened. He found nothing indicating that the world was falling apart.

He went to the living room and tried the house phone again, obtaining the same frightening results as earlier. His cell phone proved no different.

John cooked dinner, a steak, potatoes and beans with an ice cold beer. He amazed himself at how sane he'd managed to stay after the initial shock of what he'd been through. The backyard still held his family, the ground too frozen to bury them. Other than covering them with a tarp from the garage, he didn't know what to do with them. He thought of bringing them inside but if they were frozen, wouldn't they be better out there? Truly he didn't know what to do.

After dinner he tried the television. Some of the channels had shows running, others were black screens. He searched looking for news broadcasts, but found none. Not caring to watch television, he picked up a book. It was a horror novel of all things, but something to keep his mind occupied. He fell asleep some time after midnight, thinking about his family lying frozen in the yard.

The next day he decided to go searching houses again. He needed to find a working car so he could get outside of town and see what was happening. He went to the front door, and was about to open it when he saw the Doberman from the other day. It was standing motionless, foam still coming from its mouth, staring at the door as if in wait. John opened the heavy wooden front door, leaving the glass storm door closed. The dog, upon seeing him, began barking and launched itself at the storm door. The glass shook but held and John quickly shut it. It was just as he closed the wooden door that he heard glass shatter and the dog began yelping.

Opening the door a crack, he saw the animal lying on its side, a large glass shard sticking out of its ribs. Blood seeped like a fountain from the wound. The dog tried getting up when it saw John, but couldn't. He closed the door again, but a new thought had entered his mind.

He left through the garage carrying a baseball bat and a steak knife, then approached the enraged canine. Turning his head away, he bashed the dying dog in the skull with the bat, putting it out of its misery. He then headed away, tears falling down his cheeks. Thinking it was a good idea, now that he was more clear-minded, he re-checked the houses he'd visited. To his pleasure, he found what he was looking for, a gun.

He'd owned guns his whole life, but after the kids were born, Marion insisted he get rid of them. In his hands, he held a .30-30; a nice powerful rifle. A case of ammo was on the floor next to the weapon in the closet. He loaded the weapon, already feeling much safer.

Two hours later and he'd had to shoot three cats, two more squirrels and a dog. All of the animals had tried attacking him. One of the cats surprised him, managing to claw his leg pretty deeply. The one thing all the animals had in common was their foaming mouths. They must have some kind of disease that was making them crazy. It reminded him of rabies but he was no vet.

John also managed to find loads of food. He took a few items from the first two houses but knew he would have to come back for more. His hands were full with three rifles and two handguns, too. Ammo was stuffed in his pockets like bulging tumors. He was shocked to find out how many citizens had guns and wondered if maybe that was the reason the crime rate in the neighborhood was so low.

After getting back to his house, he stockpiled the weapons on the floor next to where he slept in the playroom. He couldn't carry all the ammo for all the guns, but took some for each, figuring he'd get the rest eventually.

It was while he was matching up the boxes of ammo to the proper weapons that John heard heavy breathing coming from behind him.

He spun around, grabbing the .30-30 to see a bearded man with stringy hair and beady eyes holding a cleaver from no more than three feet away.

"Give me some food," the man said.

John didn't recognize him.

"Where did you come from, friend?" John asked. The man looked furious, his face scarlet, shoulders moving up and down in rhythm with his breathing.

"I'll kill you," he said, spittle flying from his lips.

"Please, take it easy," John said in a calming voice. "I've got food. I'll give you some, just calm down." John began to lower his weapon.

"Calm down?" the man shouted. "I'm the one with the damn knife! Get me some food, now!"

John's eyebrows furrowed in confusion. Didn't the man see the gun John had pointed at him? The guy must be crazy, or was he like John but had flipped out.

"Get out of my house," John demanded. "Then I'll feed you."

The man's face turned a deep red, almost purple. His body shook with rage as if he might explode. John raised the weapon.

"Listen, mister, don't make me shoot you. Please."

The man started laughing. "With that?" He pointed a finger at the rifle. He was laughing so hard he buckled over. It was when he was bent that he lunged ahead with the cleaver raised to kill John.

John squeezed the trigger, the room filling with deafening sound, sending a bullet into the man's chest. The stranger halted with a dazed look on his face, as if reality had hit. The man's jacket was unzipped, allowing John to see the crimson flower that had sprouted on the man's white undershirt. The crazed man let out a small gasp of air before falling dead.

John ran over and checked the man's pulse but found none.

Damn, his only human contact and the guy was nuts. He'd never killed anyone before. He only did what anyone would've done. John sat down next to the corpse, feeling numb inside. After a few moments, without thinking, he dragged the body to his neighbor's yard, leaving it there. He went home, drank some beers and went to sleep.

The next day he ventured out again. More crazed animals had to be put down. John walked into a kid's room in a house at the end of the block and found two hamsters in a glass tank. One was mangled and chewed upon, very dead. The other had a bloody snout, and upon seeing John, began attacking the glass, leaving imprints of its face on the inside of the cage.

It was the funniest, yet sickest thing he'd ever seen.

He arrived home later that day to find his home without electricity. He had no internet, no lighting, and no heat.

Luckily, he'd invested in a woodstove and had it going in no time, heating up the downstairs playroom. The fridge was emptied, all the perishables placed on his back porch. The cool temperatures would help keep the food cold. He cooked dinner, drank some beers and went to sleep.

His family was still in the yard, covered with the tarp. A few times he'd had to chase or kill some animals that had come sniffing around, but otherwise he knew they were safe. He still didn't know what to do with the bodies. Truth was, he didn't want to deal with it.

It was easier to just ignore them, as selfish as that was.

The following morning he awoke to a scratching sound in the wall. Curious, he crawled over and listened. Some little critter was working frantically to get out. Pieces of the painted sheetrock began crumbling and he saw tiny claw marks appear. He heard squeaking as if two or more mice were arguing.

Damn, why couldn't they have dropped dead, too? he thought.

John went to get something to capture them in. Returning with a mop bucket, he decided to wait the little buggers out.

A short time later, a small head popped out of the hole, the creature's whiskers twitching frantically. Then the head returned inside and more of the wall began breaking. Soon the hole was the width of a softball. John held the bucket over the opening, and as soon as the mouse came out, he trapped it.

"Gotcha," he said.

Satisfied with his endeavor, he smiled before feeling something crawl under his pajamas and up his leg. Looking down, he saw four mice of various sizes, all of whom were coming at him.

One was on his foot before he knew it and he kicked it off, sending it sailing across the room. A biting pain seared his inner thigh as the mouse that had run up his leg began nibbling away at his flesh. He brought his hand down into a fist and swatted it, crushing it to death. A small spot of blood appeared on his pants, soon spreading, and he felt the moistness on his skin.

He backed away as the other three mice chased after him. Realizing he was bigger and stronger, he stopped retreating and began stomping the vermin with his bare feet.

The buggers were fast, avoiding many of the attacks. After a couple of tiring minutes he'd killed them all, including the one he'd kicked across the room and the one trapped under the bucket. When the onslaught was over, he peeled off mouse guts from his leg and washed his feet before sanitizing the floor with a household cleaner. He waited by the hole to see if any more mice would come out, but none did.

After disinfecting the mouse bite with some hydrogen peroxide, John grabbed logs from the wood pile outside and stacked them by the wood stove. He drank a cup of orange juice and ate Spam with a few browned apples he'd found at one of his neighbor's houses.

After breakfast he suited up, ready to head to more houses and see what he could find. Outside the front door, he heard howling. He went to the living room window and looked outside.

Cats, dogs, squirrels, rabbits, deer, possum, and a bear, all wandered outside his home. A few quarrels broke out among them, but a deer quickly dispersed them as if it was the leader. The backyard was full, too. Many now messing with the bodies of his family. But there were too many to stop.

All the animals were foaming at the mouths, but getting along for the most part. It was as if John were watching a sinister fairy tale unfold before his eyes. There was no way he could leave his house. He'd wind up wasting his ammo and still wouldn't have killed them all. So he decided to wait them out.

He stayed at the window, watching them like a sentry on duty, but eventually his eyes grew heavy and exhaustion took hold until he was out.

His dreams were filled with his wife and kids as they all went to the beach, built sandcastles and rode waves. Everyone was smiling and laughing until a huge tidal wave approached. The beach darkened as the wave blocked out the sun. There was no escaping it. John huddled with his family, unable to protect them, watching as the wave came crashing down.

He woke up, sweating. Looking out the window, the animals were still present. He grabbed a couple of beers and watched as some of the animals left, replaced by others, as if they were working in shifts.

A few days went by and he still wasn't able to leave his home. He'd run out of wood and was down to burning furniture to keep warm, especially at night. He read during the day to keep his mind from going insane.

Two more days passed and the animals remained. He began picking them off with his guns from the back deck, but was bombarded by birds and had to retreat inside. He sat on the floor crying. Was this his Hell? Had he died and was now being punished for something?

Five more days passed and John began losing it. He saw his family crying out for him, but he knew they were dead. The food supply had run out and the furniture had all been burned. The animals multiplied in number as if expecting something. They seemed to be growing impatient, more fights between them were breaking out.

John couldn't sleep anymore at night. His yard had become a suburban jungle, noisy and frightening. His family was gone now, dragged away by the animals; he assumed to be devoured.

One afternoon, exhausted and in a deep sleep, John was awakened by a pounding at the front door. Looking out the living room window, he saw it was the bear. It kept ramming the door, its head becoming a bloody pulp. The door finally gave in as a thunderous crash erupted through the house.

John lay on the floor, starving and hysterical. The animals charged up the stairs and surrounded him.

He knew he was mad because he heard them speaking in actual words. He laughed, realizing he must be hallucinating.

"You're the last of your kind, human," a deer said. Its mouth didn't move, but John heard the voice in his head. "You were supposed to die like the others, but you are an anomaly."

John laughed. "I'm talking to a deer."

"No, not just a deer anymore, human," the deer said. "We've evolved."

"Let's rip his head off," a possum said.

The other animals cheered. Cries of, "Kill him, kill him, kill him," were chanted.

"Enough," the deer said. "We're civilized, not like the cancerous humans who almost destroyed our planet. We were given the power to take it back, the ability to reason." The deer glanced around at the others. "After the human dies, we go back to the natural order of things, ridding ourselves of human emotion."

"I hate humans," a squirrel said. "They killed my family, and evicted us from our home. I say we kill the human."

"No, he will die, but not by our hands," the deer said. "We shall not break the pact."

John only laughed. "You'll be doing me a favor by killing me."

"We are not like you, human," the deer said and turned to leave. "We follow nature's laws."

The other animals followed the deer, leaving John alive. He lay there, starving, until he passed out.

He came to upon hearing his daughter laughing in the back-yard. Then he heard his wife pleading for him to come join them.

"It's so beautiful here, John," she said.

Smiling hysterically, he crawled to the downstairs playroom.

He loaded the .30-30 with only a single bullet before placing the gun to his head.

That was all he'd need.

THE HUM OF DEAD STARS

CHRISTOPHER J. DWYER

Moonlight dissipates into a cloud of clove smoke and my eyes adjust to the sight of an evaporating sea. Fingers tingle with the chill of another dying night as they grip the edge of a warm cigarette. Blood graces nicotine inside my poisoned heart and I wait for my skin to dry and crack under a thin layer of frost. One last drag and the remains of the cigarette fall off the balcony and dissolve somewhere between the mist and rocks below the house.

I walk into the bedroom and flip the switch next to the doorframe, killing lights showering a pretty face eager to drift back into slumber. She looks at me with a midnight gaze and flips golden bangs out of her face.

"Come back to bed," she says.

Deep breaths and I nod, ignoring the flounce of cold covering my arms and legs. I slide under layers of wool blankets and she drapes a leg over mine, stubble colliding with goosebumps. It's not so easy to fall asleep anymore, and even as I close my eyes and embrace the most beautiful woman left in the world, thoughts race to the tune of a thousand crying children. I force quiet into the most hollow portions of my brain and soon enough all I can hear are the momentary melodies of Chelsea's breaths. She's sleeping soundly and I wish I could do the same.

Wind whistles over an ocean that's seen better years and I can remember when Chelsea and I found this house, this sanctuary away from a world in which blue skies were replaced with endless nights. I force my eyelids shut and picture a summer lake glistening with sunlight. The future has become our present and what I miss the most isn't something that's within the reach of my bitter, tired fingers. Chelsea slides a hand up my abdomen, resting it on my chest. Purple-painted fingernails clash against pallid skin and a shiver of warmth glides throughout my blood.

An odd hum resonates constantly from the glitter of dead stars. It leaves us forever haunted and more than afraid of our future. The jagged corners of another dream begin to pinch me as a symphony of dying waves crash against the last bits of consciousness.

* * *

My eyes open and view an empty bed and I can hear Chelsea attempting to make breakfast in the kitchen. I yawn and catch the cold breeze from outside. Even with the few doors and windows of the house locked and barricaded, a thin rush of air always manages to seep in through unseen cracks. I swing my legs over the side of the bed and stare through the sliding doors of the bedroom.

Only a few months ago, I got used to the company of the moon and there's a small part of me that feeds off its pallid glow. Sometimes I believe I don't miss the beaming rays of sunshine anymore.

Chelsea leans into the room, tight black t-shirt and the jeans she's worn everyday for the past two weeks.

"Breakfast is on the table if you want anything," she says.

I shake my head and continue staring at the darkness of the fresh morning sky. "I'm not hungry."

She sighs and blows hair out of her face, pouting her lips. "You have to eat something. It's not going to make the situation any better if you turn against your own body. You need strength. Please, eat something, even if it's small."

"Okay." I stand up and take slow steps out of the bedroom and into the hallway. I can remember the framed pictures that once graced these walls, snapshots into the life of another family. After the earthquakes, we threw them in the trash, the ghosts of the house long forgotten. The four-second walk into the kitchen seems more like time in a coffin than anything else.

A few pieces of burnt toast adorn a plate of watery eggs. I sit and smile at Chelsea. She was never a good cook but I know deep down inside that she's been trying her best for the past few months. I shove a forkful of yellow into my mouth and chew. Chelsea sips juice out of a paper cup and asks me if I want any. I nod and she pours the last of a bottle of apple juice into her cup and slides it next to my plate. Before I notice, she's on my lap with her arms wrapped around my neck. Her tears feel like fire to my aching skin and I push her off of my torso.

She does this at least once a day and I can never blame her.

"I want to leave," she says in between deep breaths. "I don't want to be here anymore."

I force her arms to the side and gaze at a monolithic beauty, bleeding mascara over wet cheeks. "I don't want to be here either. But I'd rather be here spending my days with you than living death two hundred miles away. Home is gone."

My finger gently presses into the skin between her breasts, black fabric embracing me. "*This* is home now."

I can tell her smile is forced as she gets up and walks away. I finish my breakfast and place the soiled plate into the sink with the other dishes that neither of us has touched in days. Four or five months ago I would have yelled at Chelsea for leaving a mess in the kitchen but now I'm just grateful that we're both alive and well. Sometimes she cries for her mother and father, other days it's for her sister and the handful of friends she kept close to her heart.

I resist the urge to walk into the bedroom to comfort her and instead sit quietly in the living room, watching the anathema of blue snow fall from the sky and coat the ruins of the world outside the house.

*   *   *

Chelsea and I were engaged before the events happened. We wanted a December wedding and the quiet voices in our hearts begged us to hold true to the date. The winter air held a crisp quality and I found a charcoal gray blazer buried deep in the bedroom closet. Chelsea's hair was parted in the middle, rising roots of black fighting an unnatural swoop of blonde. She braved the cold and wore a white tank top and green-tinted jeans.

She looked at me with carcinogen eyes and mascara the color of autumn chrysanthemums. She said three words and I kissed her, standing and swaying under dead tree limbs while descending ash danced in our hair and backs. For the first time in weeks, a small sliver of pink light penetrated through the obsidian of the afternoon sky. We both smiled at this small marvel in our new world, hoping it was a sign of hope, a sign of better days.

We sat against the lone rock in the remains of the garden and held each other until the snow started to drift against the comfort of our skin, bits of vanilla radiating with only a tinge of blue. I planted my elbow in the dark crevasse below the middle of the rock and Chelsea laid her head against my chest. She perked up at the sight of two rabbits hopping through the dead trees of the surrounding forest, signs of life after nature's funeral.

We remained perfectly still and watched the animals sniff around the ground, little paws barely imprinting the ash and snow. The smaller of the two had fur as white as virgin clouds, and when it stood up, I could see a small gray spot of fur the shape of a distorted heart on its chest. Its mate, black fur and eyes like two drops of gelled seawater, nudged its nose against our feet before running back into the remains of the forest.

The white rabbit followed suit, and before long Chelsea and I had fallen asleep, each holding what was left of the world in our tired hearts.

* * *

Fuzzy vision and I hear Chelsea's voice. She's sitting next to me and I don't know how long I've been asleep in the living room. She stares straight ahead, as if entranced with the night sky. A splinter of moonlight splits her face diagonally. My hand finds its way to her lap and her fingers clasp onto mine, squeezing like she hasn't seen me in months. Her head tilts, lips gently pressing against mine. She tastes like fresh honeydew. We kiss for what feels like hours, our bodies warm with desire.

"We should make dinner," she says. "Are you hungry?"

I nod and place my lips on her head, the scent of old shampoo and daisies greeting my nostrils with eager flare. She stands up and smiles. "You stay here and relax. I'll start dinner."

I lift my legs to the other side of the couch and sigh. It's only when I catch the outline of movement against darkness that I run into the kitchen and grab Chelsea by the hand. She doesn't have to say a word; she just runs to the bedroom and slams the door shut. We've been prepared for moments like these.

"What's out there?" Her question is muffled by two inches of pine. I can hear voices outside of the walls, bodies scratching the exterior of the house. I reach into the hallway closet and pull one of the three guns resting on the top shelf. The metal is cold and all I can picture is my father teaching me how to duck hunt when I was a boy.

I rest my head against the bedroom door. "Stay in there and don't move. I'm going to check out the front of the house."

Hands and forehead drip with sweat as I peek out the peephole on the front door. I'm greeted with nothing but the violent swaying of vapid tree limbs and an everlasting gaze into the black of night. Silence breaks and my eyes burn with a quick flash of white light, fingers losing their grip on the gun. I fall to the floor and hear the banging against the door, each vivid thump pounding my spine. I close my eyes and remember that if whoever's outside gets to me, they'll get to Chelsea.

An ounce of strength finds its way into my hands and I'm pushing the door, holding it closed. The locks jingle with fright. I hear a long, winding screech and the force outside stops. I wait at least two full minutes with my heart beating as fast as a thousand horses before I stand up. My back slides against the door on the way up and part of me is surprised that it's still upright. Chelsea walks slowly into the hallway and hugs me. I hold onto her with one arm and keep the gun raised in the air with the other. "What was it?"

I shake my head and turn an eye to the peephole. A swash of black on the other side, an array of golden lights flickering in the sky. I push Chelsea away from the door and motion for her to leave the hallway. She takes tiny steps backwards until I can only see white-painted fingernails gripping the edge of the living room entrance. The locks are eased open. I'm careful to keep my fingers wrapped around the handle of the gun. The knob turns and a frosty chill sneaks into the house, the scent of sugar and ice.

I stand on the doorway, gun poised and ready for an attack. I turn my back to the night and see two streaks painted on the front door, a silver vein entwined with a splash of red in the shape of a distorted V.

END OF DAYS

The echoes of comfort fly away as I rush into the house and slam the door behind me.

* * *

The wool blanket wrapped around her, Chelsea sits silently on the couch in front of the living room window. "What if they come back? What if they break in here? What do we do?"

I've been holding the gun for almost two hours and I'm so tired I fear my fingers are interwoven with the aged metal. The truth is that I don't know what to do if someone breaks into the house.

"I don't know what to do," I say. "It was just a threat, Chelsea."

She throws the blanket to the floor, fuzzy red clashing with the vomit-colored carpet. She starts shouting and after a few minutes I can only close my eyes as a response. When she calms down, she picks up the blanket and tosses it on the couch. She's wearing tight gray sweatpants that make her legs look like knives. Before she can leave the room, I pull her into me so close that she's lifted off the floor. One deep kiss and her hands are tugging at the back of my head, slender fingers pulling brown hair.

"I'm not going to let anything happen to you," I say. "I love you. I would have rather died four months ago than know there'd be a day I'd have to live without you."

The subtle twinkle in the cavernous green of her eyes is all I need right now. She holds my hand, palms sticking together with a millimeter of sweat. Chelsea's head eases onto my chest and her eyelids open and close to the rhythm of my breaths.

"Whoever they are," I say, "they'll never get past me. Nothing will happen to you, I promise."

She presses her lips against my cheek and leaves the room. "You can't sit there all night. You need some sleep."

"I know. I'm going to sit up for a little while," I tell her.

Her footsteps in the kitchen are soft murmurs against the pink lightning storm raging outside. Cherry slices of light break through the darkness, each one shining long enough to see the outlines of every remaining star adorning the night sky. If I close my eyes, the peculiar drone beyond the living room window will fill my head. Each note is like a code, informing who's left in the world that the

Earth is evolving into something different. I can only imagine what lies beyond the balcony. And I can only imagine who left their markings on our front door. We haven't seen signs of life since the trek into the mountains nearly four months ago.

I sit up and walk through the kitchen. I haven't eaten all day and have no desire to do so now. Chelsea and I are sick of eating canned food three times a day but we both know that luck was on our side when we found a stockpile of food and bottled water in the cabinets and cupboard.

A supple ginger glow spills out of the bedroom. It makes my shadow look like a hunchback, my head and arms bent forward. My fingers slide against the wall, squishy steps on the bedroom carpet as I view the striking silhouette of Chelsea's body. She squeaks out a small "hello" with a seductive smile. She was blessed with the curves of a tattooed angel and a voice that could make a man cry.

"Come to bed," she says.

Pretty soon my clothes are on the floor and I forget that the world has ended.

* * *

I wake up alone in bed, the leftover scent of sex and lavender floating above my bare body. Chelsea was never one for sleeping in. When we first lived together, she'd wake up much earlier than me and go out for a run or make breakfast. I guess she's still in the habit even though night has eroded most of the light of every cold morning.

I swing my legs over the side of the bed and put on jeans and a t-shirt. My hoodie slouches over my shoulder as I head into the kitchen and see Chelsea sitting silently at the kitchen table, reading a newspaper. She looks up and a tiny smile curls at the bottom of her face, a sliver of delight amidst light freckles. Her head bows back to the newspaper and after a minute I realize I haven't watched the news on television or read a magazine or newspaper since the sun's rays first carved through comet dust.

Chelsea flips a page and lifts her head to me, giving me a quick kiss on the cheek. I run fingers alongside parts of her matted curls, crunching the hardened hair from day-old hairspray. She looks as beautiful as she did the night before.

I lean in and see that's she reading *The Great Falls Tribune* from March 6, 2011. She can see the inquisitive look on my face, probably the way my eyebrows flare against the pale skin of my forehead. "I haven't read anything since we got here," she says. "I just want to feel like the world is alive and breathing again." She raises the newspaper, her eyes scanning words that mean nothing now.

I nod and sit next to her, easing into the pine chair and taking a deep breath. My body wants breakfast but my mind needs fresh air. "I'm going to take a quick walk outside. Do you want to come?"

"Do you think it's safe?" She frowns.

"I think we'll be okay."

She folds the newspaper and zips up her sweatshirt. I can tell she's not wearing a bra; nipples poke through two thin layers of cloth. She reaches out for my hand and I hold on to it as we walk out of the kitchen and through the front door.

The markings on the door are behind us, neither of us mentions their creation or what they mean. We follow the small trail around the house leading up to the edge of the property, the balcony just above us. Only a small amount of light provides guidance to the end of the trail. We look over the side, cerulean mist circling above the rocks, the last breaths of a dissolving stream. Chelsea squeezes my arm, her slender fingers tightening around muscle and fabric.

"We'll go inside in a few minutes," I tell her.

I can read fear in the words lost somewhere between her eyes, unease flowing in her weary blood. A sniff of air and I know that the world doesn't smell the same without leaves and trees and animals. I used to work in the city and everyday cursed the bustle of metro life. As I take a few steps to the edge of the rocks, I realize I'd give my own soul to be lying in the apartment bed with Chelsea, a concert of blaring traffic on the streets outside.

The rocks are sturdy beneath my boots and I edge further until a blanket of mist wraps around my legs. Chelsea stays behind, standing with her arms crossed, eyes now two slits of green. When we first found the house, the sounds of crashing waves below us put our minds at ease, as if our destructive present was offset by an inkling of normality. We noticed the waters of the rivers start to evaporate only a month ago. Everyday the fog rising from the base of the mountain grows thicker and it's only a matter of time before yet another aspect of our world fades into nothing.

It's amazing to think that we haven't seen the sun in months yet the surface of the Earth hasn't frozen over. I know it's somewhere behind the blanket of obsidian, afraid to shower its old world with healthy streams of light.

Chelsea calls out to me, the trickling of her squeaky voice reaching me as I find my last step on the rocks. A gigantic breath of misty air and my lungs soothe with a comfortable taste. It's all I needed this morning. I walk back to the trail and Chelsea pulls my hand until we're pacing on the dirt.

"I don't like it out here," she says.

"Neither do I."

Before we reach the house, I look back to the lifeless woods surrounding the trail. A path of fire shoots across the horizon like a scarlet laser, piercing a constellation of stars. Chelsea puts a hand over her mouth and looks at me. We stand in awe for a few minutes, the next comet shooting across a coverlet of cobalt green, its tail withering into tiny sparks and silent explosions. I hold Chelsea's hand in mine, squeezing her fingers with each flare. The only sounds I can hear are the purrs of the remaining stars and our disparate breaths.

We walk into the house and close the front door behind us, the dead of silence greeting us with open arms. Chelsea removes her sweatshirt and tosses it to the floor. I stand behind her and rub her arms, trying to warm her skin with just my fingertips. My lips find the back of her neck, giving her a few quick kisses before she pulls away. She turns around and smiles, returning the kisses with her own.

"I love you," she says. "Every day I wake up and think I'm dreaming. I think I'm in a recurring nightmare."

"Me, too."

"What are we going to do?"

"I don't know, Chelsea. All I'm thinking about is staying alive."

She sighs and shoves her hands into her front jean pockets. "I have a horrible feeling this isn't the right place for us to be."

I close my eyes, trying to funnel the warmth from my heart into the rest of my body. "We should be dead right now. We're lucky to be here. We're lucky that we're both breathing, sleeping, eating and spending time together."

"I know. I'll just never get used to this place."

A shiver slithers up my legs and creeps into my spine. Cold dominates the room, a swoop of electric frost sticking to the windows. I look outside and the lightshow has ended, the night sky once more just an infinite coverlet of black.

*　　*　　*

Los Angeles was buried under a mile-high wave of water. Planes fell from the sky like birds hunted on a crisp autumn day. We were lucky enough to be on the road after visiting Chelsea's parents in Salt Lake City. We kept driving north until we couldn't hear the screams anymore, the chilling voices of a dying race. I can't remember the last time we saw the sun, the last time I sat outside with a smile.

*　　*　　*

The radio stopped broadcasting noise three weeks ago. Until then, I'd spend every morning scrolling through the frequencies, eager to hear even the most subtle of human voices. The FM stations were mostly all static, a few transmitting barebones silence. Chelsea would sit next to me, biting her fingernails and hoping to hear any signs of life beyond our own private world.

What startled us even more than the lack of existence was on the AM frequencies: each station played the same odd hum that fell from the stars. Its drone almost hypnotic, we sat close to each other as I fumbled through each frequency, the only sounds sneaking from the speakers making our skin crawl with terrible delight. I didn't want to know what the sounds meant, didn't want to decode the throbbing waves recoiling on each side of my brain.

I switched the dial back to FM and felt an abnormal comfort with the resonance of static.

I haven't looked at the radio since. I sit with a plastic cup filled with vodka and warm cranberry juice, staring at the dusty shelves around the basement, each adorned with cans of vegetables, fruit and beans. I know that at some point down the road we're going to run out of food, but my mind hasn't thought that far ahead into our future. I don't want to know what's going to happen the day we need to leave the house to find food and water.

Chelsea jogs down the stairs, her boots clicking against the aged wood. "Are you okay?"

"Yeah, I'm fine. Just wanted to sit somewhere for a bit where there were no windows."

"Dinner's ready. Why don't you come upstairs and eat with me?"

I force a smile and finish my drink, crumbling the paper cup and tossing it to the floor. It lands next to a lawnmower covered with grime. I follow Chelsea up the steps, closing the basement door behind me and locking it.

We eat a mix of baked beans and creamed corn, each of us filling our glasses with one of the many bottles of wine that were hidden away in the kitchen cabinets. Chelsea's cheeks fill with red spots and I know she was drinking while she cooked dinner. Her eyes are watery, broken emeralds shimmering with a thin layer of tears. I don't ask if she's okay. I finish my plate and split it in half, paper snapping us out of our quiet trances.

With Chelsea still at the table, I leave and open another bottle of wine. A big gulp flowing down my throat, I head into the living room, plopping down on the couch like I've worked a twelve-hour day. Long sips and long gazes pass the time before I'm lost somewhere in the fuzzy confines of slumber.

*   *   *

Chelsea's scream floats from the corners of a dream world, hiding the urgency. My eyes open to the reality of her desperate pleas, and before I realize it, I'm on my feet and running into the kitchen. Chilly air flows freely from the broken kitchen window, angora curtains shifting from side to side in a violent motion.

Chelsea is huddled in the corner, hair draped over her face like she's hiding from the outside world. I grab her by the arm and pull until she's running behind me. We run into the bedroom and slam the door.

"Stay in here. I'm going back out there."

I pull the closet door open and snatch the gun on the shelf, clicking the safety off and glaring at Chelsea before leaving her. She reaches for the shotgun under the bed and crawls into the corner of the room. It all happens in slow motion. I ease my steps from the hallway to the kitchen, careful to not let my boots squeak against the wooden floor.

The gun aimed in front of me, I swing into the kitchen and see a black figure hop from behind the table and into the living room. My breath panicked and heavy, I follow it until the shadow disappears. All I can see is a figure draped in black, not an inch of skin peeking from its clothing. A quick burst of red and I'm on the floor, pain wriggling the nerves in my face, gun thrown too many feet away from me.

Through hazy vision, its legs scuttle past me and I hear the breaking of glass.

I roll over and onto my feet and hurry into the kitchen, leaving the gun on the carpeted floor behind me. With nothing but the hurried stream of air sliding against my face, I lean over the sink and look out the broken window, careful not to scrape my chest on the battered glass. The night whistles with uncertain glee, the intruder long gone by now. The blood dripping from my nose leaks into my mouth and it tastes like tinfoil.

I knock twice on the bedroom door, Chelsea barely opening it. I see a bit of dirty blonde hair, fingernails digging into the door. "Stay in here," I say. "I need to board up the kitchen window." I can't hear what she says before I turn the knob to me and pull with all of my force.

Two markings are engraved into the kitchen table. A silver streak crosses a longer stripe of red, making an upside-down **V**. I shudder and force myself to walk away.

The basement is darker than the skies outside. I stumble down the stairs, nearly tripping over my feet.

Fumbling through the trash on the floor next to the generator, I find a piece of wood much larger than the size of the window. I don't have time to keep searching so I throw it by the bottom of the stairs and find the toolbox we keep on top of the old refrigerator. Another crash upstairs, not nearly as loud as the one before. A gunshot rings and blows past the silence of the basement. I let out a muffled scream, the moan of a frightened child.

I reach the top of the basement stairs and see my love covered in blood, crimson spots dancing on her white t-shirt. Smoke glides from the hot barrel and disappears into the ceiling. Chelsea falls to the floor, dropping the shotgun. The sound of her crying is the loudest noise I've ever heard in my life.

The body is crumpled against one of the kitchen chairs, its legs curled. I can see it's an older man with hair the color of polished brass. His eyes are open and his chest is absent of breaths. Black and torn fabric reveals multiple patches of freshly penetrated skin.

"He pushed open the bedroom door," Chelsea says. "I shot him, Konrad. I had to shoot him."

I reach for her hand and she grips it harder than she ever has before. Holding on to her, I reach for the man's wrist. His heart has stopped beating, his cold, dead body leaving this world with a filthy stare at my wife.

"Go get a towel and clean off. *Now.*"

She runs to the bathroom. I push the man's eyelids down, flaps of skin covering the coldest stare to grace this lonely house. His arms are heavy as tree trunks and it's tough to pull him out of the kitchen. I let the body fall down the basement stairs, watching the skull smack the concrete wall, bits of blood smearing the marine-blue stone. I trot along the steps, finding the toolbox and sheet of wood.

Running back upstairs, I drop it on the kitchen floor and slam the basement door behind me. Chelsea is in the bathroom, wearing a lacy pink bra. She sits against the sink, head down and solemn. Her soiled t-shirt is crumpled in the trash barrel amidst a mess of wet paper towels. I put my arms around her and press my lips against her forehead. Her sweat is sweet, like sugar water.

It only takes me five minutes to board up the window. When I'm done, I take a swig of wine and drink until it spills out of my mouth and drips on my shirt and the floor. It takes me a few moments to collect myself and realize what has happened over the last ten minutes. I ease into one of the kitchen chairs and finish the bottle of wine before letting my mind calm to the tune of the nighttime's ambient melody.

*   *   *

Chelsea stands next to the living room window, her hands gracing the shotgun like it was a sleeping child. She watches the trees sway back and forth, waiting for any sign of movement in the darkness surrounding the house. I drift in and out of consciousness, my eyes following her in the silent filmstrip of my mind. Before long, I sit up and she's gone, leaving me with a square portrait of absolute black. The wine leaves pulses of tenderness beating just behind my eyes, the remains of a violent evening.

I slip out of the living room, ignoring patterns of candlelight dancing against the hallway floor. Footsteps are gentle and slide against the linoleum floor in a seamless motion. I stand before the basement door and take a deep breath before opening it. The steps come slowly, my boots lending weight until the wood creaks with an awkward moan.

The intruder's body is slouched at the bottom of the stairs. His eyelids are still closed, the fury once raging in his arms and legs now dormant in insipid skin. I poke his chest with a bitter finger and wince, part of me expecting the corpse to return to full life. His pants are thick and soiled and smell like fresh dirt. I search his two pockets and find nothing. The head tilts to the side when I remove my hand. I jump back in reaction, each thud of my heart nearly popping through my ribcage. I stand up and notice the black marks on the left side of his neck. Leaning down, I see the amateur tattoo scrawled into the skin. It's a sideways **V** and at this very moment all I can picture is Chelsea crying in her room, clutching the eggshell white blankets while trails of veins fill with anxious blood.

I kick the body once, twice. It doesn't move. Curses fill the air and my eyes start to water. I wipe away the discharge, running up the basement stairs and letting the cool indoor air graze past my cheeks as it shoves the door shut behind me. With ovals of light my guide, I follow them until I reach the bedroom door. Chelsea sleeps on the very edge of the bed, like a frightened dog. I'm careful not to startle her as I kick off my boots and fall into the mess of pillows and blankets.

The world rages on outside of our house, and all I can do is let the tears flow as I nestle my head next to the golden curls of my wife's hair.

*　　*　　*

Two days have passed and neither of us has ventured outside. It's only now that I've learned to accept the radiance of noise crinkling in the night sky, its mellow drone sliding into my ears in hypnotic fashion. Chelsea lies naked under the sheet and says she can't hear it anymore.

"How?"

"All I can hear is the shotgun blast," she says. "The weight of his body slamming against the kitchen chairs."

I nod and understand that to kill someone is to accept seeing the person's face every time you close your eyes. Chelsea turns to me with a look of desperation, eyes eager to confess their sins with only a single glance. The bed sheets barely cover her body up to her chest.

"This isn't going to last forever," she says.

I won't answer her. Instead, I stare at the collection of stains on the bedroom ceiling; follow the collection with my hand as more words creep out of her mouth. I say nothing and get out of bed, waiting a moment before putting on my jeans and t-shirt.

"Please listen to me," Chelsea says. "We have to think about leaving. I don't want to die."

Head down, I let my toes curl against the carpet. It takes all of my willpower to stay silent, but only a phrase escapes my lips. "We're not going anywhere."

I blow out the candle on the dresser and find my boots, ignoring the waves of sound pounding on my skull. Chelsea closes the door after I leave. I sit at the kitchen table, my fingernails trying to pick off the dry chips of black and red paint. I don't know the interpretation of the symbol but every time I see it I know that

Chelsea's right. It's not safe here anymore, but leaving the mountains will only guarantee that both of our lives will end under harsh
circumstances.

It's only a matter of time before whoever's outside will break in
again.

It's only a matter of time before death comes knocking again.

I find another bottle of wine buried behind rows of canned
vegetables. Jade glass covers blood red liquid, and before I pop
open the cork, Chelsea grabs the bottle from me and smashes it to
the floor. Tiny shards split and waltz into the air, drops of merlot
splashing against banana-colored linoleum. She's taking deep
breaths, small breasts sulking under a thin layer of purple fabric.
She shakes her head, disappointment rising from white knuckles.

She clenches her teeth and leaves the kitchen. For a moment
her aura floats behind her, a simple pattern of translucent lace
crawling into the air. I rub my eyes, letting leftover sleep dig into
my retinas. "Chelsea…"

She doesn't answer and within a matter of seconds I hear the
bedroom door crash with unbridled might. I sigh and start to clean
up the mess on the kitchen floor. Paper towels soak up the dirty
residue of wine, leaving a trail of orange spots on the kitchen floor.
I'm on my knees, dropping the towels into one of the last plastic
trash bags we have left when Chelsea walks back into the kitchen,
pallid skin drained of every drop of emotion.

Her lips curl and I ask what's wrong. She just turns her head
back to the bedroom, a simple motion that beckons me to follow
her. I take her hand and she leads me through darkness and into
the bedroom where our bodies are lit by an array of lights. I step
away from Chelsea and edge closer to the bedroom window, my
hand shoving away the few inches covered by curtains. The moon
hovers amongst the night sky, a bright eye looking down upon a
scarred planet. In a matter of moments, the moon's center pops in
a vivid flash. It looks like a giant orange rose set to fire, purple
streaks entwined with space glitter and tinges of silver.

Chelsea presses her body against mine but I barely notice. "Oh
my God," she says. She squeezes the loose ends of my t-shirt,
tugging on the cloth like a child clutching its father. We stand for
what feels like hours, watching the celestial destruction unfold in

the sky. Gold light spills into the room, and for a moment I look away, my vision locked on Chelsea's tranquil face. The green in her eyes mixes with shimmering moonlight, like emeralds floating in a sea of melting bronze.

I pull Chelsea to the bed, my hands on her hips. Breaths of sorrow take flight from my lips as flickers of dust begin to drop from the remaining stars. Chelsea lies next to me and a frightening calm creeps into my chest, every heartbeat forcing hair to stand on end. With her body nuzzled against me, we eventually drift into a dreamless slumber, an outline of igniting flowers burnt to the backdrop of our eyelids.

*   *   *

I sit up in bed, alone and tired. The blankets are crumpled by my feet. I reach over to the opposite side of the bed, expecting my hand to be greeted with the warmth of Chelsea's skin but my fingers find nothing but cool sheets and my own shadow. My stomach growls, feeding off the remains of sleep. I force myself out of bed and close the curtains.

I stumble out of the bedroom and walk into the kitchen. The large board surprises me and after a few seconds I remember what happened a couple nights ago. Chelsea isn't in the kitchen or the living room. After checking the bathroom, a chilly wind lurches into my bones. The front door is wide open, the air barely able to rustle its sturdy frame. In a moment of panic, I grab the gun from our bedroom, dress quickly, and run outside, my boots scraping against the dirt trail. The moon is nowhere to be found, replaced by a swash of stars the color of morning bruises. I see her hair tossed by a winter wind, whorls of curly locks spattered in multiple directions. With the gun stuck inside the back of my jeans, I jog to Chelsea and stop just a few feet away from her.

She stands with her arms covering her stomach. I take a step next to her and whisper into her ear. "Chelsea, honey, are you okay?"

She closes her eyes in response, violet eyeliner gleaming with spatters of glitter. She inhales and takes a step forward, closer to the edge of rocks. Ashen swirls of mist circle around us, and when I try to slide a hand into her crossed arms, she pushes me away. "We can't live like this any longer. It's not worth it."

"Chelsea, please. Come back inside the house and we'll talk."

She shakes her head, moving her arms to the side and opening her eyes. "No, I don't want to go back in there. I'm not going to waste away in there."

Chelsea steps further, her pink sneakers now hugging the slab of gray rocks. Another few inches and she could fall. She starts to speak again but my arms are already around her waist, lifting her into the air. She kicks away the mist rising from the decaying mountain stream, screaming at the top of her lungs. The noise rattles the bones in my face. She attempts to fight her way out of my grip the entire walk back to the house. I set her down at the set of four concrete stairs at the bottom of the front door.

"Calm down...please."

She lets her head drop low and starts to cry, thick tears falling from her face and smacking the stone beneath our feet. I kneel in front of her, placing my hands on the sides of her head, soft rumples of hair touching my skin.

"What's wrong?"

Chelsea sniffles and looks at me, smudges of mulberry wet with salt and sorrow. Her frown is almost icy and I have to look away. She holds onto my hand and I can barely hear what she says under the whine of my own thoughts.

"I'm pregnant."

Blood in my heart quickens and in seconds Chelsea's eyes glow with the reflection of scattered fireflies.

*　*　*

Chelsea sleeps with her head on my chest. I can remember the first night we slept together. She was twenty-three years old and it took every ounce of resistance to keep myself from proposing after only a week of dating. Only a couple of years later, we're sitting alive after the Earth's funeral with a baby baking in her womb. She said it wouldn't be fair to raise a child in this new world; wouldn't be fair to bring life into a world so filled with death.

She wanted to end her life to avoid creating a new one. She said I was the reason she didn't jump into the remains of the river. I was the reason why she wanted to continue to live.

I ease myself out of her grasp and head into the kitchen, careful not to wake her. The wine calls out to me but even in celebration I know the sweet taste of alcohol wouldn't be respectful. I pour a small glass of water and sit at the kitchen table, wondering if the ideas running through my head were the same ones my own father experienced so many years ago.

The liquid soothes my throat. I sit for a few minutes more; trying to ignore the remains of the intruder's etching scrawled into the surface of the kitchen table. My palm slides over the markings and a slight chill runs up my arm and into the muscles. I finish the water and drop the glass into the sink next to a growing pile of filthy china.

"Hey, baby," Chelsea says.

I'm alarmed at the tinny peep in her voice and turn around with a fist.

"Sorry, I didn't think you were awake," I say.

She smiles and sits at the table, rolling the sleeves of her sweater past her wrists to the middle of her hand. "It's okay. We've been on edge since we found this place."

I sit next to her and she immediately curls her fingers over my hand. Her cheeks are as red as poinsettias. "We're having a baby," she says with a grin. "*A baby.*"

"I know." My voice twinkles with the type of delight that neither of us have experienced before.

I'm just about ready to ask Chelsea what she wants for dinner when I hear a screeching bang in the living room. We both stand up, the light of terror sprinkled in our eyes. "Not again," I say.

I rush to the bedroom, Chelsea behind me, and grab the shotgun. It hasn't been touched since she shot the intruder just days ago. It feels powerful in my arms, almost a living, breathing entity soaking up the weight of my arms.

"Stay here, I'll be right back."

Chelsea closes and locks the door behind me. Long strides to the living room turn into a full run, another snapping crunch striking the walls. The front door is shoved off its hinges before I'm there, bolts and screws tossed into the night air. Three figures stand before me, each dressed in black. I raise the shotgun, but before I can pull the trigger I'm brought to the ground by someone behind me. His hands knock the shotgun across the living room floor and in only a second I feel the clout of a wooden plank against my face.

"Get the girl," one of them says.

Springs of pain rush into my eyes, my cheekbones. My breaths are panicked and all I can see are flickering spots of white. The man keeps his arms on mine, movement stifled by his grimy body. The three other shapes walk past me and into the kitchen. I can barely see them now, only wads of black against the blood dripping into my eyes. Chelsea's apocalyptic scream pierces the air and everything is starting to fade away.

The last thing that comes across my vision is my wife's body dragged across the carpeted floor, her golden hair now just a distant memory.

* * *

Jarring flashes of pewter poke me out of sleep. I turn over to see the shotgun leaning against the loveseat in the corner of the living room. My tongue finds a small hard object in my mouth. I spit it out and see it's one of a few teeth that are missing from my jaw.

Moonlight drips into the room through the broken living room window and I say one name before shouting as loud as I've ever had before. *"Chelsea!"*

I frantically run to each part of the house. She's not here and after a few seconds I remember the figures dragging her across the floor.

My wife, my love. Gone.

My father used to say that men's tears were a different color than women's. I look in the bathroom mirror and see a torrent of salty water shooting from my eyes, each arc of every tear burning the bruises and cuts in my battered face. They look darker, as if my glands started producing secretion as black as motor oil. I can't feel my heart beating and I could die right here in the bathroom, clutching my heart while calling out the names of everyone I've ever known.

There's only one name I need to hear and I don't have the strength to speak it out loud again.

I leave the bathroom and stagger into the kitchen; try to picture Chelsea cooking at the stove, a tight white t-shirt cut just below the belly button. My eyes closed, I walk into the living room and feel the chill of a winter breeze. The front door lies on the floor, digging into the carpet. The outside air is cold and unforgiving and when I see their symbol splattered against the front entrance's landing I drop to my knees. They took my wife but I wish they had taken me instead. My child could be breathing, unknowing of the world outside its mother's skin.

Leaving the house, I take a few steps along the sandy trail, kicking dirt into the air. The ethereal hum of the stars is gone, replaced by lifeless silence. I walk around the house twice before going back inside, stepping on the front door as I enter. I expect to see Chelsea leaning into the living room, swinging by one arm gracing the edge of the entryway.

I'm greeted by nothing except a blood-stained carpet and regret.

A familiar shine hops across the kitchen walls and I remember the nights when Chelsea would read by candlelight, her legs crossed and head perched by a fist. Her hair would hang over her eyes and I would always ask how she could see in between the long, frosty curls.

The bedroom smells like burnt cinnamon. I notice the tip of something small and brown placed in the center of the bed. It's a bag made of burlap, tied with dirty brown string. It feels like two squishy marbles and I drop it to the floor, not wanting to open it. Deep breaths eclipse a wearied heart and I force myself to pick it up.

The string comes undone with a simple twitch and the bag falls apart in my hands, each corner easing open. What I hold is something I've stared at for too many months. What I hold is the beautiful siren that lured me to my wife in the very beginning. What I hold convinces me that she's far away and dead.

I bring my hand to my face and Chelsea's eyes glare back at me, devoid of life and filled with the lost echoes of hope. Red strands of muscle squiggle out of the bloody sheath and I drop them to the ground, hoping that my skull will collapse and fill my brain with the music of the departed.

I just held my wife's lifeless eyes in my hands and now I know that I'll never see her again. Her life was wasted in this new world.

Bed sheets holding my body, I slide into the pillows and try to remember Chelsea's voice. I can only hear it if I close my eyes. Lips kiss the edge of the pillow, my drool spilling onto the soft fabric of my wife's pillow. It still smells like her. With a last ounce of vigor, my legs find the bedroom floor and I blow out the candle, the syrupy aroma of butterflies arousing the air around me. Through the darkness, I make my way into the closet, throwing her jeans and old blouses aside. The handgun is cold to the touch. I wrap my fingers around the handle and shut the bedroom door, forever leaving the scent of her behind me.

*   *   *

The stars mock me as I walk along the trail at the front of the house. I look to the sky with eyes of rage, blaming them for the demise of life and love. The only sound penetrating the night air is the scraping of my boots against dirt and rock.

The gun is jammed in the back of my jeans. I wait until I reach the back of the house to pull it out, holding it high in front of me, both hands aiming it towards the moon. I stand before the rock where Chelsea and I confirmed our love for each other, the exact spot where we were married. I toss the gun to the ground and it lands in a bed of lifeless flowers, slate gray metal slamming against the only withered petals that hadn't blown away in the wind.

I kneel into the rock, my face pressed against the lone crevasse in the middle of the weathered stone. A steady flow of tears falls and coats the rock.

I cry for my mother and father, my little brother who was in college when it all went to Hell. My grandparents were deep beneath the ground and were spared the wrath of destruction. I think of Chelsea and the tears stop. I remember the promise I made to her and realize I have broken it into a million little pieces. Wiping my face, I reach over and pick up the gun, gaze at it for a minute. I never owned a weapon until we found this house.

Wind whips at my back, my thin jacket flapping and smacking against the skin. I peel it off and throw it to the side, watch it drift against the edge of rocks and fall over; the outline of my soul descending with it as it disappears into whatever is left of the river below the mountains.

I kick off my sneakers; shake the dirt and sand out of the soles before I throw them over the side of the mountain. The black rubber blends with the darkness and soon they're out of sight. Sitting on the rock, my toes push away a pile of dead leaves. They crumble into a pile of dark green dust and blow away.

With my legs hanging over the front of the rock and my back to the open air and the river below, I shove the gun in my mouth, teeth clamping down on the barrel. My tongue licks the bottom of the metal, a strange flavor that reminds me of overcooked coffee. Bits of rain descend from whatever clouds lurk behind a wall of black static. They hit my swollen face and the wetness comforts the cuts and bruises.

I hum a song to say goodbye, the last tune of my life will be built on my own accord. Chelsea's voice joins me and my finger rests against the trigger. I can feel the rising mist sneak up my t-shirt, colliding with sweat and sticking to my back.

With eyes open to take a final view of the world, I can see Chelsea walk along the trail. She's wearing all white, a skirt ending just above the knee. She smiles, the blurry appeal of death asking me to just pull the trigger. Her silhouette disappears as slivers of lightning begin to pierce the horizon. I'm left with just my shadow.

I scoot over closer to the edge of the rock, hoping that when the bullet shatters the back of my skull, gray matter and bits of bloodied bone will tumble down the mountain and hit the ground before my body does.

I'm ready for it. I'm ready to do this.

Just when I'm about to end it a fluffy shape of white enters my vision. It comes closer, stopping at the edge of the woods before I can see what it is.

The rabbit, fur as virginal as a summer morning, with a gray blotch shaped like a heart on its chest. It scoots over to me, only an inch away from my toes. It sniffs the bottom of my foot and for a moment I swear its tiny eyes glance up at me.

I look up to the sky, say her name only once. Wherever she is, I know she's smiling. I know she's holding our child, giving it a kiss on the forehead for me.

Lips grow cool from the barrel of the gun and I pull it out of my mouth to gently rest it on my lap. The rabbit scampers away, hops into the woods and disappears. A smile finds its way across my face.

Standing up, I turn to the edge of the mountain. Fog makes way for the gun as I toss it as far as I can, watching the little black dot fade into a cloud of incandescence. I imagine the sun setting for Chelsea and me, a veil of gray embracing the remains of a world that took everything away from us.

This is only the beginning.

THE COST OF SURVIVAL

MICHAEL SIMON

The steady drip of water echoed off the rusted girders and concrete walls as Conor leaned his body across the rail and slowly raised his night vision goggles. Puddles of stagnant water stretched into the darkness, fuelling the growth of millions of blood sucking insects that swarmed every inch of exposed flesh. But Conor ignored the buzzing insects just as he ignored the cold seeping through his tattered jeans and worn flannel shirt... just as he ignored the smell of decay that oozed out of every crevice in his bitter, dark world.

Instead he focused on the largest pool of fuel-stained water in front of the rail car. Through his goggles, the world was locked in a green hue, its edges fuzzy and distorted.

"It's there," he whispered. "Looks like it caught a big rat."

The figure beside him, leaning back against the moisture laden concrete, didn't answer but quietly slid the rifle's safety to the *off* position. With only one arm, he balanced the barrel between his legs and checked the muzzle before passing over the weapon. Conor carefully affixed the goggles to the scope before taking aim. It wasn't the most accurate way to hit a target but the prey was close and they had more ammunition than they could use in a lifetime. A normal lifetime.

As Conor positioned the gun, the other figure automatically tried to straighten the worn, cloth collar around his neck. It was his last one, and although properly stained and frayed, it was a point of pride that saw him put it on every morning.

It was his last link to a previous existence.

Conor didn't bother to check the gun. The priest had proved to be as efficient as he was loyal. As soon as the bullet left the barrel, the man would have a second waiting in his outstretched palm.

He aimed where he thought the head should be and the shot was an explosion of light and sound in the confined subway tunnel, shock waves bouncing off walls and mercilessly hammering human eardrums. The creature jerked and thrashed as Conor reloaded and fired again. It took five bullets to kill it.

Conor waited for the echoes to fade before turning around.

"Call the girls," he said. "Tell them we're having take-out tonight."

*　　*　　*

Living in constant hunger, month after month, taught them to eat anything. Gone were the days when the liver and heart were automatically thrown out. The organs may have smelled bad and tasted worse but they supplied calories and minerals and, in the end, that was all that mattered.

Jenny was slick with a knife. She could skin a rat in two minutes flat and gut a crocodile in under twenty. DJ and the little one, Sarah, were slower but adequate when the group wasn't pressed. In the tunnel however, Conor was letting Jenny do the work. It wasn't safe to loiter this far from home as the vermin and the dogs were getting hungrier and bolder every day.

"More light," Jenny whispered as she dug into the cavity of the crocodile's stomach. DJ, clutching the small flashlight, dutifully moved closer, almost burying the light in the hole. Blood and vicious fluids dripped off their arms and hands.

"How are the batteries holding up?" Conor asked as he patrolled the darkness with his night goggles.

Standing off to one side, Sarah held up two double-A batteries. In the angle of the light, she looked like a tiny gnome. "We're down to twenty," she said. "Another month and they'll have drained out, too."

Conor's smile was cold. "And we'll be down to using candles. Look how far we've come."

*　　*　　*

Crocodile meat is an acquired taste, one that is made infinitely easier by the lack of other options. In their perpetual dark world they ate their fill when possible. Without a fridge or icebox, the chances of meat lasting more than a few days was highly unlikely. In the underground tunnels it was too cold to survive without fire but not cold enough to keep food from spoiling.

John tossed a couple of table legs into the oil drum and for a moment they watched, mesmerized, as a sheet of sparks shot skyward. He retreated to his spot in the corner and Conor noticed when he unconsciously rubbed his stump.

"How's it doing?" he asked.

The priest, embarrassed at getting caught, shrugged it off. "Good, actually. I only feel it once in a while now."

A blatant lie, Conor suspected. No one lost a limb and forgot about it.

"What about the pus?"

"All gone, thanks to DJ." His gaze found the redhead stripping a section of rib bare with her teeth. "The antibiotics she found in the shops made a huge difference."

Conor grunted and went back to eating. The priest didn't need to be told he was a tough SOB. Two months back, when a section of girder fell from the ceiling and pinned the man's arm to the floor, everyone thought he was dead, everyone except John. The gaunt, forty-year-old must have been fused from horse leather because he actually talked Conor through the process of finishing the amputation job the angled steel had begun. With hands shaking and sweat pouring off his brow, Conor cut through the remaining muscle and tendon and even applied a heated blade to staunch the bleeding. It was only then the man passed out.

The infection set in soon enough but because of DJ, eight weeks later there was a flap of shiny pink skin covering the hole. The redhead noticed the priest looking at her and she smiled between mouthfuls.

Sarah finished her plate and looked up. "Tastes like chicken," she said and everyone sitting round the fire groaned. It was an old joke. She turned to Conor. "I found two boxes of crackers this morning and left them in front of the locker."

Conor nodded. If the twelve-year-old weighed sixty pounds it was because she had fallen into a puddle. The ballerina could probably squeeze into a glove box if need be, which was good because the collapsed shops in the pedway that ran above the subway lines didn't allow for much wiggle room and yet Sarah's daily chores included scrounging through the debris in the hope of finding something useful, food being the top priority.

Conor knew the others didn't like it. Forcing a kid to risk her life everyday wasn't something they were raised to condone. But he didn't mind being a bastard; in fact something in him quite relished the role.

John finished his plate and leaned back. "Does anyone know what day it is?" he asked.

Jenny glanced up through a mat of tangled blonde hair. "Ah, the day Conor let's us go topside for a shower?"

The other two girls giggled.

"Smart ass," Conor whispered.

"No seriously," John said. "Did anyone else remember it's been exactly one year since the Cataclysm."

The others stopped immediately and looked at him.

"One year since the first asteroid strike or since the air changed?" DJ asked, her smile shattering on the sharp edge of memory. Dredging up those feelings wasn't a pleasant experience. Everyone lost somebody.

But John wasn't put off. "April seventh, the day that changed the world forever," he said.

Jenny's eyes took on a faraway cast. "First one hit outside Richmond. It killed twenty-thousand."

"I was outside Mexico City," DJ recalled quietly. "Ten million in ten minutes. There were over a hundred impact sites…"

"They were still counting the dead when the big one arrived," John said. "It landed in the Atlantic and produced a tidal wave that destroyed everything on the east coast."

"Tell me something I don't know," Conor interjected sarcastically. "It was on the television." He resumed eating.

DJ nodded. "The world kept moving, the stations kept reporting until…"

"The air turned into poison," Jenny finished, slowly putting down her plate. "Some kind of toxin that the asteroids unleashed." She paused, remembering her moment. "I fell through a fault in the pavement when it happened. I watched my friends die…" She rubbed at some tears that suddenly appeared in the corners of her eyes. "They were trying to save me when they collapsed choking and gagging."

"The heavier, colder air below the street level saved your life," John said. "It prevented the poison from spreading below the city."

"Everybody above ground died," Sarah continued in her tiny voice. "Across the world, they died…" She hugged her legs tight and leaned against Jenny.

Nobody noticed as John made the sign of the cross with his remaining hand and mouthed a silent prayer.

Conor finished his plate and gestured towards the girls. "Are you guys going to eat that?" he asked.

*   *   *

DJ moaned softly in her sleep and Conor, lying beside her on the thin mattress, couldn't suppress a grin. The moaning the redhead did in her sleep was probably more genuine than the sounds she made during their hurried lovemaking. He was never very good at that sort of thing; then again he wasn't very good at many things before the Cataclysm. It was only afterward that he found his true calling, the ability to survive. Since day one he'd instinctively found the safe places to stay, the right things to eat and even made the hard decisions that defied the odds. John recognized it the moment they met as did the girls. And sleeping with him was probably a small price to pay for staying alive.

He fancied DJ lately, with her quick wit and penetrating green eyes. Her red hair was matted and streaked with grime as none of the girls had much success maintaining their pre-cataclysm level of personal hygiene. The clean water was saved for drinking while the fuel-tainted, smelly stuff was used for everything else. Then there were the sewer lines that were rusted and leaked daily.

But, as far as women were concerned, Conor's standards weren't very high to begin with.

They had the presidential suite; a glorified janitor's closest just off the main platform that served as their home base. The other three huddled in their sleeping bags just outside the door, far enough away to permit the illusion of privacy and yet close enough to maintain protection in their dangerous underground warren.

He had been pumping gas in a small hick town in Vermont, one step ahead of the ex-wife's blood-sucking lawyer, when the first rock struck.

Conor's grin widened. The bitch was dead now as was that piece-of-shit lawyer, along with most of the planet. That would have included him as well except that he decided to take a trip back to the coast as soon as the waters started to recede. He could smell an opportunity as well as the next guy and the valuables scattered around the wasteland of what used to be the east coast, or in this case, New York City, would be substantial. With his experience growing up in the projects, it was a joke to slip by the police and the National Guard.

The city was a different story; it was a mess, a virtual wilderness of destruction. Familiar landmarks were gone, hell, all the landmarks were gone, and buildings crushed and demolished like a child's Lego set. Because the tidal wave had destroyed everything, Conor was forced to travel underground. That was exactly two days before the air turned into yellow death.

He was lucky. He'd made all the right decisions.

* * *

DJ carefully sniffed the remains of the meat as the rest of the group waited expectantly.

After a minute she nodded. "Still good."

Sarah took out her small knife and began cutting small pieces that she dropped into the pot. Jenny added some spices rescued from the shops, two levels below the street. The pot was set on a crudely fashioned holder just above the flames.

"Two days in a row," John remarked. "I might actually get tired of fresh meat."

"It's the last time," DJ replied. "It'll be bad soon."

The priest nodded and padded her arm appreciably. No one questioned DJ's nose. She could track a scent half a mile down the tunnel but more importantly, and the reason Conor let her join, was her uncanny ability to detect when food was bad.

"You going back out today, Conor?" Sarah asked, her gaze flickering to the gun leaning against the wall.

186

"Naw," He shook his head. "There's some packaged stuff in the locker that's past its expiry date. We should eat those tonight." He hesitated as a thought struck him. "What's the latest on the shopping levels?"

Sarah stopped cutting and tilted her head. "Been everywhere on the second level and there's nothing left. To go further would mean tearing down that wall of debris I showed you last week."

Conor shuddered. The tight places he had to squeeze through to follow the little girl still gave him goose bumps. He wasn't claustrophobic per say but the close confines topside made him feel like he was buried alive.

"What about the first floor?"

She grimaced and the others averted their eyes. None of them liked the fact Conor kept forcing Sarah to check the top floor, the one that was still filled with the poisonous air.

"I could only get halfway up the stairs before my eyes started to water," she said. "And Jenny told me to come back."

Conor's jaw tightened and he turned towards the blonde.

"Hey." She threw her hands up defensively. "It's the same symptoms I felt when I scrambled into the subway entrance. The vomiting and seizures come next and I didn't think you wanted her dead."

Conor was about to snap back when DJ interjected. "It's better than last month, remember. We couldn't even get the door to the stairwell open without gagging."

"Absolutely," John echoed the sentiment. "Maybe the air is starting to clear up."

They all looked at Conor expectantly. His upper lip curled and he growled at Jenny. "Get that meat cooked." Then he got up and stomped off.

DJ let out her breath. "That was close."

Sarah, eyes wide in sudden realization, grabbed Jenny's hands. "I'm sorry, Jenny," she whispered. "I shouldn't have mentioned you. I should have just said I got sick!"

"It's all right, little one. He'll get over it."

John took a few pieces of meat and dropped them into the pot. "Unfortunately he has a point. We are running out of food and the stores on that floor are our best option...if we can get to it. I just wish he'd let me go."

"And what exactly could you do, Father," Jenny asked, her words mildly sarcastic. "With one arm and a body twice as big as Sprite here?" They had all seen the destruction, collapsed walls, shattered glass and all manner of debris wedged together like a collapsed mineshaft.

John smiled. "At least it might spare your shoes."

At the mention of last week's episode all three girls broke out laughing and Jenny unconsciously looked down at her stained hush puppies. When Conor pushed Sarah to try the stairs again the fumes had made her violently ill. Jenny, first in line to pull her out, had been practically bathed in vomit, her shoes taking the worst of it.

"It smells like cinnamon," Sarah said when the laughter faded. "It leaks down from the street."

DJ nodded. "I can smell it, too. Sometimes in the morning it's in the air down here in the tunnels."

John raised an inquisitive eyebrow. "So what's the answer? Is it dissipating above or just spreading to other areas?"

No one had an answer.

*   *   *

Conor made sure the girls were busy before he took John to the food locker. When the priest first told him about the girls' nickname for the room, Conor had laughed. It make him wonder what they thought was actually inside the closet-sized storage room.

John waited several steps back as Conor produced the key to the huge padlock and dialed up the combination to the second lock. He may *lose* the key but no one else knew the combination and they had yet to find a file capable of sawing through both hasps.

"Everything all right?" John asked.

"Fine, it's just a little rust."

"You might have noticed," John deadpanned. "It is a little close down here in the tunnels."

"Given a choice between the air in the street and the humidity down here, I'll take the latter," Conor replied as he straightened the night goggles and opened the steel door.

John stepped forward, carefully angling the flashlight away from Conor. He stopped in front of the shelves.

"What do you think?" Conor asked.

John splayed his light across several rough looking shelves. With nails sticking out and each shelf a different shape, the priest couldn't restrain a smile.

"It looks like somebody isn't going to make it as a carpenter."

Conor snickered. "Would you believe I was kicked out of shop class in school?" He didn't add the fact it was for punching his teacher in the face.

"Actually I would," John muttered, half to himself.

"I had to put them together quickly," Conor explained. "The first flashlights I found were dying. Several days later I found the goggles."

"Yeah, can't wait until they die," John said. He hesitated as he glanced over the shelves and did some quick calculations.

"How much has it gone down this past week?" he asked.

"About ten percent."

John unconsciously rubbed his stump. "I can see why you've been so stingy about dolling it out."

"Even with the occasional fresh meat, five is a lot of mouths to feed," Conor said. "Sometimes I wonder..."

"Don't go there, Conor," John interjected quickly. "There are lines we don't want to cross."

Conor peeled off his goggles and turned to face the man. The rush of air was cool on his face but the stench was still there.

"In wars and times of stress, people do what is necessary to survive. Sometimes the ends supersede the means," Conor said.

John let his flashlight dip as he took a deep breath. They could barely make out each other's features and the expressions were hidden in shadow. It only seemed that they were talking about subtle things.

"Civilization has come a long way, Conor. We've developed ethics and laws that dictate our lives now, written and unwritten rules that define who we are and what meaning our lives will convey to the next generation."

"What if there is no next generation, John? What if the poisonous air up there has killed everyone else and we're all that's left?"

The priest shook his head slowly from side to side. "We must stand up to the challenge, Conor. We have learned to modulate and control our instincts, to recognize a higher calling."

"Funny thing, John, is that I don't recognize anything here but a diminishing stack of food. And my instincts tell me we're going to need a lot more of it or we're all going to die."

The priest panned his light across the packages. "If that is our fate, so be it. But don't sacrifice our humanity along the way, Conor. Don't let a millennium of struggle come undone during our last days on this planet."

For a long minute Conor didn't say anything. Then he put his goggles back on.

"Nice words, Father," he said. "Very nice words."

* * *

Sarah was the first to hear the sounds. She flicked off her light and waited quietly in the darkness until it was repeated and then she climbed down to the platform to find Conor.

"Could it be animals?" he asked.

The girl shook her head. "It's coming from the first level, right below the street, and the air is still bad up there."

The next day he went with her and sat in a cave of destruction on the second level but heard nothing. On the third day it returned, a low-pitched grating that echoed through the pipes and dribbled dust like a minor earthquake.

"It's from the street," Conor confirmed to the group that night.

"What's causing it?" DJ asked. "Is it just debris shifting?"

Conor shook his head. "No, there's a pattern to it, something artificial."

"Are you saying it's manmade?" John asked.

Conor looked at him with an unreadable expression. "We'll have to wait and find out."

*   *   *

The next morning they heard a crash.

The girls immediately huddled around Conor and John had the gun loaded and ready.

"Stay behind me," Conor hissed. Then to John. "How far do you figure?"

The priest aimed his light into the darkness. "I'm guessing a couple of hundred yards. Any ideas?"

Conor shook his head and took the gun before walking down the platform. "No good ones."

As they advanced into the tunnel, John swept the light back and forth. The girls followed but their nervous whispering prompted an icy glare from Conor and they quickly lapsed into silence.

The light was a tiny beacon in an ocean of night, the tunnel swallowing them whole as they slowly crept forward. Conor kept to the middle, John and the girls on one side of the rail line. Except for the echo of water drops the only sound was the crunching of loose stones beneath their feet and an errant wind whistling off the walls.

John stopped abruptly, his light centered at a spot between the rail lines.

"What is it?" Conor whispered.

"On the rail," John pointed. "A figure slumped across the line."

His eyes focused on the spot and Conor nodded. He raised the gun.

"Wait," the priest whispered. "He's not moving."

Conor hesitated and took his finger off the trigger. "Show me the ceiling," he said.

John swung the light up and Sarah let out an audible gasp when the light revealed a gaping hole in the concrete. And a thick rope hanging down.

Without prompting, John followed the rope down until...

"Another one," DJ breathed. "They both must have fallen through!"

The second figure, dressed in similar nondescript clothes, dangled lifeless at the end of the rope. With his arms and legs splayed outwards, he looked like a marionette at the end of a string.

"DJ, check the one on the ground," Conor ordered as he kept his gun trained on the prone figure. "You other two run back and get me a knife to cut the other one down."

DJ crept forward and rolled the body over. "He's alive," she said. "But he's pretty beat up. His leg is busted."

Conor relaxed the grip on the gun as John leaned in. "Aren't you glad you didn't shoot first?" he asked.

Conor just shrugged. "We'll see, Father. Right now I'm not inclined to decide anything."

* * *

Their uniforms were standard army, coated in dust and dirt, and each carried a nine millimeter handgun, water flask, a backpack of rations and a funny shaped respirator with a two inch filter.

"How's the injured one?" Conor asked the priest.

John glanced over to where DJ was talking to one of the soldiers by the fire. His comrade was lying nearby, a dressing over the left side of his face and an improvised splint holding his right leg in position.

"He's out. DJ gave him a shot of morphine before we straightened the bones."

He exchanged a look with Conor. They both knew how many ampoules of morphine they had rescued from the pharmacy and you could fit them all in the palm of one hand.

Conor took another look at the handgun before walking over to the fire. The soldier immediately stood up and extended a hand as Conor approached.

"Sergeant Brian O'Shea, sir. I want to thank you for saving me and the corporal."

Conor slowly took the man's hand and they shook.

"I'm Conor. I see you already met the rest of the group. You're the first people we've seen in over a year. I guess we're not the only survivors after all."

O'Shea wiped a dirty hand across a dirtier chin. His young face carried three-day-old stubble and a jagged scar ran down the left side of his jaw.

"A few, sir. We've been holed up in Cheyenne Mountain. The Executive Branch was evacuated there initially but opened its doors to the civilians when the air turned. Probably about four-thousand all together."

"What about the rest of the US or the world?" John asked.

O'Shea shook his head. "We haven't picked up any signals on the radio bands, sir, err, Father."

"So, how did you get back to New York?" Conor asked.

"Orders, sir. We were a recon team tasked to find a safe place for all the people to hunker down until the air clears."

"What's wrong with where you are now?" Conor asked.

"We're running out of fuel to supply the air purifiers and without them the poison will start leaking in. Our job, like I said, was to scout out potential shelters. New York, with its extensive subway system, was the best choice. The cold air down here keeps the poison out."

"But how are you going to get everyone here?" John asked. "That's a lot of people."

"We have the transports and the resources to make a one way trip, Father. The roads are a mess in places but keeping people secure in airtight compartments is safe enough. We estimate it'll take three weeks to get everyone here."

Conor gestured to the pair of masks. "Is that why you use those?"

He nodded. "They've been modified and they work most of the time. Only when a storm comes up the coast and the particle count jumps do we have to find shelter."

"Are there many storms?"

"You probably don't know, sir, but ever since the last asteroids fell and released all those toxins there's been a bitch of a climate pattern, acid rain, ferocious storms, basically unpredictable weather. That's what happened to the corporal and me. A storm suddenly blew in and we jumped into the first hole we found in the street. He fell through and I was trying to climb down when the walls caved in." He absently rubbed his bruised side. "The next thing I remember is DJ over there putting a cool cloth on my forehead." He smiled at the girl and Conor noticed her blush.

"And the air is clearing?" John asked.

O'Shea pursed his lips. "They say it's going to take another eighteen months, give or take," he said. "But the people should be arriving here in about six months." He glanced around. "With all the supplies and materials they'll be bringing, this place will look like a hotel in no time."

Conor picked up a respirator. "And these work pretty good?"

"Used to," O'Shea said. "Until the corporal fell on his and crushed it and mine got a big crack in the shield."

"But your unit knows where you are, right?" the priest asked.

"Oh, yeah, we radioed in about two hours before the storm hit. Doesn't matter though since they don't have the resources to get us." He gave a self-deprecating laugh. "Hope you guys don't mind a couple of new roommates for the next six months."

*   *   *

Conor unlocked the door and stepped aside as John slipped in with his light. The beam flashed across mostly empty shelves.

"How much longer?" John asked.

"I had figured about five, maybe six months if the hunting was good," Conor replied. "For the five of us. Even then we'd be little more than walking skeletons. Throw in two more mouths to feed including an injured man..."

John raised a hand, forestalling any further explanation. "I did my own calculations and came to the same conclusion. With seven we'll starve to death in three months." He paused. "Finding them was a death sentence."

"No, Father, feeding them is."

*   *   *

"That's a nice weapon," Conor commented as O'Shea cleaned the nine-millimeter. "And," he gestured towards the foil wrapped bundle. "It looks better than that. What do you call it, an MER?"

O'Shea chuckled. "The gun probably tastes better, too." He shoved the clip in and handed it to Conor. "Reliable, accurate and never jams. Not so good for hunting but good for protection." He glanced at Conor's rifle leaning against the wall.

194

"DJ tells me you bring in a lot of food with that rifle. Is that because you're partial to vermin or you don't have enough supplies?" His cool green eyes seemed to evaluate Conor.

"Naw," Conor replied nonchalantly as he examined the gun. "I was just trying to stretch out what we got. Until you two showed up I wasn't sure how long we'd be stuck down here."

O'Shea's expression relaxed into a smile. "I understand. Don't worry, in six months you'll have all the food you need."

* * *

John found Conor by the food locker. He didn't bother to shine his flashlight; he already knew Conor was checking the gun.

"Is that the corporal's?"

In the near darkness Conor nodded. "I pocketed it after everyone went to bed last night." When John didn't speak, Conor continued. "I sent the girls up to the second level to test the masks. They didn't like it but I don't really care."

"The soldiers are still sleeping," John said. "DJ gave the corporal our last vial of morphine. He'll be in hell when he wakes up."

"I know," Conor said. "They both haven't recovered from the fall." He straightened and slid the safety off.

John put a hand on his arm. "You don't have to do this."

Conor didn't resist. He read the inflection in the priest's tone. They had spent over a year in the dark, cold confines of Hell together, scratching out a meager existence.

"It comes down to a simple decision," he said. "I made all the right ones so far and we're still alive. They may despise me but they see the alternative. I'll leave it to you, Father. You may choose faith but I'll stick with instinct; the instinct to survive at all costs."

He allowed the priest's hand to fall.

"And remember," Conor said, "this decision involves not just you and me. Your judgment affects DJ, Jenny and little Sarah. Would you condemn them, too?"

He waited but the priest said nothing more. He turned and walked away.

Conor stood in the dark for several minutes, listening to the sound of his heart beat and the patter of water dripping relentlessly in the tunnels. Relentlessly, just like his drive to survive.

He knew the priest had to walk past the sleeping soldiers on his way out. He would either wake them and warn them or quietly slip by and join the girls on the second level.

He slipped on his goggles and silently approached the platform. Pausing momentarily, he could hear John's faint footsteps walking down the tunnel and the heavy breathing of the slumbering soldiers.

ABOUT THE WRITERS

B. L. Bates received a BS in electrical engineering and worked for several years in industry before a head injury left her blind. After raising three step-children and two of her own, she turned to writing horror, fantasy and science fiction to stay sane. She lives in southeastern Massachusetts with her biologist husband. When not reading or writing, she enjoys the outdoors and cooking. Her other works have been published on SNM Horror and on two other sites now defunct.

When **David Bernstein** isn't writing some type of horror, he can usually be found reading or watching it. He's been published in a number of horror magazines and anthologies, many of them zombie oriented, and is almost finished with his first zombie novel. It would've been done a lot sooner, but he keeps getting ideas for short stories and has to write them. He believes, and now knows, that hard work pays off. He lives in the NYC area.

Christopher J. Dwyer is a writer from Boston, MA. His work has appeared in Twisted Tongue Magazine, Red Fez, Sex and Murder, Troubadour 21, Gold Dust Magazine, Colored Chalk, and numerous fiction anthologies. He is currently the writer-in-residence for online literary magazine Dogmatika.
He can be contacted through his official website: www.christopherdwyer.com.

Anthony Giangregorio is the author and editor of more than 25 novels, almost all of them about zombies. His work has appeared in Dead Science by Coscomentertainment, Dead Worlds: Undead Stories Volumes 1, 2 , 3, and 4, and an upcoming anthology (Zombology) by Library of the Living Dead Press and their werewolf anthology titled War Wolves. He also has stories in End of Days: An Apocalyptic Anthology Volumes 1 & 2
Check out his website at www.undeadpress.com

Joseph Giangregorio is the son of Anthony Giangregorio and a horror writer as well. He co-wrote the book "*Visions of the Dead*" with his father and has a few stories in the coming zombie anthology "*Family of the Dead*" by Living Dead Press as well as Dead Worlds: Undead Stories Volume 2.
He is attending college for his associates' degree and from there will be moving on to his bachelors. He's also a promising welder who is in the process of becoming certified.

Kelly M. Hudson grew up in the wilds of Kentucky and currently resides in California. He has a deep and abiding love for all things horror and rock n' roll, and if you wish to contact Kelly or find links to other stories he's had published, please visit www.kellymhudson.com for further details. Kelly thanks you for reading his dumb old story and wishes you and yours a very happy day!

Lance Looper is a copywriter in Austin, Texas and spends his days writing about the marvels of modern technology for his corporate overlords. His nights are spent with his wife Donna and their two loving but schizophrenic boxers.
Contact Lance at lancelooper@yahoo.com

Pasquale J. Morrone makes his home in Maryland with his wife, Kathleen. His novels and short stories are promoted on the web. His two novels, Spook Rock and The Lazarus Culture are available online as well some of the other bookstores. He has numerous short stories published in a variety of anthologies. Known to most people as Pat, he writes mostly in the horror genre. His blog can be found at: dabsinfiction.blogspot.com, which is a helpful writer's guide for new writers.

G.R. Mosca was born in Birmingham, England and is a graduate of Bard College. He currently resides in Thomasville, Pennsylvania with his companion Annalisa and their five cats. Contact G.R. Mosca at gmosca@aol.com.

Perry P. Perkins is a novelist, blogger, and award winning travel writer. He is a stay-at-home dad who lives with his wife Victoria and their two-year-old daughter Grace, in the Pacific Northwest . A student of Jerry B. Jenkins Christian Writer's Guild, his novels include Just Past Oysterville, Shoalwater Voices, and The Light at the End of the Tunnel. Perry has written short stories for numerous magazines and anthologies, and his inspirational stories have been included in twelve Chicken Soup anthologies.
Examples of his published work can be found online at:
www.perryperkinsbooks.com, and on www.pdxdads.com

Alva J. Roberts lives in Western Nebraska with his wife and their two dogs. He has been published in Dead Worlds 3 and has works scheduled for publication in Zombology IV, The Scroll of Anubis, and Bards and Sages Quarterly. When he isn't writing, he works as a librarian.

Jessy Marie Roberts lives in a "haunted" house in Western Nebraska with her husband, Alva, and their two dogs, Tucker and Snags. She grew up in Morgan Hill, California, where she did a three year stint as a Mighty Acorn. When Jessy isn't busy writing, she enjoys cooking, gardening, and watching scary movies.

Michael Simon lives and works in eastern Canada with his wife and three children. Published works have appeared in Apex: Science Fiction and Horror, Andromeda Spaceways Inflight Magazine, The Sword Review, Ragged Edge, Drabble, Mindflights and Art and Prose. He has been shortlisted for the AEON Award and Writers of the Future and has contributed to several anthologies including Travel a Time Historic, Tall Tales and Short Stories, The Unknown, Dead Worlds: Undead Stories (Volume 1,2 and 3) and Book of the Dead. Nonfiction articles have appeared in Stitches Magazine, The Physician's Chronicle, Physician's Review, Caregiver Magazine, The Medical Post and Hockey Net.

Marc Wiggins has been an avid lover of post-apocalyptic fiction ever since he saw his first zombie movie in seventh grade. He has always loved the written word and favors zombie novels over movies. Though it has been years since he has written creatively, he was recently inspired to write again after encouragement from a good friend. Marc lives with his loving wife and kids in Southern California. This is his third story published, the others being in Dead Worlds: Undead Stories Volume 1 and 2.

DEAD MOURNING: A ZOMBIE HORROR STORY
by Anthony Giangregorio

Carl Jenkins was having a run of bad luck. Fresh out of jail, his probation tenuous, he'd lost every job he'd taken since being released. So now was his last chance, only one more job to prevent him from going back to prison. Assigned to work in a funeral home, he accidentally loses a shipment of embalming fluid. With nothing to lose, he substitutes it with a batch of chemicals from a nearby factory.

The results don't go as planned, though. While his screw-up goes unnoticed, his machinations revive the cadavers in the funeral home, unleashing an evil on the world that it has not seen before. Not wanting to become a snack for the rampaging dead, he flees the city, joining up with other survivors. An old, dilapidated zoo becomes their haven, while the dead wait outside the walls, hungry and patient.

But Carl is optimistic, after all, he's still alive, right? Perhaps his luck has changed and help will arrive to save them all?

Unfortunately, unknown to him and the other survivors, a serial killer has fallen into their group, trapped inside the zoo with them.

With the undead army clamoring outside the walls and a murderer within, it'll be a miracle if any of them live to see the next sunrise.

On second thought, maybe Carl would've been better off if he'd just gone back to jail.

DEAD TALES: SHORT STORIES TO DIE FOR
By Anthony Giangregorio

In a world much like our own, terrorists unleash a deadly disease that turns people into flesh-eating ghouls.

A camping trip goes horribly wrong when forces of evil seek to dominate mankind.

After losing his life, a man returns reincarnated again and again; his soul inhabiting the bodies of animals.

In the Colorado Mountains, a woman runs for her life, stalked by a sadistic killer.

In a world where the Patriot Act has come to fruition, a man struggles to survive, despite eroding liberties.

Not able to accept his wife's death, a widower will cross into the dream realm to find her again, despite the dark forces that hold her in thrall.

These and other short stories will captivate and thrill you.

These are short stories to die for.

DEAD SALVATION
BOOK 9
by Anthony Giangregorio

Henry Watson and his band of warrior survivalists roam what is left of a ravaged America, searching for something better.

HANGMAN'S NOOSE

After one of the group is hurt, the need for transportation is solved by a roving cannie convoy. Attacking the camp, the companions save a man who invites them back to his home.

Cement City it's called and at first the group is welcomed with thanks for saving one of their own. But when a bar fight goes wrong, the companions find themselves awaiting the hangman's noose.

Their only salvation is a suicide mission into a raider camp to save captured townspeople.

Though the odds are long, it's a chance, and Henry knows in the land of the walking dead, sometimes a chance is all you can hope for.

In the world of the dead, life is a struggle, where the only victor is death.

RANDY AND WALTER: PORTRAIT OF TWO KILLERS
by Tristan Slaughter

Randy Barcer lived his life the way he wanted to, joyfully slaughtering innocent women and children.

But sometimes he did much worse to them and those that died would be considered the lucky ones.

That is until he met Walter Brenemen, and he soon found out that this man who claimed to be his brother, was far more dangerous than Randy could ever hope to be.

"I'll give you the name of a woman and tell you where to find her. Then we'll see which one of us can get to her first. If you win, I'll leave you be. But if I win...well, I guess we'll just have to wait and see."

With those words, Walter changed Randy's life forever.

It was a simple game.

Whoever kills the most, wins; with a small town caught in the middle.

Forget what you know or think you know about horror. Let go of everything you've ever been taught about serial killers. Step into the world of Tristan Slaughter and discover what it is that makes a killer.

This is not your typical slasher novel.

This is:

Randy and Walter: Portrait of Two Killers.

You will never look at a man the same way again.

Welcome to a world of despair, desire, cruelty, punishment, pure evil and most of all...Death.

REVOLUTION OF THE DEAD
by Anthony Giangregorio
THE DEAD SHALL RISE AGAIN!

Five years ago, a deadly plague wiped out 97% of the world's population, America suffering tragically. Bodies were everywhere, far too many to bury or burn. But then, through a miracle of medical science, a way is found to reanimate the dead.

With the manpower of the United States depleted, and the remaining survivors not wanting to give up their internet and fast food restaurants, the undead are conscripted as slave labor.

Now they cut the grass, pick up the trash, and walk the dogs of the surviving humans.

But whether alive or dead, no race wants to be controlled, and sooner or later the dead will fight back, wanting the freedom they enjoyed in life.

The revolution has begun!

And when it's over, the dead will rule the land, and the remaining humans will become the slaves...or worse.

KINGDOM OF THE DEAD
by Anthony Giangregorio
THE DEAD HAVE RISEN!

In the dead city of Pittsburgh, two small enclaves struggle to survive, eking out an existence of hand to mouth.

But instead of working together, both groups battle for the last remaining fuel and supplies of a city filled with the living dead.

Six months after the initial outbreak, a lone helicopter arrives bearing two more survivors and a newborn baby. One enclave welcomes them, while the other schemes to steal their helicopter and escape the decaying city.

With no police, fire, or social services existing, the two will battle for dominance in the steel city of the walking dead. But when the dust settles, the question is: will the remaining humans be the winners, or the losers?

When the dead walk, the line between Heaven and Hell is so twisted and bent there is no line at all.

RISE OF THE DEAD
by Anthony Giangregorio
DEATH IS ONLY THE BEGINNING!

In less than forty-eight hours, more than half the globe was infected.

In another forty-eight, the rest would be enveloped.

The reason?

A science experiment gone horribly wrong which enabled the dead to walk, their flesh rotting on their bones even as they seek human prey.

Jeremy was an ordinary nineteen year old slacker. He partied too much and had done poorly in high school. After a night of drinking and drugs, he awoke to find the world a very different place from the one he'd left the night before.

The dead were walking and feeding on the living, and as Jeremy stepped out into a world gone mad, the dead spotting him alone and unarmed in the middle of the street, he had to wonder if he would live long enough to see his twentieth birthday.

DEADFREEZE
by Anthony Giangregorio

THIS IS WHAT HELL WOULD BE LIKE IF IT FROZE OVER!
When an experimental serum for hypothermia goes horribly wrong, a small research station in the middle of Antarctica becomes overrun with an army of the frozen dead.

Now a small group of survivors must battle the arctic weather and a horde of frozen zombies as they make their way across the frozen plains of Antarctica to a neighboring research station.

What they don't realize is that they are being hunted by an entity whose sole reason for existing is vengeance; and it will find them wherever they run.

DEAD WORLDS: Undead Stories
A Zombie Anthology Volume 1
Edited by Anthony Giangregorio

Welcome to the world of the dead, where the laws of nature have been twisted, reality changed.

The Dead Walk!

Filled with established and promising new authors for the next generation of corpses, this anthology will leave you gasping for air as you go from one terror-filled story to another.

Like the decomposing meat of a freshly rotting carcass, this book will leave you breathless.

Don't say we didn't warn you.

VISIONS OF THE DEAD
A ZOMBIE STORY
by Anthony & Joseph Giangregorio

Jake Roberts felt like he was the luckiest man alive.

He had a great family, a beautiful girlfriend, who was soon to be his wife, and a job, that might not have been the best, but it paid the bills.

At least until the dead began to walk.

Now Jake is fighting to survive in a dead world while searching for his lost love, Melissa, knowing she's out there somewhere.

But the past isn't dead, and as he struggles for an uncertain future, the past threatens to consume him.

With the present a constant battle between the living and the dead, Jake finds himself slipping in and out of the past, the visions of how it all happened haunting him.

But Jake knows Melissa is out there somewhere and he'll find her or die trying. In a world of the living dead, you can never escape your past.

THE NEXT EXCITING CHAPTER IN THE DEADWATER SERIES!

BOOK 7

DEAD VALLEY
by Anthony Giangregorio

Untouched Majesty

After nearly drowning in the icy waters of the Colorado River, the six weary companions come upon a beautiful valley nestled in the mountains of Colorado, where the undead plague appears to have never happened.

With the mountains protecting the valley, the deadly rain never fell, and the valley is as untouched as the day it was created.

But the group is soon captured by a secret, military research base now run by a few remaining scientists and soldiers.

On this base, unholy experiments are being carried out, and the group soon finds themselves caught in the middle of it.

Mary, Sue, Raven and Cindy are taken away to be used as breeders, the scientists wanting to create a new utopia, which the living dead can't reach, but the side effect of this is the women will lose their lives.

Henry and Jimmy, now separated and captured themselves, must find a way to save them before it's too late; the scientists unleashing every conceivable mutation at their disposal to stop them.

In the world of the living dead, the past is gone and the future is non-existent.

ROAD KILL: A ZOMBIE TALE
by Anthony Giangregorio

ORDER UP!

In the summer of 2008, a rogue comet entered earth's orbit for 72 hours. During this time, a strange amber glow suffused the sky.

But something else happened; something in the comet's tail had an adverse affect on dead tissue and the result was the reanimation of every dead animal carcass on the planet.

A handful of survivors hole up in a diner in the backwoods of New Hampshire while the undead creatures of the night hunt for human prey.

There's a new blue plate special at DJ's Diner and Truck Stop, and it's you!

DEAD WORLDS: Undead Stories
A Zombie Anthology Volume 2
Edited by Anthony Giangregorio

Welcome to a world where the dead walk and want nothing more than to feast on the living.

The stories contained in this, the second volume of the Dead Worlds series, are filled with action, gore, and buckets and buckets of blood; plus a heaping side of entrails for those with a little extra hunger.

The stories contained within this volume are scribed by both the desiccated cadavers of seasoned veterans to the genre as well as fresh-faced corpses, each printed here for the first time; and all of them ready to dig in and please the most discerning reader.

So slap on a bib and prepare to get bloody, because you're about to read the best zombie stories this side of Hell!

THE DARK
by Anthony Giangregorio
DARKNESS FALLS

The darkness came without warning.

First New York, then the rest of United States, and then the world became enveloped in a perpetual night without end.

With no sunlight, eventually the planet will wither and die, bringing on a new Ice Age. But that isn't problem for the human race, for humanity will be dead long before that happens.

There is something in the dark, creatures only seen in nightmares, and they are on the prowl. Evolution has changed and man is no longer the dominant species. When we are children, we're told not to fear the dark, that what we believe to exist in the shadows is false.

Unfortunately, that is no longer true.

SOULEATER
by Anthony Giangregorio

Twenty years ago, Jason Lawson witnessed the brutal death of his father by something only seen in nightmares, something so horrible he'd blocked it from his mind.

Now twenty years later the creature is back, this time for his son.

Jason won't let that happen.

He'll travel to the demon's world, struggling every second to rescue his son from its clutches.

But what he doesn't know is that the portal will only be open for a finite time and if he doesn't return with his son before it closes, then he'll be trapped in the demon's dimension forever.

FAMILY OF THE DEAD
A Zombie Anthology
by Anthony, Joseph and Domenic Giangregorio

Clawing their way out of the wet, dark earth, these tales of terror will fill you with the deep seated fear we all have of death and what comes next.

But if that wasn't bad enough to chill your soul, these undead tales are penned by an entire family of corpses. The zombie master himself, Anthony Giangregorio, leads his two young ghouls, his sons Domenic and Joseph Giangregorio, on a journey of terror inducing stories that will keep you up long into the night.

As you read these works of the undead, don't be alarmed by that bump outside the window.

After all, it's probably just a stray tree branch...or is it?

DARK PLACES
by Anthony Giangregorio

A cave-in inside the Boston subway unleashes something that should have stayed buried forever

Three boys sneak out to a haunted junkyard after dark and find more than they gambled on.

In a world where everyone over twelve has died from a mysterious illness, one young boy tries to carry on.

A mysterious man in black tries his hand at a game of chance at a local carnival, to interesting results.

God, Allah, and Buddha play a friendly game of poker with the fate of the Earth resting in the balance.

Ever have one of those days where everything that can go wrong, does? Well, so did Byron, and no one should have a day like this!

Thad had an imaginary friend named Charlie when he was a child. Charlie would make him do bad things. Now Thad is all grown up and guess who's coming for a visit?

These and other short stories, all filled with frozen moments of dread and wonder, will keep you captivated long into the night.

Just be sure to watch out when you turn off the light!

THE MONSTER UNDER THE BED
by Anthony Giangregorio

Rupert was just one of many monsters that inhabit the human world, scaring children before bed. Only Rupert wanted to play with the children he was forced to scare.

When Rupert meets Timmy, an instant friendship is born. Running away from his abusive step-father, Timmy leaves home, embarking on a journey that leads him to New York City.

On his way, Timmy will realize that the true monsters are other adults who are just waiting to take advantage of a small boy, all alone in the big city.

Can Rupert save him?

Or will Timmy just become another statistic.

The Lazarus Culture

by Pasquale J. Morrone

Secret Service Agent Christopher Kearns had no idea what he was up against. Assigned on a temporary basis to the Center for Disease Control, he only knew that somehow it was connected to the lives of those the agency protected...namely, the President of the United States. If there were possible terrorist activities in the making, he could only guess it was at a red alert basis.

When Kearns meets and befriends Doctor Marlene Peterson of the Breezy Point Medical Center in Maryland, he soon finds that science fiction can indeed become a reality. In a solitary room walked a man with no vital signs: dead. The explanation he received came from Doctor Lee Fret, a man assigned to the case from the CDC. Something was attached to the brain stem. Something alive that was quickly spreading rapidly through Maryland and other states.

Kearns and his ragtag army of agents and medical personnel soon find themselves in a world of meaningless slaughter and mayhem. The armies of the walking dead were far more than mere zombies. Some began to change into whatever it was they ate. The government had found a way to reanimate the dead by implanting a parasite found on the tongue of the Red Snapper to the human brain.

It looked good on paper, but it was a project straight from Hell.

The dead now walked, but it wasn't a mystery.

It was The Lazarus Culture.

BOOK OF THE DEAD
A ZOMBIE ANTHOLOGY

Edited by Anthony Giangregorio

This is the most faithful, truest zombie anthology ever written, and we invite you along for the ride. Every single story in this book is filled with slack-jawed, eyes glazed, slow moving, shambling zombies set in a world where the dead have risen and only want to eat the flesh of the living. In these pages, the rules are sacrosanct. There is no deviation from what a zombie should be or how they came about.

The Dead Walk.

There is no reason, though rumors and suppositions fill the radio and television stations. But the only thing that is fact is that the walking dead are here and they will not go away. So prepare yourself for the ultimate homage to the master of zombie legend. And remember... Aim for the head!

DEADFALL
by Anthony Giangregorio

It's Halloween in the small suburban town of Wakefield, Mass.

While parents take their children trick or treating and others throw costume parties, a swarm of meteorites enter the earth's atmosphere and crash to earth.

Inside are small parasitic worms, no larger than maggots.

The worms quickly infect the corpses at a local cemetery and so begins the rise of the undead.

The walking dead soon get the upper hand, with no one believing the truth.

That the dead now walk.

Will a small group of survivors live through the zombie apocalypse?

Or will they, too, succumb to the Deadfall.

ANOTHER EXCITING CHAPTER IN THE DEADWATER SERIES!

DEAD CITY
by Anthony Giangregorio
BOOK 3
NEW PERILS IN AN UNDEAD WORLD

After narrowly surviving an attack by a large pack of blood thirsty, wild dogs, Henry and his companions stumble upon an enclave that has made its home in an abandoned shopping mall.

Hoping for a respite from the perils of the walking dead, Henry and the others plan to settle down for the winter, safe in the company of fellow survivors of the zombie apocalypse.

But unknown to the group is the dark secret the enclave keeps, a secret that could threaten to destroy the companions and anyone else unfortunate enough to be caught in the trap.

In a dead world the only thing still living... is hope.

SEE HOW IT ALL BEGAN IN THE NEW DOUBLE-SIZED EDITION!

DEADWATER: EXPANDED EDITION
by Anthony Giangregorio

Through a series of tragic mishaps, a small town's water supply is contaminated with a deadly bacterium that transforms the town's population into flesh eating ghouls.

Without warning, Henry Watson finds himself thrown into a living hell where the living dead walk and want nothing more than to feed on the living.

Now Henry's trying to escape the undead town before he becomes the next victim.

With the military on one side, shooting civilians on sight, and a horde of bloodthirsty zombies on the other, Henry must try to battle his way to freedom.

With a small group of survivors, including a beautiful secretary and a wise-cracking janitor to aid him, the ragtag group will do their best to stay alive and escape the city codenamed: **Deadwater.**

DEAD END: A ZOMBIE NOVEL
by Anthony Giangregorio

THE DEAD WALK!

Newspapers everywhere proclaim the dead have returned to feast on the living!

A small group of survivors hole up in a cellar, afraid to brave the masses of animated corpses, but when food runs out, they have no choice but to venture out into a world gone mad.

What they will discover, however, is that the fall of civilization has brought out the worst in their fellow man.

Cannibals, psychotic preachers and rapists are just some of the atrocities they must face.

In a world turned upside down, it is life that has hit a Dead End.

DEAD RAGE
by Anthony Giangregorio

An unknown virus spreads across the globe, turning ordinary people into bloodthirsty, ravenous killers.

Only a small percentage of the population is immune and soon become prey to the infected.

Amongst the infected comes a man, stricken by the virus, yet still retaining his grasp on reality. His need to destroy the *normals* becomes an obsession and he raises an army of killers to seek out and kill all who aren't *changed* like himself.

A few survivors gather together on the outskirts of Chicago and find themselves running for their lives as the specter of death looms over all.

The Dead Rage virus will find you, no matter where you hide.

DEADTOWN: A DEADWATER STORY
BOOK 8
By Anthony Giangregorio

WORLD OF THE DEAD

The world is a very different place now. The dead walk the land and humans hide in small towns with walls of stone and debris for protection, constantly keeping the living dead at bay.

Social law is gone and right and wrong is defined by the size of your gun.

UNWELCOME VISITORS

Henry Watson and his band of warrior survivalists become guests in a fortified town in Michigan. But when the kidnapping of one of the companions goes bad and men die, the group finds themselves on the wrong side of the law, and a town out for blood.

Trapped in a hotel, surrounded on all sides, it will be up to Henry to save the day with a gamble that may not only take his life, but that of his friends as well.

In a dead world, when justice is not enough, there is always vengeance.

ANOTHER EXCITING CHAPTER IN THE DEADWATER SERIES!

DEADRAIN
BOOK 2
By Anthony Giangregorio

Welcome to the New America, population: 0

When a bacterial outbreak contaminates America's lower atmosphere, the resulting rain mutates into a deadly conduit for death.

Human's all over America are exposed and within a matter of days society has crumbled and the walking dead rule the land.

The America we know is gone, replaced by a new order; where the dead walk and humans are the prey.

Henry Watson and his small group of companions travel the country, searching for someplace better, someplace where the rain is safe.

In the New America the rules have changed; survive or perish.

THE PLACE TO GO FOR ZOMBIE AND APOCALYPTIC FICTION

LIVING DEAD PRESS

WHERE THE DEAD WALK

www.livingdeadpress.com

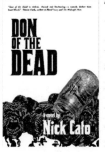
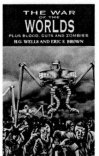